He came out of the shadows...

and slowly descended the stairs, becoming visible. Boots, black jeans, a wiry frame. His tread was slow, measured, designed to intimidate. But Victoria was not easily intimidated.

"Why have you come here, Miss Summers?" His voice was deep, and chased a shiver across her heated skin.

"I—I need you...your help."

In fascination, she watched him walk toward her, trading shadow for dusty light. He was lean and sinewy, and his hair was brown and long, thick and curling. But it was his face that was truly captivating. His intense blue-green eyes, his well-shaped mouth, the stubble on his chin and upper lip... His gaze was so steady and so penetrating that she felt as though he was touching her physically; she even felt a tingling sensation on her arms. And then she saw the scar—the slash through his eyebrow and along the curve of his cheek.

And she had only one thought: If he was the man who could save her, she didn't want to think about the one who was after her....

D0036669

Dear Reader,

They're rugged, they're strong and they're *wanted!* Whether sheriff, undercover cop or officer of the court, these men are trained to keep the peace, to uphold the law. But what happens when they meet the one woman who gets to know the man *behind* the badge?

Twelve of these men are on the loose...and only Harlequin Intrigue brings them to you—one per month in the LAWMAN series. This month, meet Torbel, a dangerously enticing private investigator with unusual methods.

Be sure you don't miss a single LAWMAN coming to you in the months ahead...because there's nothing sexier than the strong arms of the law!

Regards,

Debra Matteucci
Senior Editor & Editorial Coordinator
Harlequin Books
300 East 42nd Street
New York, NY 10017

Sweet Revenge
Jenna Ryan

Harlequin Books

TORONTO • NEW YORK • LONDON
AMSTERDAM • PARIS • SYDNEY • HAMBURG
STOCKHOLM • ATHENS • TOKYO • MILAN
MADRID • WARSAW • BUDAPEST • AUCKLAND

To Kathy, sister and friend.
To Bill and Kay, my parents.
To Rod, who has helped me in his own special way.
To Bonnie, Alice and Shauna.
Thanks for everything.

ISBN 0-373-22393-5

SWEET REVENGE

Copyright © 1996 by Jacqueline Goff

This edition published by arrangement with Harlequin Books S.A.

® and TM are trademarks of the publisher. Trademarks indicated with ® are registered in the United States Patent and Trademark Office, the Canadian Trade Marks Office and in other countries.

Printed in U.S.A.

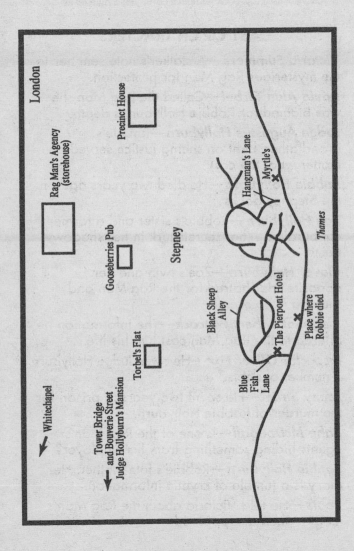

London

Rag Man's Agency
(storehouse)

Precinct House

Gooseberries Pub

Stepney

Hangman's Lane

Myrtle's

Black Sheep
Alley

The Pierpont Hotel

Place where
Robbie died

Thames

Whitechapel

Tower Bridge
and Bouverie Street
Judge Hollyburn's Mansion

Torbel's Flat

Blue
Fish Lane

CAST OF CHARACTERS

Victoria Summers—A stalker's note sent her to the mysterious Rag Man for protection.

David Alun Torbel—Called the Rag Man, he was blamed for Robbie Hollyburn's death.

Judge Augustus Hollyburn—Robbie's grandfather, bent on seeing justice served no matter what the cost.

Robbie Hollyburn—He died two years ago on the Stepney docks

Zoe Hollyburn—Robbie's sister and a former cat burglar. What secrets lurk in her shadowy past?

Clover Hollyburn—Zoe's twin and her opposite. Her hatred for the Rag Man and Victoria is no secret.

Sergeant Robert Peacock—The information he offered to the Rag Man cost him his life.

Inspector Oliver Fox—He owes Judge Hollyburn a number of debts.

Lenny Street—He spent two years in prison for the murder of Robbie Hollyburn.

Rahn McDougall—Is one of the Rag Man's agents hiding something from his employer?

Sophie Hollyburn—Robbie's late mother. Her diary is a jumble of cryptic information.

Boots—He told Victoria about the Rag Man's magic—then disappeared.

Prologue

"I'd have sold my soul to see my grandson's murderer punished." Augustus Hollyburn's fists hit the polished mahogany mantel. "I said that two years ago, Scratch, and I meant it, I swear to God I did."

His longtime friend, Lucius Scranton, hid a smile behind the rim of his glass. "Yes, I remember. Then you should be pleased. Justice was served."

"The hell it was!" Augustus's tumbler shattered against the fireplace grate. Two ounces of Napoleon brandy caused the flames to surge up, blue and angry. "Damn that Rag Man, Scratch. Damn him to hell and back. He's as slippery as an eel, as cunning as a fox and, on top of that, he has horseshoes up his—"

"Asperity," Scratch interrupted smoothly, "is a very unhealthy thing." Sipping his Scotch, he sat back in the plump-cushioned chair and stretched his leather-shod feet toward the fire. "You really shouldn't get so worked up, Goggy. Not good for the blood pressure at our age."

Scowling, Augustus regarded his gnarled hands. "Eighty-one years old and look at me, shaking like I've been chased through Stepney by spooks. Damnation!" His head reared up. "Why did I say Stepney? You see, Scratch? You see what he's done to me?"

"This Rag Man, what's his name—Torbel?"

"More like 'Trouble,'" Augustus muttered. He shuffled, not walked, he thought in disgust as he slid his arthritic feet across the carpet to his pipe rack. He owned a Georgian mansion in the posh Mayfair district of London. He had money in the bank, plenty of it, plus shares in collieries and shipyards. In his time, he'd been up there with the finest high-court judges in England, respected and, yes, by God, even feared by his peers.

Grimacing, he massaged a persistent sore spot on his chest. Bloody spring fog. Thick as turtle soup, that's how his grandson—his late grandson—Robbie would have described it.

The pain deepened, causing Augustus to flinch and Scratch to frown in concern. "You all right, Goggy? Maybe you should sit down. You look a bit peaky."

Good old Scratch. He never changed. They'd been through a lot since those days at Oxford, when Augustus had been wild and unrestrained, with few cares or scruples. Then the war had come, and he'd been forced to settle down—or at least give the appearance of doing so. No Hollyburn ever truly settled down.

A shudder strong enough to rattle his old bones ran through him. If only circumstances had been different and Robbie hadn't gone down to the Stepney pier on that foggy night. If only he'd never heard of the notorious Rag Man. If only...

His chest pain subsided to a dull ache.

Leaning forward, Scratch warmed both his Scotch and his hands before the flames. "Who is this Rag Man anyway?" his old friend questioned.

Augustus glanced sideways out of canny blue-green eyes. Scratch was always calm, of the gentry, born and bred. Distinguished, that was the word for him, not frail and wizened as Augustus had grown.

Trembling, Augustus raised his pipe, puffed in agitation, then shuffled slowly to his chair. "He's responsible for my grandson's death, that's who the Rag Man is, the son of a bloody whore." He flapped a cranky hand. "You're not completely unfamiliar with the seamy side of London. You must have heard of him."

Sufficiently warmed, Scratch sat back again. The firelight reflected off the rich amber liquid in his glass. The entire hearth area glowed golden red in the otherwise darkened parlor. "Why don't you tell me the details, Goggy?" he suggested. "All of it, the whole story, start to finish. Of course, I know Robbie was murdered on the docks just over two years ago. The man convicted of the crime was recently released from prison—I know that, too. But everything else is just bits and pieces. In any case, I can see you're not satisfied with the outcome.''

No, dammit, he was not satisfied.

Augustus's mind drifted backward as the smoke from Scratch's slender cigar floated past his eyes. The aches in his old body faded momentarily, replaced by a stab of anger that carried with it the sour taste of spite. He was the devil, that Rag Man, and justice was his private joke.

But the recent spate of events hadn't started with Torbel. This latest nightmare had begun three weeks ago in West London with the beautiful American solicitor, Victoria Summers. . . .

Chapter One

Late May in England . . .

To Victoria Summers, it meant flowers and fog and the promise of a well-deserved vacation away from London. To her da, it would mean a change of occupations. Muffin man turned vegetable seller, or maybe trinkets for the tourists to buy. Visitors to England were hungry lately for color, and nowhere could they find more of that than in a Whitechapel market, or wherever else her father might choose to park his ancient wares cart.

Noting a tiny sound behind her, Victoria glanced back for the tenth time in two minutes.

The law offices of Bock, Press and Woodbury commanded the entire third floor of Talbot House, a venerable building close to St. Paul's Cathedral in the heart of old London. The romantic in her loved the location, plus the fact that the place shouted *Mary Poppins* at her. With darkness and shadows spreading out in murky black pools, Talbot House could have been the bank where George Banks had paid his fateful late-night call.

Victoria smiled faintly at the memory. The thought of George brought her back to her da. Alfred Summers was a colorful Yorkshireman, his ex-wife Lily an American singer-poet, his aunt Prudie an eccentric British-American flower seller. Which made Victoria a hodgepodge, she supposed. A solicitor prone to searching for ghosts and gremlins yet too firmly rooted in reality to invent them on a whim.

Halfway across the polished marble floor, she halted and brought her head around again, biting her lower lip. She'd definitely heard something like a furtive footstep, discernible to her instincts more than to her ears. But who'd made it? As far as she knew, she was the only person here—except for Caffy, the seventy-three-year-old night watchman.

Hitching her shoulder bag up a notch, Victoria studied the welter of shadows in her wake. Tendrils of fear coiled in her stomach, but she knew better than to acknowledge them right now. You couldn't illuminate mausoleums like this properly. They always came out stark and eerie, smelling of time measured in centuries rather than decades.

Her eyes scanned the darkness. Caffy's name flitted briefly through her mind, but she dismissed it. He had his good points, but stealth wasn't one of them.

Curling her fingers around the strap of her bag, she started walking again, through shadows half the size of her apartment. The door wasn't far. And 11:30 p.m. wasn't overly late by London standards. There'd still be cabs going by.

The cavernous central hall went on forever, an echoing black void. Images of masked murderers, Victorian maidens, dark coaches, fog and empty alleyways flitted through her head, but she stopped them cold. Alfred Summers's daughter could stand up to cowardly pranksters with the best of them. On the other hand, who knew if the person back there was a coward or a prankster.

Dammit, where was that door? It must be…there! She spied it twenty feet ahead, past a trio of Roman columns and up four marble stairs.

The heels of her Italian shoes clicked on the polished floor. The clock ticked sonorously—like a bomb, she reflected grimly. There wasn't much traffic on the street beyond the smoked-glass panels. There was fog, though, plenty of it, thick and white and floating past the windows in freakish waves.

Victoria controlled a strong urge to bolt as she recalled the three phone calls she'd received recently. One last Sunday and two more on Wednesday. Today was Friday.

The brass door handle gleamed in the muted streetlight. She reached for the latch—then stifled a scream as a man's large hand clamped down hard on hers.

Jerking free, she spun around. Fear turned to relief and then to annoyance when she viewed Caffy's sleepy, bearlike features.

"I'm supposed to let you out." His voice held an unmistakable slur. "You should have buzzed me."

Victoria blew out a deep breath. He was stealthier than she'd realized. "I did. You never answered."

"I was in the men's room," he explained, twisting ineffectually on the lock.

"You were drinking. I'm not stupid. Oh, here, let me do it."

His hands dropped. His bleary eyes did not. "I never . . ."

The stuck bolt clicked, and she pulled the door open. "Save your excuses for Bock and Press, Caffy. I'm not a rat." She paused, her gaze straying into the darkness beyond his shoulder. It hadn't been him she'd heard; she was sure of it. "You didn't see anyone lurking around back there, did you?"

He flexed his fingers one by one. "Tom and Tabby."

"People, Caffy, not cats."

"You want me to turn up the lights?"

She started to nod, then shook her head instead. "Never mind. I'm probably imagining things."

"Maybe it was me you heard."

"Maybe." The suggestion was preferable to the alternative that had been trying to hammer its way into her mind for the past five minutes. A crank caller might telephone once or twice, but he wouldn't risk being apprehended after-hours in a building where high-profile barristers Edward Bock, Steven Press and Ernest Woodbury kept their offices. Not unless he was incredibly stupid. And Victoria didn't sense stupidity. She sensed deliberation, calculation and a third emotion she could only define as malice.

Her uncertain eyes probed the darkness one last time. Yes, it was malice she felt. It crawled over her skin like an army of ants. But what could she possibly have done to incite it?

Jamming her left hand into her jacket pocket, she considered the question, then glanced down as her fingers brushed up against a folded piece of paper. Withdrawing them, she opened it—and felt the blood drain from her cheeks. With a momentary sense of horror, she read the words taped there in letters cut from magazine and newspaper headlines.

Scotland Yard can't help you.
Even the Rag Man can't protect you from me.
I'm out here, Victoria.
I'm waiting....
I'm watching....

"YOU SENT SOMEONE up the river you shouldn't have," her father said with a shrug. He was a grizzled man of sixty-four, spry and patchwork, a colorful, lovable character whom Victoria's legal friends dubiously likened to Eliza Dolittle's father.

She ignored those so-called friends. Alfred Summers wore a cap and a baggy wool jacket, suspenders he called braces and work boots with holes in the soles. He was currently arranging vegetables on his cart. Ever the crafty merchant, he instinctively placed the best produce on top.

"You send people off enough times, lass, and some of 'em'll come back for you. Bound to happen."

Perched on an empty barrow in her torn and faded jeans, her battered leather boots and the World War II army jacket Prudie had given her on her eighteenth birthday, Victoria sorted celery bunches. "I'm a solicitor for the defense, now, Da," she reminded, snapping off the wilted ends and tossing them to his collie.

He wrinkled his nose. "What's that mean?"

"It means," she replied prosaically, "that I don't send people off anymore. I try to keep them from going."

"Maybe you didn't try hard enough."

"Huh." She broke off half a stalk, holding it out for the keen-eyed dog. "In that case, anyone whose defense I messed up would still be serving time. Besides, Bock's never let me handle anything really big.''

"Yet," her father finished for her. She caught the twinkle in his eyes but refused to laugh.

"Know-it-all," she retorted. "This celery's awfully ratty, Da. You should have a chat with Mr. Bock. He adores lawsuits, even ratty veggie suits. Winning is a point of pride with him. He's a snooty old stick-in-the mud.''

"About law or bad celery?''

"Both.''

"Sounds like a proper gentleman.''

"More like a two-faced twit, actually.''

Snorting, her father dumped onions into one of the bins. "So why do you stay on if Bock's a git and you never get the big cases?''

"Because the head of almost every law firm I know in London is a git. They all hoard the big cases. Except Mr. Woodbury. We've gotten way off topic, though, Da. I want to know what you think of this note.''

"What can I say? Someone's trying to scare you.''

"It's working." She hopped from the wagon, wiping her hands on the backside of her jeans. "Morning, Mrs. Grundy,'' she said to a woman passing by with a cart of breadstuffs.

"Morning to you, lass. We don't see you hereabouts very often.''

"She works on Bouverie Street now." Alfred pronounced the street name with an equal measure of pride and disdain. "Near the Temple.''

"Posh." Setting down her cart, Mrs. Grundy thrust a large tea cake at Victoria.

"Oh, no, really, Mrs. Grundy, I couldn't— Thank you. Uh, tell me, do you know anyone called the Rag Man? Da thinks he's heard the name, but he can't place it.''

The old woman screwed up her face. "Rag Man. Sounds familiar. Lives down Stepney way, I think. Don't get down there much meself. The local peelers might know.''

"That's what Da figured. I'll ask them. Thanks, Mrs. Grundy—for the bun, too.''

"Always welcome." She started off in her slow but sure fashion. "Don't be a stranger, missy. Lot of big mouths on Bouverie Street, but most with hearts no bigger than pebbles."

Victoria nodded politely, struggling not to choke on a crumb that had lodged itself in her throat.

Wordlessly and without lifting his head, her father passed her his old navy canteen. Victoria took a grateful sip, then choked. "There's vodka in this lime juice, Da."

"I ran out of—"

"Rum, I know."

"You live how you like, lass, and I'll live how I like. A wee nip now and then never hurt anyone. No lectures. As for that note of yours, Mrs. Grundy's right. Go to the Stepney peelers if you're curious about the Rag Man. Meself, I'd be more curious to know who wrote the thing. Your Mr. Bock got anything to say on that score?"

"Nope. But Mr. Woodbury does, and he's right. Everything about my note is too common and readily available—the paper, the cutout letters, even the tape, all drugstore stuff. And the phone calls are even less concrete, since I'm the only one who heard them. Until I'm attacked, I'm not in official danger."

"Sounds like the law and all. Do the cauliflower for me, will you, lass? And stop sneaking bits of bun to the dog. She's had her breakfast."

Victoria abandoned discretion and simply gave the dog the bun. Her father saw entirely too much, whether he said so or not.

He was proud of her accomplishments—she didn't doubt that for a minute—but the life that went with it, no, that he didn't like. Nor did he understand why she'd chosen it.

But that was irrelevant right now. She had a far more pressing problem—and only one direction, it seemed, in which to turn.

"The Rag Man." She tested the odd name on her tongue. "Why put something like that in a threatening note? The name does have a familiar ring to it, but I'm positive I don't know any Rag Man."

"The person after you might," her father said shrewdly. "I've bumped into a note writer or two in my time. Not a wholesome lot overall. Sometimes they're harmless, but it only takes one who's twisted in the head and you got yourself a whole lot of trouble."

Victoria heaped cauliflower on the growing mound. "What have I got, Da?" she asked softly. "Tell me what you think—the truth."

His weathered hands shook slightly as he picked up the note she'd brought. "I think," he replied in a voice she seldom heard him use, "that this one's as twisted as they come. My old senses say you got trouble, lass, serious trouble."

VICTORIA HAD an excellent view of Tower Bridge from her fourth-floor flat off Tower Bridge Road. She had deep, comfortable sofas, oil paintings on the papered walls, an antique coffee table and a computer she seldom used. Her wardrobe ran the gamut from Catherine Walker and Ralph Lauren to the faded jeans and T-shirts she wore whenever she worked her father's cart. In short, she had everything she needed, except for—and only due in part to the recent threats she'd received—that elusive thing called peace of mind.

It was late when she returned from Brixton Market, dark but clear and warm, muggy for London in May. She dropped her leather backpack on the floor by the door and headed automatically for the answering machine. No flashing red meant no messages. So much for being in demand.

Well, she wouldn't be, would she? she thought impatiently. She couldn't make up her mind what she wanted, not only from life—although she thought she'd figured that out years ago—but also from the people she might have called friends. She moved in legal circles these days, yet whenever she attended a related social function, she invariably found herself wishing she were in a Lambeth pub instead. It made no sense.

With a grunt, she flopped into the nearest chair, undid her ponytail and shook out her near-black hair until it fell in a mass of loose waves and curls about her shoulders. She didn't need a mirror to know that she looked like a blue-eyed Gypsy. Her mother had actually considered calling her Gypsy Blue. Thankfully her father's saner will had prevailed. "Victoria" might not be unique, but it was better than "Gypsy," especially when your goal in life was to become a lawyer.

"Yeah, right," she murmured to her Yorkshire terrier, Rosie, who was jingling into the living room. "A lawyer with a psychopathic note-writer on her case." Her normally smooth brow furrowed. "I wonder if I did screw up, Rosie. Maybe when I worked for the crown attorney's office."

Rosie yipped twice, but only because the phone was ringing.

Victoria's instincts kicked in automatically. She made no move toward the table, just watched in silence and waited. The answering machine cut in on the fourth ring.

At first she thought the caller had hung up. But then the same raspy whisper she'd heard on two previous occasions greeted her. It started with a chuckle that sent icy chills across her skin and had Rosie hopping fearfully into her lap. The dog's cold nose on Victoria's arm jolted almost as badly as the cleverly disguised voice when it whispered, "I know you're there, Victoria. I know because I watched you today, just as I watched you last night in Talbot House. I saw you looking for me. I saw you read my note. The Rag Man can't help you, Victoria."

Another chuckle...another twist of fear deep in her stomach.

"Maybe he wouldn't help you anyway. You're going to die, Victoria Summers. Count the hours until justice is served. Until you are as dead as your former employer—and the one whose murderer you helped to set free."

Oliver Twist...

The Dickens title sprang to mind long before Victoria located the building out of which the Rag Man worked. He was a private investigator these days, but he'd worked for Scotland Yard ten years ago. Undercover, Sergeant Robert Peacock of the Stepney Precinct had informed her. The Rag Man was in reality one David Alun Torbel.

Now, that name Victoria did recognize, although it had taken several minutes and more than one prompt from Sergeant Peacock and his superior, Inspector Oliver Fox, for her to place it.

Her former and recently deceased employer, Crown Attorney Lord Hugo Hobday, had been in charge of a case involving Torbel and another man whose name she couldn't recall.

"The Robbie Hollyburn murder trial," Inspector Fox had reminded her. He was a tall man, not as ramrod straight as Sergeant Peacock, but formal and undeniably authoritative, despite the fact that he was at least fifteen years Peacock's junior.

"I recall the case," Sergeant Peacock put in. He had big brown eyes, graying brown hair, narrow features and a neat little David Niven mustache. On his jaw was a small, kidney-shaped birthmark. When he spoke, he kept his hands firmly clasped behind his back. "Young Robbie Hollyburn was knifed in the back on the docks two years ago." He surveyed her with open skepticism. "You say you worked on that case, miss?"

Victoria dismissed the question. She'd run into similar attitudes throughout her career. No point trying to teach an old dog much of anything, especially a pompous old dog. "I worked behind the scenes," she told them. "Lord Hobday and his assistant worked the courtroom. Torbel and the other man—"

"Lenny Street," Sergeant Peacock supplied with a small smile of contrition. "He was one of Torbel's men back then."

"They were charged with second-degree murder." She frowned. "As I recall, Lord Hobday didn't think the evidence warranted the charge. He got it reduced to manslaughter. I did the paperwork. Street was sentenced to two years."

"He was released three weeks ago," Inspector Fox confirmed. "Torbel's detective's license was suspended indefinitely, but of course he got it back in short order."

A young woman in uniform with tightly coiled red hair, pale features and grimly set lips passed behind the inspector carrying a clipboard. Victoria glanced at her but addressed her question to Sergeant Peacock. "I know the victim's grandfather was Augustus Hollyburn. I saw him in court before he retired. He was a well-respected judge. Tough but fair, Lord Hobday used to say. I heard he didn't take the crown's decision well at all."

"Yes, that's fine, you can go, Clover," Inspector Fox said loudly to the woman. He cleared his throat. "Judge Hollyburn wanted first-degree murder. Impossible under the circumstances, but understandable considering his relationship to the victim. At any rate, you wanted to know about the Rag Man. We've told you all we can. His name is high profile hereabouts—the man himself is not. Would you recognize Torbel if you saw him?"

Victoria thought back. "We never met."

"In that case," Sergeant Peacock said stiffly, "you'd best be on your guard."

Victoria would have pressed the matter, but both men had seemed so uncomfortable all of a sudden that she decided it might be simpler to discover the truth about the Rag Man for herself. She wasn't an impeccable judge of character, but she noticed details. Not on the level of Sherlock Holmes, but sufficiently well to recognize that the female officer whom Inspector Fox had called Clover had been the source of the men's discomfort.

All thoughts of the Stepney police, however, flew from Victoria's mind the moment she entered what Sergeant Peacock had termed "the Rag Man's domain."

The entire neighborhood could have been plucked out of a Charles Dickens novel. Old-fashioned shops huddled along the narrow Stepney streets, shabby structures for the most part, but authentic down to their beetle-browed roofs and moldering foundations. There was the usual assortment of establishments—a butcher shop, a bakery, a pharmacy, a pub called Gooseberries and a bookstore with heaped bargain bins on the sidewalk.

Victoria longed to explore the entire street, but she settled for a glimpse, partly because she wanted to get this meeting over with and partly because she was hot. The temperature had climbed to an uncustomary eighty-three degrees with a humidity level high enough to turn her usually wavy hair into a riot of long dark curls.

She should have put it up, she thought, pushing damp strands from her forehead. She also should have worn cooler clothes. Her sage-colored linen skirt suit and matching pumps didn't fit either the unseasonal temperature or the area.

But she'd had to talk to two sets of police that day, one near her apartment about the phone message she'd received last night, and the second here in Stepney. Not that professional clothing had made a speck of difference in the first instance. Her caller's voice was disguised, the threat considered so much bluster until accompanied by a criminal act.

That was the legal system for you, Victoria reflected with mild cynicism and a deeper shiver of apprehension. All for the perpetrator, nothing for the victim. She'd been a lawyer long enough to understand if not accept that unpleasant truth.

People stared as she cut across the crowded street toward the cluttered side road where the Rag Man's agency sat. Slyly, but they followed her every move.

Aware of the interest she'd aroused, Victoria left the shops behind and started down one of the less populated side streets—assuming you could call the collection of rough, tippy cobbles a street.

"A horse could sprain all four ankles in these potholes," she muttered, picking her way carefully over the broken stones.

Perspiration slid down her back, so she slipped off her jacket. Pulling her black silk tank top away from her midsection, she stared at the collection of old buildings around her. Some were constructed of wood and stone; all were smeared with great patches of mortar. They were attached mostly, like row houses with absolutely no uniformity. Tall, narrow structures adjoined long, squat ones. The stone-and-mortar staircases appeared solid enough but tilted precariously to the side and often had the added detriment of no handrails.

Checking the address Sergeant Peacock had written down, she shaded her eyes and regarded the building directly across the street. It had *Little Dorrit* written all over it. Despite her reasons for coming here, Victoria allowed a smile of delight to curve her lips. Nothing like this existed in her great-aunt Prudie's Florida bayou.

Shoulders squared, she took a deep breath and started toward the collection of brick, stone and ancient timber. Better to plunge in than stand around contemplating. That wouldn't accomplish a thing.

There were more people on foot than in vehicles down here. Victoria noted the ones that scurried rather than walked and tightened her grip on her purse. She heard babies crying, children shouting and men and women plying their wares in a nearby lane. She thought briefly of her father, then blocked the memory. A chat with the Rag Man, that was her goal, not to prowl through an open market.

A pawnshop stood next the Rag Man's agency. Both buildings had rough plaques swinging from the eaves, but only the pawnshop owner watched her mount the stairs to his neighbor's door.

No sign said Enter. However, in Victoria's experience, you didn't knock on business doors unless they were run out of private homes. With a display of confidence she didn't feel, she reached for the handle.

"Oy! What you about, then?"

Victoria's heart leapt into her throat. The speaker was so close behind her, she could almost feel his breath on her neck.

Controlling her reaction, she turned. "I'm—" Oh, God, he was only a kid, seventeen at most, with squarish features and straight dark hair that hung in his eyes. She relaxed. "I'm looking for the Rag Man. I was told I'd find him here."

The boy's eyes narrowed. His straight, prominent brow gave him a vaguely Neanderthal look, but at least he wasn't carrying a weapon. "Does he know you, then?"

"I doubt it."

"D'you know him?"

Victoria didn't flinch. "No. Is he here?"

"Could be." He surveyed her with an insolence that had one of Victoria's fine eyebrows arching in a mild challenge. His lack of response rankled but didn't daunt her.

"Is this a detective agency or not?" she asked when his gaze continued to rake her.

"We take cases," he replied in an offhanded tone.

He looked too young to be an investigator. On the other hand, this so-called child possessed what her mother would term old eyes. Seventeen in literal years likely translated to thirty-seven in experience.

After another candid appraisal, the boy reached around and pushed the door inward. "Come on, then," he said, and led her in.

She had expected a fairly mundane scene—the usual lobby with potted plants, a reception desk, a filing cabinet and someone halfway respectable to greet potential clients. She encountered none of those things. This was a huge old English storehouse, littered with stacks of papers, overflowing barrels and unsealed cartons. Some of the barrels contained fruits and vegetables, others had books with threadbare bindings, still others held patchwork bundles of cloth. Fagin would have loved it. Victoria wasn't sure how she felt; she merely tried to take it in.

A black cat lounged beside the telephone, which was perched precariously atop a stack of yellowed directories. Exotic green-and-purple ferns grew in little clay pots shoved into obscure wall niches. A variety of ancient tools hung on hemp ropes from timber beams, instruments for cutting, possibly eavesdropping and long-distance viewing. There were actually two desks positioned at right angles to each other with empty chairs wheeled haphazardly out in front of them.

Victoria counted four work areas, partly screened off: the central one where she stood, which might loosely pass for a reception area, and three others—one to the left, one to the right and one directly ahead. These so-called offices seemed in much the same state as the main area, cluttered and disorganized. Old movie posters nailed to the redbrick walls added color to an already vivid jumble. *Frankenstein*—the latest version—*Rob Roy,* the entire Basil Rathbone collection of Sherlock Holmes, Miss Marple and, of course, *Oliver.* Evidently someone's pride and joy, the posters had been mounted, framed and hung with an aesthetic eye. Victoria felt alternately charmed and disconcerted. Who was this enigmatic Rag Man?

Bodies emerged from dark patches like curious rats. None of them resembled her associates on Bouverie Street, and all wore expressions similar to that of the boy beside her. Suspicion bordering on open mistrust.

One of them, a tall, strapping man with longish brown hair, strong, vaguely poetic features and gentle hazel eyes strode past his cohorts and over to her. "Who's this, Oswyn?" he asked. Deep voice, Irish-English accent, pleasant manner.

Victoria held out her hand. "My name's Victoria Summers. I've come to see the Rag Man."

The man's clasp was firm. "Keiran McLehr. Do you have business with Torbel, Ms. Summers?"

"Possibly."

"I'm his partner. Can you talk to me?"

"I'd rather talk to him."

"Is it personal, then?"

"It's difficult to explain, Mr. McLehr. Is he here?"

For an answer, Keiran nodded at the boy. "Fetch him down, Oswyn." His gaze, faintly amused, returned to Victoria's face. "Tell him he's wanted by the law."

Chapter Two

The law . . . !

How could he know—or did he? Victoria regarded him through veiled eyes. "I'm not a cop, Mr. McLehr."

He smiled. " 'Keiran', and close enough. You're a solicitor."

"But how do you—?"

"He recognizes the name, Ms. Summers."

It wasn't Keiran who spoke this time, but a man on the stairwell straight ahead. Victoria hadn't noticed him. The slant of afternoon shadows made him visible only as a pair of black jeans, boots and a wiry right forearm that looked at once slender and deceptively strong.

She caught a flash of red as he began to descend. His tread was slow and measured, designed, she felt certain, to intimidate.

But Victoria had seen live alligators in Prudie's bayou. She had also come up against several of her da's crusty East End friends. She was not easily intimidated. On those rare occasions when she was, she did her level best not to let it show.

She watched in increasingly fascinated silence as the Rag Man traded shadow for dusty light. He wasn't as tall as Keiran, six feet at most, nor was he as strapping. His was a leaner, more sinewy build, feline to Keiran's canine, she decided. His hair was brown, on the long side, thick and deeply curling. She would have called those curls a mop except the word didn't fit this man somehow.

Aware of a tingling sensation on her skin, she shifted position. She couldn't be reacting to him; it wasn't possible. She tried for a more objective view.

There was nothing disheveled about the man. He wore a red jersey with the three upper buttons undone and the sleeves pushed up. His black jeans were faded but untorn, and his boots spoke both of good workmanship and hard wear.

Yet she knew it was the Rag Man's face that had truly captivated her, his intense blue-green eyes, his prominent cheekbones, his well-shaped mouth, the rough stubble on his chin and upper lip and his strong nose. But even more than his arresting features, she noted the scar, a livid slash that started just above his right brow and ran along the curve of his cheekbone almost to his ear.

Pressing a hand to her fluttering stomach, she forced herself not to stare. How on earth, she wondered, fighting an odd spate of breathlessness, had he managed to avoid losing his eye?

He continued to descend, his gaze steady and so penetrating that she felt as though he were touching her physically. A light shiver chased itself across her heated skin. No one spoke, not the Rag Man, not Keiran or Oswyn, not any of the ten or more men and women now lounging about.

"Why have you come here, Ms. Summers?" Torbel broke the silence to inquire.

Before he reached the bottom of the stairs, he walked out onto a stack of wooden crates and, crouching, appraised her far more thoroughly than Oswyn had done.

His wrists were beautiful, she noted, but they wouldn't look amiss with shackles around them. She wondered distantly how his fingers would look curled around her own wrists....

Collecting her composure, Victoria replied firmly, "If you're Torbel, I want to talk to you."

One dark brow went up. "You don't recognize me?"

"Not your face. But I knew your name when I heard it." Meeting his stare with difficulty, she added a forthright "I worked under Lord Hobday on the Robbie Hollyburn murder trial. I realize that you might resent me—"

"I don't resent people, Ms. Summers. Why have you come here?"

Obviously privacy was out of the question. Just as obviously Torbel understood that she could be mulish when she wanted to be, although it was no easy feat when her mind kept conjuring up images of him moving in on her like the predator he undoubtedly was.

A full thirty seconds passed before he made a subtle gesture with his head. As if by magic, the unsavory group of observers, presumably people who worked for him in one capacity or another, dissolved into the shadows.

He regarded her across the large room. "Unless you want to shout and defeat your own purpose, you might try coming a little closer."

With a trace of dry humor, Keiran murmured, "He only bites people his own size and sex. You'll be safe enough."

Victoria had serious doubts on that score, but she approached the Rag Man anyway. Not surprisingly he kept his advantage, staring down at her from the stack of crates.

Victoria forced herself to confront his unwavering gaze. She'd never encountered such disturbing eyes before. Lord Hobday's professional glare would have paled by comparison to this man's.

Reaching into her purse, she withdrew the note she'd received Friday night and handed it up. "I was hoping," she said in her most precise legal tone, "that you might have an idea about the person who wrote this."

The Rag Man's gaze lingered on her face, then switched to the paper. A slight frown furrowed his brow as he read.

"Problem?" Keiran inquired.

Victoria thought he'd left. She hadn't seen him leaning against a stone pillar.

He accepted the note Torbel tossed him, scanning it swiftly. " 'Even the Rag Man can't protect you from me.' What's this sh—?" He glanced at Victoria, then up at Torbel. "Who'd write a piece of rubbish like this?"

"A crank," Torbel replied with a shrug.

Victoria's hackles rose. "Not a crank," she countered. "He's threatened me three times ón the telephone. I taped one of the calls."

"This is a matter for the police, Ms. Summers," Torbel said flatly. "I don't run a protection agency."

English heavily tinged with Irish—she placed the accent immediately. "Your name's been mentioned twice, Mr. Torbel. That might not mean anything to you, but it does to me, particularly as I'm the one against whom these threats are being directed."

"You think there's a connection between your threats and me?"

"They're not *my* threats, and yes, I do. So does whoever's behind them."

"The Robbie Hollyburn trial ended two years ago. It's a very loose connection at this point."

He really did have beautiful wrists, Victoria observed. If such things could be considered sexy, then he had sexy ones. Sexy hands, too. And a nice mouth—except for the words that came out of it and the dismissing tone he used to utter them. He appeared to have no interest in the note or in her.

Tilting her head back made her neck muscles cramp, but she wouldn't talk to him unless she could look him straight in the eye. "Lenny Street was released from prison recently," she said. "That could be significant."

Through hooded eyes, he studied her, as if she were some new and strange specimen. "If the note is linked to the Robbie Hollyburn trial, why threaten a secondary player like you? Why not someone closer to the case?"

Victoria refused to be goaded. It was what he wanted, and she'd be damned if she would give him the satisfaction. "Possibly," she retorted, "because Lord Hobday passed away six months ago in Essex. Quietly, out of the public eye—and out of the press. As for his one-time assistant, Aaron Bolt quit law sixteen months ago after getting into some legal trouble. His stepfather's big in shipping. He sent Aaron off to Turkey. No one's heard from him since."

"Aye, so you win by default," a large man with a Scottish accent concluded. He had shorn black hair and a big belly that hung over his waistband. Victoria had spotted him earlier. He'd left with the others. She hadn't seen him return.

"I consider it a loss myself," she murmured, her eyes on the Rag Man. "I also think these threats are bona fide."

The Scotsman made a doubtful sound in his throat, then grunted at Torbel. "Call for you, from the pub."

"Deal with it, Ron."

The big Scotsman turned, muttering under his breath. Torbel motioned at Keiran, who shrugged and followed the man called Ron toward the phone.

Which left Victoria alone with the Rag Man for the first—and she sincerely hoped last—time.

Before she realized what he was doing, Torbel rose, hopping from the crates in a single, agile bound. In two-inch heels, Victoria was almost as tall as him. Funny, she didn't feel it. Must be his presence that loomed larger than life, because the man himself certainly didn't.

It intrigued her that his gaze never wavered. She felt heat and dust swirling around them as he regarded her at disturbingly close range. "You're convinced the note writer wants to harm you, is that right?"

"I can't imagine he'd be threatening me for the good of his health, Mr. Torbel."

"Just 'Torbel,' and I've known a few cranks in my life. They're a gutless lot for the most part. What makes you think yours is the genuine article?"

"Because he's been following me. He wanted me to come to you."

"Yes, I sensed as much."

Not quite sarcastic but close. "You make talking difficult, Torbel. I want to find out who this person is. I think it's a man, but I could be wrong. You're a private detective—I'm a prospective client. Don't you think between those two things we might find some common ground?"

He lowered his lashes slightly. "So you came here to hire me—to expose the person after you."

Although that wasn't exactly what Victoria had had in mind, it did seem the most viable solution. Not wise, considering the man she'd be dealing with, but if he could get the job done, then the result would be worth the risk.

As if reading her thoughts, the Rag Man advanced on her. Victoria recognized the tactic, designed to unnerve her, and held her ground. It wasn't an easy task. Torbel was a frighteningly sensual man, more male than she'd ever dealt with. And all the scar did was heighten the mystery that surrounded him.

"I want this person caught," she said. He continued to advance, so she added a vexed "I also don't appreciate feeling trapped."

He understood. A small smile touched the corners of his mouth. "You're a fighter, then."

"No more than most people, but I do it when I have to." She sent him a challenging look. "Will you help me, Torbel? It could prove as beneficial to you as to me."

"Cranks don't worry me, Ms. Summers."

She was tempted to punch him. "My name's Victoria, and this is no crank. You say you've dealt with note writers in your time. Well, so have I, and in a not very pleasant legal capacity. I don't sense a cry for help here. This feels like revenge, not the threat of it but the act itself."

"Because of Robbie Hollyburn."

"We have no other common bond, do we?"

"None."

Damn him, he closed in like a cat, eyes focused, stride smooth and unerring. He halted at last, but not until he'd drawn to within two feet of her.

His eyes glinted with a light she couldn't read. "If I do agree to help you, lady, it'll be on my terms, not yours."

Irritated, Victoria retorted, "Back off, Torbel. I'll be paying the bill. You have no right—"

"My terms," he repeated flatly, "or no deal."

She opened her mouth to protest, then closed it as a saner instinct prevailed. She wasn't wrong about this, but neither was she stupid. Pride was an admirable trait; foolish stubbornness could cost her her life.

Voice low, she said, "What terms?"

He looked neither smug nor triumphant. In fact, his expression didn't alter in the slightest. "You stay down here."

"In Stepney?"

He must have mistaken her shock for revulsion because he said dryly, "It isn't the underside of hell, you know."

"I didn't—"

"You can share with Zoe. She has a flat above Gooseberries."

"Who's—"

"She works here. She also knows a thing or two about stalkers."

"But I'm not—"

"Being stalked?" The Rag Man's eyes glittered unnervingly. "What would you call him, then, Victoria? Someone who says he's out there watching and waiting."

Her temper flared, partly because of what he'd said and because of what he wouldn't allow her to say. "Would you mind letting me finish a sentence?" she demanded. "I've never been stalked before. It isn't a comforting thought. Now, on top of that, you want me to move in with a woman I've never met. What does Zoe do here? Is she one of your agents?"

Again that disturbing glint in his eyes, perhaps humor, but she couldn't be sure. "She is now."

Implying that she hadn't always been. Victoria voiced the expected question. "What did she do before that?"

Torbel's lips definitely quirked this time. "She was a cat burglar. Her full name is Zoe Hollyburn."

"YOU'RE A BASTARD, Torbel," Keiran remarked without rancor. "What did you expect her to do, faint or fly away?"

"Neither." Torbel headed for the alley, followed by his lanky partner. "She's not a fainter, that one. And she's not about to leave without one hell of a fight."

He stepped into the lane, welcoming the blast of hot, muggy air that wafted over him. Sunlight filtered through a vast array of chimneys, dappling the cobbles, a stray Dalmatian and his own small black cat, who was currently draped across the dog's back.

The Rag Man's alley, he reflected, half-amused as he surveyed his surroundings. That's what they called this place. The child of a charity worker who herself had been a charity case in her middle years. "Son of the rag lady," they'd called him in Dublin. They'd called him a few other things, too, he mused, his thoughts darkening. It was funny how labels stuck—and how feelings of rancor could flatly refuse to die....

Squinting, he located the sun. Four o'clock or thereabouts. He had a case to clear up later, but little else on his plate. He could have offered to accompany Victoria back to her flat to collect her belongings. Could have but hadn't been in the proper frame of mind to do so.

Behind him, Keiran chuckled. "Why didn't you tell Victoria about Zoe?"

Torbel slanted him a knowing look. "I told her enough. She'll figure out the rest on her own. She had a chat with Fox and Peacock earlier. Maybe she talked to Constable Clover Hollyburn, as well."

"Zoe's sister isn't the problem, Torbel. You're asking a woman of substance to live with a former cat burglar, one whose grandfather just happens to be Augustus Hollyburn and whose younger brother was the person you and Lenny were accused of murdering. I don't think you told her enough."

"She's bright and, I suspect, reasonably adaptable. She'll tough it out."

"Do you think there's anything to that note of hers?"

"Could be." Nudging open one of the cellar windows with his boot, Torbel let the cat inside. "I'll have to— Oh, hell. It's Street."

"Where? Ah..."

His stance deceptively relaxed, the Rag Man waited for the man he'd spotted down the alley to approach. Lenny Street, released from prison after two years and now full of bluster, sauntered toward him. Even at a distance, Torbel could see that he'd deteriorated badly in confinement.

"Afternoon, Torbel—Keiran. Were you hoping I'd stay away?"

"You've been out for three weeks, Lenny," Torbel replied calmly. "You haven't been around yet. Why now?"

Lenny Street's attitude had altered drastically. Grim before, he was positively surly now. He was a tall, spare man with long arms and legs, coarse black hair, a mottled growth of black whiskers, a beak for a nose and eyes that could pass for bits of flint. Three of his front teeth were chipped—and he smelled like a brewery.

"I missed me old friends, of course," he answered with an unconvincing swagger.

He kept his distance, Torbel noticed with a glimmer of disgust.

"I hear there's a pretty lady been asking about the Rag Man," Lenny went on, propping a thin shoulder up against the storehouse wall. "Word is she looks like a Gypsy, tall, dark haired and blue eyed. Polished, too, I'm told."

"By whom?" Keiran questioned.

Lenny shrugged an indolent—or more likely an insolent—shoulder. "It's all over the street. I heard she's cozy with the cops."

"Thanks for the warning," Torbel replied with a lack of inflection that was his trademark. If people didn't know what you were thinking, you might just stay a jump ahead of them. The lesson had come hard in his youth, but he'd learned it well ever since.

A muscle in Lenny's jaw twitched, though he made no threatening moves. Torbel wondered if he'd be as reticent if Keiran weren't about. Keeping his eyes on Street, he said to his partner. "See how Victoria's making out with Zoe, will you?"

Keiran glanced from Torbel to Street and back again. "You want me to go with her to fetch her things?"

Torbel pictured Victoria's wild dark hair, her vivid blue eyes and her long-limbed body. She had a light tan, slender curves, a tongue to match his Welsh-Irish grandmother's and an obstinate nature, which he simultaneously admired and avoided like the plague. Too bad, he reflected, that she had a brain to go with all that beauty. He'd have had no trouble dismissing an air-head.

So, no, he didn't want Keiran to go and fetch her things, but he'd let him do it anyway. Then he'd sit down and try to convince himself that it really had been necessary to insist she take up residence here.

He nodded at Keiran but continued to stare at Lenny, who had the same expression on his face that he'd worn all through the trial. He believed Torbel had murdered Robbie Hollyburn. Well, he certainly wasn't alone in that belief.

"You should have been inside with me, Torbel," Lenny said when Keiran was gone. "It's as close to hell as you can get."

"I know what prison's like, Lenny. Make your point."

Torbel suspected it wasn't his words so much as his scar, coupled with his reputation before, during and after his years at Scotland Yard, that had the man edging backward. He would kill; he would, he could, and he had. For all that Lenny didn't know, that much he understood clearly.

"No, point, Torbel," he mumbled, his Cockney accent ripe. "Just came to see the pretty lady lawyer is all. Least I can do, considering she's one of them what sent me up."

"You know about her, then."

"I know about all of them. Hobday, Bolt and her. The first two are dead."

Torbel's eyes narrowed. "Bolt, too? Where'd you hear that?"

"In the hole. You can learn a lot by asking the right people the right questions."

"Why were you asking about the crown attorney's office?"

Safely out of range, Lenny gave his chin a belligerent thrust. "Curiosity. I stuck a knife in their throats every night I spent there."

His expression level, Torbel started forward. "Did you also stick a note in Victoria's pocket on Friday night?"

Lenny had shifty eyes, and these days a devious brain to match. "Wouldn't be in my best interest to say so if I did, now would it? Anyway, you're a fine one to be acting high and mighty. No one really knows what you're about, do they? Not the cops, not the cons, not even those that work for you. I never figured you out, Torbel, but you're no bloody saint, that's for sure.''

Torbel felt his temper rising, a dangerous sign. "Who wrote the note, Street?"

"Maybe I don't know. Maybe I do and I just don't want to say."

He slowed his retreat for that taunt. Torbel caught it and pounced with a swiftness that left Lenny gasping. His fingers clawed at the hand that was suddenly wrapped like an iron band around his throat.

"Don't..." he choked, but Torbel ignored him. With a mighty thrust, he slammed Lenny against the brick wall of the storehouse and pinned him there. Eyes glittering, he moved forward until less than six inches separated their faces. "If you're behind the note, Street, I'll find out about it. And when I do, you'll answer to me. You got that, boyo?"

Lenny made a sound like a strangled yes, and Torbel stepped away. He released the man slowly, aware that beneath his timorous surface Lenny Street was seething. He might also have written that note; a show of compliance meant nothing from a man who'd sunk to the level of a sewer rat.

With a sideways motion of his head, Torbel said, "Get out of here, Lenny. And don't go spreading tales if you want to live in peace."

Rubbing his sore throat, Lenny stalked wordlessly away. He glowered at Torbel from the corner but kept his mouth firmly shut. Head lowered, he disappeared into the late-afternoon shadows.

That might not have been a smart thing to do, Torbel reflected, shaking out the tense fingers of his right hand. Street had played cons before with fair success, using scams of his own invention on people who should have been bright enough to spot the lie. He'd have to make sure that Lenny was closely watched.

Torbel closed his eyes. He had a job to finish. He also had a beautiful female attorney somewhere in the vicinity who likely resented him as much as Lenny Street did.

Life was hell, he concluded, turning for the rear door. The last thing he needed was another complication. God help him, though, he had one. Her name was Victoria Summers—and chances were good that, one way or another, she'd be the death of him.

Twinkle, twinkle, pretty star,
You know who and what you are,
Up above the law so high,
Ruby knife points in the sky.
Ruby red, like blood when spilled,
The night that Robbie H. was killed.
Keep the twinkling star in sight,
Time now to put this wrong to right.
To those who long have lived the lie,
Time now for justice . . . Time to die!

Augustus Hollyburn's hands trembled as he read the note, or rather, the photocopy of *a* note, delivered to his home anonymously ten minutes ago. Every word burned itself into his brain. Revenge for Robbie's murder—that's what it sounded like, because that's what it was. Justice at last at the hands of a phantom.

The old man let out a long, shaky breath. He must telephone the police, of course. That was proper, and he was, after all, a high-court judge, possibly on the verge of a knighthood. Still, he could cheer in silence for the writer of this note. Too bad he had to turn the photocopy over to the authorities, but he daren't risk his knighthood over a scrap of evidence that would ultimately do no damage to anyone.

"Chivers." Flapping the paper at his watchful butler, he pointed at the telephone. "Bring me that, then find out if anyone saw who delivered this note."

The butler nodded, brought him the phone and departed. The old judge repeated the last two lines as he dialed:

To those who long have lived the lie,
Time now for justice . . . Time to die!''

A clipped voice answered on the first ring. "Stepney Precinct. Sergeant Faber. How may I help you?"
Taking a deep breath, Augustus Hollyburn began to speak.

Chapter Three

Zoe Hollyburn, former cat burglar, was Robbie's sister and Augustus's granddaughter. This had to be the twist to end all twists, Victoria decided as she accompanied her soon-to-be-roommate down a series of sooty back alleys to Gooseberries, a pub also owned by the Rag Man, which she had spotted en route to his agency.

Zoe, a tall woman with a mass of fire red hair as riotous as Victoria's, glanced doubtfully in her direction. "You don't look overly hardy, Vickie. You sure you're up to a flat over the pub?"

Victoria had been told numerous times that her features possessed the delicacy of a Renaissance statue. Height not-withstanding, people tended to underestimate her stamina—Zoe included, it appeared.

"I'll manage," she said politely. She followed that with a frank "You remind me of someone." And not Robbie, either, she thought, because she'd seen pictures of him during the trial. He had curly brown hair, big, puppy-dog brown eyes and narrow features. Zoe had striking blue-green eyes and freckles. She was pretty and surprisingly sophisticated, but far from narrow featured. She looked like...

"That woman at the precinct house," Victoria exclaimed suddenly. She laid a forestalling hand on Zoe's arm. "Inspector Fox called her Clover."

Zoe halted, glanced at the hand on her arm, then across at Victoria's suspicious face. "You get around, don't you? Clover's my sister, my twin, actually."

"Your twin sister's a cop and you're a cat burglar?" Victoria was stunned. "How did that happen?"

Zoe's laugh had the same melodious sound as her West London accent. "Don't kid yourself, Victoria. It happens more often than you think. My mother's cousin was a vicar, righteous down to the tips of his toes. My mother never set foot in a church after she married my father for fear she might burst into flames, or whatever other judgment God might see fit to lay upon her for her sins."

What could she say? Victoria's hand fell away. "I see."

"No, you don't, but then you didn't know Sophie." Zoe started walking again, picking her way over sprawled dogs and ducking under laden clotheslines. "She was a tramp, and I'm being kind. Not that you'll ever get Clover or old Goggy to admit it. They thought—well, let's just say they insisted she was pure as the driven snow. They weren't alone. Sophie was a consummate actress. And she knew the art of discretion."

Victoria dodged a low-hanging planter crammed with colorful snapdragons. "How do you know she wasn't?" An indelicate question, but straight talk was preferable to conversations couched in euphemisms. Victoria had inherited that belief from her da and Prudie. Her mother found such candor horrifying.

Evidently Zoe had no problem with bluntness, for she laughed again. "Because unlike other members of my family, I'm not an ostrich." She stopped before a small door and pushed. "They're always burying their heads for the sake of...I don't know what."

"Pride, maybe?" Victoria suggested.

Wedging her hip and shoulder hard against the plank door, Zoe made a gesture of possibility. "With Augustus, though, it's more a question of control. He refuses to acknowledge my existence, has done for years, but not until he'd tried everything in his power to dominate me. What he can't dominate, he simply hates and, trust me, that hatred is strong."

The door creaked open under protest. "Come on, then," she invited with a wicked grin, "if you're still determined." She pointed into the black void. "We have to climb, and it's a closed staircase. I hope you're not claustrophobic."

She was, actually, but since there seemed no way to avoid this, Victoria gritted her teeth and ducked under the low frame.

With the door shut and not so much as a thread of light to guide her, she almost panicked. Fortunately Zoe gave her no opportunity to do so. "Up," she ordered, and pushed her firmly forward. "It's only ten stairs. So what did you think of Torbel?"

Truthfully she was trying not to. Victoria counted steps. *Six, seven, eight...* "I thought he'd be older. He looks like he's had a hard life."

"You noticed the scar."

"Your grandfather and sister might be ostriches, but I'm not. How did he get it?"

"I don't know. We don't ask, and he wouldn't tell us if we did. A private man is our Torbel. He leads, we follow—it works. Simple as that."

Victoria doubted it was anywhere near that simple, but she let the subject slide in favor of giving the door she'd bumped into at the top of the stairs a determined shove.

It opened into a surprisingly broad hallway, poorly lit but complete with hand-woven rugs and a picture of the current monarch. Rough laughter and music that sounded a bit like drunk Herman's Hermits drifted upward from the pub.

"Surprised?" Zoe asked over her shoulder.

"A little," Victoria admitted. "I'm more surprised that you'd work for the Rag Man after all that's happened. I don't suppose you want to talk about that."

"Maybe later." Zoe led the way to the only other visible door. "Do you like Sherlock Holmes?"

The abrupt change of topic had Victoria mystified, but only until Zoe ushered her across the threshold. Then she understood.

The flat was Baker Street to a T, right down to the overflowing bookshelves, the rolltop desk and dining table, the deep, comfy chairs and the ugly fringe swag lamp near the window. The floor was badly scarred oak, strewn with area rugs. Movie posters adorning the paneled walls explained the similar collection in the Rag Man's storehouse. Plants, both hanging and potted, filled every available corner and ledge, and the open shades revealed an area of London rich in history and teeming with life. Teeming with street vendors, too, Victoria realized with rising delight.

Zoe joined her at the window. "You're not offended, I hope. They're just people making a living."

She might be a reformed cat burglar, but she was lousy at reading people. "I should go and get my things," Victoria said absently, her eyes devouring the market scene below. Her da would adore this.

"The commute's going to be a pain for you," Zoe said. "You sure you want to do this? I don't mean to push you out the door, but life's not cushy in the East End."

"I'll manage," Victoria countered evenly. She was getting heartily sick of people making assumptions based on her clothes and professional bearing—although to be fair, what else could they base their ideas on? They didn't know about her da or Prudie, or even her mother, who lived like a hippie yet maintained a bank balance few Gypsies could ever hope to boast.

Zoe must have misread her long silence, because she chuckled and, tossing her red hair, started for the small kitchen. "I can't imagine what Torbel was thinking. I'll make us a pot of tea, and you can tell me all about your note—and ask me again why, when he was convicted as an accessory to my brother's death, I would work at his agency. It'll take your mind off your surroundings."

Victoria swatted at her unbound hair with a faintly exasperated hand. While she thought she might come to like Zoe in time, she resented her current condescending attitude.

"Sugar?" Zoe called out. "Oh, hell, I've lost my watch."

Immediately contrite, Victoria uncurled the fingers of her right hand and regarded the ticking object in her palm. Prudie would be proud of her. Well, reproachful first, but proud after that.

Zoe poked her head out of the kitchen. "Have you seen it?"

Victoria hesitated, then let it slide to the carpet. She didn't have it in her to mock a possible new friend. "No," she lied straight-faced. "I'm afraid I haven't."

TORBEL DIDN'T TRUST HER. She could tell by the way he watched her all the way from Stepney to her flat near Tower Bridge.

He drove fast but well, and refused outright to let her bring her Toyota Celica back.

"There's nowhere safe to park it," he told her, halting his black Nissan Pathfinder near the curb.

Victoria undid her seat belt. "I'll take my chances, Torbel. I need my car. I can't afford taxis every day for God knows how long."

A warning rumble of thunder had her glancing at the blackened sky. Clouds had been massing over the dome of St. Paul's for the past two hours, ever since she'd arrived at Zoe's flat. Her new roommate had just finished locating her watch on the floor by the window when Oswyn had appeared with the news that Keiran was tied up and so Torbel would accompany her to her apartment.

It had sounded dangerously like a summons to Victoria; however, for the sake of peace and a swift resolution to her problem, she'd finished her tea and returned to the storehouse with Oswyn.

Rain began to fall in big, fat drops as she and Torbel started up the short walk to her flat, which was really the upper third of a quaint eighteenth-century townhouse.

"Cherry trees and Georgian architecture," Torbel remarked in disgust. "You Sloanies are all the same."

Victoria stopped. "I'm not a Sloanie. I'm an Amer—" At his elevated brow, she sighed. "American. It isn't the same thing."

"Mmm, I thought I detected a mixed accent." Reaching around her, he pushed the door open. "What part of America?"

"Florida mostly. And a little Connecticut." He slanted her an unfathomable look but offered no comment. Damn, but he was standing too close, and he was too sexy by far. Victoria's breath tightened in her chest as his forearm brushed her bare upper arm.

She controlled another sigh. You'd think she was a sex-starved adolescent the way her body reacted to him. If she planned to spend any time at all with this man, she would need to summon up her most rigorous self-control and wear it like a coat of mail.

It took her twenty minutes—most of them fumbling thanks to Torbel's ever-watchful gaze—to pack two suitcases and suspend her daily delivery of the *Times,* another ten to take Rosie to her neighbor downstairs and say goodbye. She heard deepening rumbles of thunder beyond the softly papered walls.

Rain fell in buckets now, streaming down the outer windows. Unfortunately the temperature and humidity remained suffocatingly high.

Torbel prowled like a panther. He reminded her strongly of a Celtic warrior. She didn't know why, since she'd never seen one, but the description just seemed to fit.

She managed to get out of her clothes in private, exchanging her skirt and silk top for a pair of cream-colored jeans, suede boots and a deep coral cotton tank top. None of it was especially new or expensive, so why, Victoria wondered, did Torbel's frown deepen when he turned from the living-room window and spied her? More mistrust—or something else? She opted not to dwell on the possibilities.

"Is that the lot?" He indicated the stylish luggage she'd hauled from the bedroom.

"Since you didn't tell me how long I'll be away, I thought it best to assume the worst." Her cool tone gave way to a more uncertain one. "Do you have any idea who it could be, Torbel?"

Hands in the pockets of his black jacket, he made a final survey of the room. "One or two. Nothing concrete."

"Lenny Street?"

"Maybe."

"That isn't very helpful." A trace of impatience crept in. "What about Zoe's twin sister or her grandfather?"

Torbel's chuckle was ironic. "I wouldn't pin my hopes on Goggy. For one thing, he's too old and arthritic."

"He could have hired a legman."

"He's up for a knighthood. He wouldn't allow even hatred to jeopardize his chances."

"I'd have thought that having a former cat burglar for a granddaughter might have done a fair bit of damage already."

Torbel reached for her bags. "Feels like bloody bricks in here," he muttered.

"I brought my weights."

He stared at her, frowning.

"For keeping in shape, Torbel." His eyes moved to her sleek arms. "I'm twenty-nine. Prudie says it's all downhill for muscle tone after twenty-five."

"Who's Prudie and what kind of bull has she been feeding you?"

"It isn't bull," Victoria shot back. "Prudie's my great-aunt on my da's side. She lives in Florida now, and she knows more about the workings of the human body than most doctors."

"Does she also know how much strain it takes to do in a back?" he inquired, exaggeratedly polite.

Victoria controlled her irritation, grabbing one of the cases and dragging it out the door. She'd never be able to work with this man. They'd be at each other's throats in no time.

On the other hand—she cast him a covert glance—being at each other's throats might be preferable to the alternative.

The house had no lift. It took them several hot, stuffy minutes to navigate the stairwell to the ground floor.

Victoria was soaked to the skin halfway to her car, which was parked ahead of his at the curb. Knowing he would try to dissuade her, she kept well ahead of him.

She was negotiating a soggy patch of grass when she caught a glimpse of something flying through the air. Her peripheral vision was good but not sharp enough to identify the airborne object. Not that it made much difference, since a moment later she was flying, as well.

The impact jarred, blurring her vision. From somewhere beneath her, she heard Torbel swear. The landing had knocked the breath from her lungs and most of the awareness from her brain. What on earth was going on?

One thing she knew—Torbel had tackled her. She was currently sprawled on top of him. His arms about her waist held her fast against his body even as he reversed their positions.

The object that had whizzed past must have triggered the action. Victoria made no attempt to struggle despite her instincts which cautioned that he was too close, and her senses were taking far too much notice of it.

"Torbel . . ." she whispered.

But he silenced her with a terse "Quiet." His intent gaze darted into and around the nearby park.

Heart racing, Victoria followed his probing eyes. She saw rain and neatly trimmed trees, grass and shadows.

"Are you all right?" he inquired at length. His eyes continued to comb the surrounding area.

"Fine." She did want up and away from him quite badly, though. Being this close made her skin tingle.

"Did you see anyone?" he asked.

"No. Can I get up now?" She began to squirm, pushing discreetly on the hands that continued to circle her waist.

He took one last look around. "Yeah. Whoever it was is gone."

Victoria held her breath while he helped her to her feet. Danger had an understandable appeal, but the concept of the predatory male had never fascinated her. Why now? She must be more frightened by the note writer than she cared to admit.

She watched his eyes move in a slow arc from street to park and back again. "What was that thing that flew past us?"

For an answer, he crouched, hunting absently through a sodden bush. Eyes still fixed on the park, he extracted a weapon that could have come straight out of the Middle Ages.

Victoria stared at the length of sturdy wood with its lethally spiked head. "That's a flail, isn't it?"

"Mace." Curling his fingers about her wet upper arm, he nudged her toward his Pathfinder. "No more arguments. It missed you by less than a foot."

Victoria's eyes fastened themselves in morbid curiosity on the ancient weapon. "He wants me dead," she whispered, unbelieving.

"I think," Torbel said grimly, "he wants a little more than that."

THE STOREHOUSE WAS a veritable rabbit warren of short stairwells, low ceilings and oddly shaped rooms. One of those rooms, half a flight up from the ground, contained a fridge, a stove and a collection of mismatched cupboards. Keiran called it a kitchen; Victoria called it a page out of a Grimm's fairy tale, Hansel and Gretel to be precise.

Despite the stifling heat and a cup of coffee spiked with brandy that the Scotsman Ron had concocted, she was shivering. Torbel leaned against the heavy wood table, examining the mace as if it were a Chinese puzzle. That he also examined her from time to time was the only reason Victoria managed to maintain her composure.

"You didn't see anyone?" Keiran asked from the counter.

"A shape," Torbel said without inflection.

Aware of a vague alcoholic tingling in her limbs, Victoria set her cup on the table. "Don't you think," she suggested prosaically, "that you should stop handling that thing and call the police? There might be fingerprints."

"The shape I saw was dressed in black from head to toe. There won't be any incriminating fingerprints, Victoria."

"There won't be now," she agreed. She fought the tremor that ran through her. She should go to Zoe's flat and change out of her wet clothes. Instead, she veiled her eyes and said, "You still haven't told me what you meant when you said he wants more than my death."

"What's more than death?" Keiran demanded.

Torbel sent them a meaningful look. "Two deaths."

Comprehension dawned, slowly because of the alcohol, but now something he'd said earlier struck Victoria with force. "He missed me by less than a foot, right? And the mace flew past me on the left. You were behind me and slightly to my left, weren't you?"

Keiran swore softly as he let a collection of cats and dogs in from the lane.

Torbel shrugged. "It could have been a bad throw."

Victoria's blood chilled. "Whoever's after me wants you dead, too." Fear flowed unhindered through her mind. "He directed me to you, and now he'll try to kill both of us."

Torbel shot Keiran a glance, then, passing the mace over, started toward her. "Don't go off half-cocked, Victoria."

She stood. The brandy burned in her stomach; it must have been a hundred and eighty proof. She wobbled but caught herself and faced him resolutely. "I never go off half-cocked. I'm not naive, Torbel, and I'm certainly not stupid. He wants me dead and he wants you dead, too. And what's worse, he's crazy...or she."

Her bravado wavered as he drew closer. She didn't want him to touch her. Well, maybe she did, but she wouldn't allow it. She stepped away, dragging the chair between them, not caring what significance either man might place on her action. "Admit it, Torbel. This is big and horrible and dangerous, because no one who uses medieval weapons to attack people could possibly be considered sane."

Torbel's face was an implacable mask. He'd halted several feet in front of her. He made no further move to close the gap. Very lucky, she reflected in retrospect, that he didn't.

With no forewarning whatsoever, something crashed through the window, shattering the pane to Victoria's left.

"Son of a..." Torbel grabbed at her, but instinct already had her on her knees. "Get back!" he urged, pulling her arm.

She scrambled for the wall. The crash had resembled the report of an elephant gun. The hole in the window seemed to confirm that. Except...

"Torbel—" she began urgently.

"Keep your voice down."

She hadn't realized he was directly beside her.

"Do you see anything?" Keiran demanded in a low voice.

Torbel gave his head a shake and Victoria a firm push on the head with his hand. "Stay below the level of the window." He regarded Keiran, who was on his haunches across the room. "Take the front. I'll cover the lane. You," he told Victoria, "wait here until we get back."

His breath stirred the dark hair lying across her cheek. She tucked the loose strands behind her ear and tried again. "I really don't think—"

"No arguments." Torbel gave Keiran a barely perceptible nod.

"But it isn't . . ."

He'd stopped listening. With a sound like an exasperated grunt, he made for the door. Keiran headed for the front of the building. Victoria considered trying one last time, then decided to let them go. If they wanted to be brave, that was their business. Hers lay some fifteen feet ahead in a dark, cobwebbed corner near the stove.

It was an old trick, overused but effective as hell, she thought as she crawled cautiously forward. A note, wrapped in a stone and launched through a window.

Sounds from the city street accompanied her across the stone floor: the moan of cargo ships, a Cockney couple shouting, the singsong voice of a hawker plying her wares in the rain—plastic raincoats, cheap umbrellas and live flowers.

She'd almost reached the rock when a voice in her ear nearly made her jump out of her skin.

"I told you to stay put."

She counted to five before turning to glare at him. "You told me to stay down. I am down."

"You're also in full view of anyone who might be lurking outside the window."

"It wasn't a shot, Torbel. It was a rock." She picked up the rock, cobwebs and all. "I saw it before you and Keiran took off, but you wouldn't listen to me."

He slanted her a suspicious look from under his lashes. "You didn't try very bloody hard to stop us."

"No," she answered honestly. She had the strongest urge suddenly to touch his face. The Rag Man wasn't classically handsome, yet every one of his features spoke of strength, determination and force of will. He was a leader, pure and simple, and something about that and him excited her on the most elemental level.

She shouldn't do this, though, entertain fantasies where Torbel was concerned. It must be the heat and high humidity affecting her judgment, prompting a sexual craving that had no basis in logic.

She offered no protest when he took the rock from her and broke the string.

"Well?" she demanded as he skimmed the note. "What does it say?"

He handed it back to her. Against her will, she began to read, "Twinkle, twinkle, pretty star..."

THE SCRAGGLY chimney sweep, wearing baggy pants and a jacket whose sleeves hung several inches too long, slogged from puddle to puddle, along a narrow alley and down a cracked set of stairs to the unfurnished room that contained a battered metal sea chest, an overturned crate, sweep's tools and absolutely nothing else—unless you counted the pair of rats that scurried away every time the door opened.

Must change, thought the begrimed sweep. *Must not be caught. Too much at stake for that. Justice, that's what I am, the angel of death, instrument of revenge.*

The sweep gave an evil chuckle. Off with the jacket, pants and leaky boots. Discard the strategically placed padding. Back into normal street clothes. No more putty, wig and cap— goodbye gloves. Wipe off the soot and brush out the hair. Was that all of it? A good-sized mirror, that's what was needed. Mustn't overlook any detail that might betray the game.

But this was not a game. It was payment. Two years had crawled by, two years of watching and waiting. Of plotting. They could all be gotten now, big and small. They had no right to live, not after what they'd done.

A painful memory stirred, as vivid now as the night Robbie Hollyburn had died: the victim lying on the wet pavement, the mournful wail of a passing ship—and something dreadfully wrong, an image that must be blocked.

One man had run. Another had been captured. But the one captured had not been the one to stick the knife in Robbie's back. The sweep flinched, then straightened. Robbie's killer had had the luck of the Irish on his side. He'd fled like a jackrabbit.

Fox, rabbit, weasel, snake—Torbel was all those things and more. He must die, and the woman, too, because she was the only one left alive to punish.

Caution now, thought the transformed sweep. No need to rush. Lock the chest, straighten the clothes, slip out the door and into the drizzly shadows. Think of the guilty ones under torture. Dream of that. Quote the eerie, poignant rhyme:

I wish I may, I wish I might,
Get the wish I wish tonight....

Chapter Four

"The call came in a few hours ago," Sergeant Peacock explained from his seat in the storehouse kitchen. "Naturally we took pains to contact Ms. Summers immediately. When we couldn't do so, Inspector Fox sent me here. His—our feeling was that she had likely come to you for help."

His voice trailed off to a cough as he ran uncomfortable fingers over the mark on his cheek.

Who wouldn't feel distressed under scrutiny from the Rag Man, Victoria thought in sympathy? The worst of her fears had subsided when Torbel had returned with Sergeant Peacock. The discomfort within her had not.

"Who was this warning call from, Sergeant?" she asked.

"Er, Augustus Hollyburn, actually."

Torbel's dark brows came together. "Are you sure?"

The sergeant stiffened. "I took the call. He wanted to speak to Clover, but her shift ended two hours ago. I relayed the message at once to Inspector Fox. It was Judge Hollyburn's contention that Ms. Summers might be in danger."

Torbel eyed him doubtfully. "How did Judge Hollyburn know the note was intended for Victoria? For that matter, how did he get hold of it in the first place?"

"He said it was delivered anonymously to his home. His butler found it. The envelope had no postage stamp, only Judge Hollyburn's name. Apparently it was pushed through his mail slot sometime after the regular delivery."

"And from that lot of rhyming babble, he was able to determine that it was meant for Victoria?"

"It was only a copy, Torbel. I gather the original note came flying through your window rather later."

"That's ridiculous," Victoria said. A small black cat that had been rubbing her head on Victoria's calf strolled over to wrap herself around Torbel's ankles. "Why would whoever's behind these threats send a copy of a note intended for me—well, all right, Torbel and me—to Augustus Hollyburn before he delivered the original here?"

The sergeant shook his graying head. "All I know is that I was finishing my beat and, upon checking into the station, was instructed by Inspector Fox to proceed at once to the Rag Man's agency."

Sergeant Peacock's large brown eyes had quite noticeable pouches beneath them, due either to a lack of sleep or heredity. Still, he possessed a distinguished air, something between David Niven and Prince Philip, leaning more toward David than Philip in Victoria's opinion.

His tone reproving, he said, "I'll take your note, your rock and your mace down to headquarters and see what the boys—I beg your pardon—the people in the lab can do about locating some useful fingerprints."

Scooping up the cat, Torbel set her where she wanted to be, atop a high oak cupboard. "There won't be any prints, Peacock. Whoever this prat is, he's not likely to make a mistake like that."

"It has been known," Peacock replied, offended. "You might not have operated by the book at the Yard, Torbel, but the rest of us are obliged to. May I have the articles, please?"

Torbel cast him a sidelong look, then, with a second glance at Victoria, reached into his pocket and withdrew the paper. "The rock and mace are behind you on the counter. You won't find any prints."

"Except yours, of course."

The cat meowed. A smile Victoria could not interpret played on the corners of Torbel's mouth. "Don't count on it," he murmured cryptically.

The sergeant bristled but made no further comment. Using his handkerchief, he picked up the evidence and dropped it into a plastic bag. He paused only briefly when Zoe sauntered in. She must have been outside, because her hair was wet and her makeup smudged.

"Evening, Sergeant," she greeted in her husky, melodious voice. "What brings you out on such a foul night? If Fox is interested in that bugger-with-the-butcher-knife case I'm working on, he's elusive as hell, probably ex-foreign legion."

"I'll pass that on, er, Zoe." Avoiding her eyes, the sergeant rose, touched his cap to Victoria and exited through the rear door.

Zoe poured herself a cup of coffee, caught her reflection in the teakettle and stifled a shriek. "Waterproof mascara, my Aunt Fanny. Hi, Smudge." Reaching up, she scratched the cat's chin. "What was Peacock doing here?"

"Being a pompous ass." Torbel shoved back his chair and took his cup to the sink.

Victoria watched him. "He wasn't wrong, you know, Torbel. One stray fingerprint might have solved this case."

"You live in a dreamworld if you think that. We're not dealing with a fly-by-night here, Victoria. Someone's been planning this for a very long time. Probably waiting for Street to get out of prison so he could either pin this whole thing on him or go after him, too."

Since she couldn't refute his remarks, Victoria subsided in her chair. "Has anyone seen Lenny Street lately?" she mused out loud.

Zoe wiped her eyes and balled the tissue between her palms. "I have—he looks like hell. He's not very happy with you, either, Torbel. He figures you got off too easy by comparison. He's turned into a rat, that one. Forget framing him—he might very well be your culprit. I wouldn't trust him if he had both hands on the Bible."

"You wouldn't trust your own grandmother if she were an emissary to the archbishop," Torbel remarked with a glance out the window.

Zoe lowered her catlike body in the chair opposite Victoria. "My grandmother married old Goggy, then promptly gave birth to a slu—to Sophie. Would you trust someone who had no better sense than to tie herself to an out-of-date, sexist tyrant with delusions of knighthood? No wonder Sophie went off."

"What happened to her?" Victoria asked.

"She died shortly after Robbie was born."

"Complications?"

"Alcohol and a fast car. She was streaking pell-mell for Shannon Airport. She must have stopped at a pub on the way. If you don't know Ireland, they brew a lethal poteen."

"Whiskey," Torbel translated. Victoria decided that the glint in his blue-green eyes might also be described as lethal.

"This must have happened a long time ago," she remarked, counting backward. "Almost twenty-three years."

"Nineteen seventy-three," Zoe confirmed. "I was sent packing, so to speak, shortly thereafter. Eight years thereafter, actually, but it was a living hell before that with Goggy threatening to have Scratch—that's his lawyer, Lucius Scranton—change his will. As if I cared. I could never have lived up to Clover's shining example of grades, groveling and general subservience. 'Go into law,' Goggy told her, so she became a police officer. 'Go into law,' he told Robbie. 'Go to hell,' Robbie told him back. Thank God the kid had spunk. It wasn't easy with grandfather pushing and prodding him at every turn. Robbie was it, you know, the last legitimate male in the Hollyburn line."

Her words jogged a memory. "Robbie planned to go into law until he met, uh—" Victoria glanced at Torbel. He seemed unperturbed, albeit fully aware of her meaning.

"Robbie did what he wanted to do. I never offered any inducement."

"But he did want to join your agency." Although that might have had something to do with Zoe's presence, she supposed. "Would you have let him?"

"Probably."

She pushed the hair from her cheeks. The air felt sticky and cloyingly hot. "I think Judge Hollyburn would have made life very difficult for you if you had. Not that I imagine you'd have cared."

Fishing a rubber band out of her jeans pocket, Zoe used it to confine her hair. "One thing you learn early on is that you can't let old Augustus intimidate you if you want to retain your individuality. Too bad Joey didn't live. It might have taken the pressure off the rest of us. God knows, we heard enough about it, Clover and me, that is. Joey was our third, you see."

"You were triplets?" Victoria asked, surprised.

"Yes, but Joey was feeble. He died when he was six weeks old. Grandfather would have given anything to get him back. He'd have sacrificed Clover and me in a minute. He'd have cut off his right arm—I think he'd have sold his soul if he thought it would have worked. Then, just when he'd given up all hope, along came Robbie, and he was over the moon."

"Nice man," Victoria muttered.

"He's not alone in his thinking," Torbel commented dryly.

Her head came up. "My da's not like that. He was happy with a daughter."

One dark brow rose. "Does your da own an ancestral home?"

"Of course not. And if ancestral homes make jerks out of men, then I'm glad he doesn't."

"Ancestral homes, ancestral names. Did you know that we were all named for some ancestor or other? My mother had a great-aunt Zoe. I'm not sure about Clover and Robbie, but I think Clover might have been Goggy's second cousin."

"Sounds complicated," Victoria said.

"Extremely." With a final check of her face, Zoe started for the door. "I'm off to search for a loon with a butcher's knife." She stabbed a finger at her employer's chest. "I want an illicit affair next time, Torbel. No more kooks bearing weapons. I was a cat burglar not a cutthroat. Oh, by the way." She paused, her gloved hand on the door frame. "Ratz has been looking for you. The phone's out, so if you happen to be heading that way, you might want to pop in to the pub. See you later, Vickie."

Rain drummed monotonously against the roof and walls. A man with a ponytail had boarded up the broken window. The cat, Smudge, settled into a contented black ball atop the tallest cupboard, her stare unblinking on Victoria.

She considered asking Torbel to regale her with the sordid details of the night Robbie had died, but thought better of it when she realized that she was shivering. In fact, it was all she could do to keep her teeth from chattering.

"You look all in," Torbel noted.

"Thanks," she murmured. "A gentleman might have noticed, but he wouldn't have mentioned it."

A smile played on the corners of his sensual mouth. "I never claimed to be a gentleman. Come on." He pushed off from the counter. "I have to go pubside. I'll walk you to Zoe's and buy you a muffin on the way."

Although Torbel's thoughtfulness surprised her, Victoria didn't jeopardize it by saying so. She simply strapped on her leather hipsack and joined him at the door.

They walked in silence for a time. The rain stopped as they neared the end of the lane. Not that it made much difference. Few people prowled the streets at this time of night; fewer still seemed willing to leave the relative anonymity of the shadows.

"Raisins?" Torbel asked out of the blue.

"What—? Oh, muffins." Victoria smiled at the fat vendor who'd parked his cart across from Gooseberries. "Yes, please."

"Two," Torbel told the man.

Victoria studied his face in the misty streetlight. His eyes fascinated her. In constant motion, they searched alleys and doorways, street corners and stairwells. She wondered how he'd lived before he went to work for Scotland Yard. However, "Why do you have a cat burglar working for you?" was as direct a question as she dared put to him right then.

"Zoe's a friend." His eyes continued to move while he handed her a hot buttered muffin. "Oswyn was the son of a friend, and Tristan just showed up one day."

"You have three cat burglars on your staff?" Some inner instinct told her she shouldn't be shocked. "What about the others? Are they criminals, too? Keiran? Ron? The guy who boarded up the window?"

"Every one."

"And you trust them?"

"They wouldn't be around if I didn't."

She broke off a piece of soft bun but didn't eat. "You're taking a big chance, aren't you, Torbel? I know some criminals can be reformed, but others aren't open to it. What if one of them crosses you?"

Again that enigmatic half smile. "What you really want to know is, do I think one of them is behind all of this? The answer is no."

"You're too trusting, Torbel."

"I know my people, Victoria."

Her nerves were beginning to settle, but only, she suspected, because her mind was otherwise occupied. For a rough-edged man, he was too attractive by half. To offset that, she'd been prodding him deliberately. It was not a smart thing to do. She was in no rush to see an open display of his temper. Perhaps wisely, she backed off.

"Maybe," she allowed. "But I still wouldn't—"

She broke off as someone rushed past in a hurry. Victoria spied thin, wiry limbs and felt a tiny bump against her arm. The man muttered something unintelligible and veered off.

Her fingers went automatically to her hipsack—rather, to where it should have been. Alarm coursed through her. "He took my pouch!" she exclaimed.

Give him his due, Torbel was off before she could think of an outraged expletive. He caught the smaller man in three strides, grasping his arm so hard he nearly yanked the would-be purse snatcher off his feet.

A layer of smoke from the pub momentarily obscured Victoria's vision. "Not so fast, Tito," she heard Torbel snarl.

"What?" The little man's startled expression turned to one of relief. "Oh, bloody nightmare, I thought you was a cop, Torbel. I mean, I know you was a cop once and all, but...who's the lady then?"

"Pouch, Tito."

"Yeah, sure, no harm done. Sorry, miss." He gave an uncomfortable laugh. "I didn't know you was with Torbel. Don't worry, it's all there."

Cockney down to his scruffy-sneakered toes. Victoria would have been amused if she hadn't been busy counting credit cards and pound notes. She heard sloshy footsteps, then a deep bass voice boomed out, "Problem, Torbel?"

She looked up—and up and up. The stranger with a bald, shiny head and tattoos on his forearms was the largest human being she'd ever encountered.

"Nothing I can't handle, Ratz." Torbel released his small, sticky-fingered quarry. The situation brought to mind a picture of *The Lion King*'s odd couple, Puumba and Timon.

The purse snatcher stayed cockily close, flashing her a yellow smile before turning his attention to Torbel. "What's that, then?" He flapped a hand at the envelope Ratz was handing over. Two gold rings gleamed in the lamplight. "You on the take, Torbel?"

"Shut up," Ratz growled. "Bad news?" he asked Torbel.

"It's from Street."

Immediately interested, Victoria fixed her hipsack in place and poked her head over his shoulder. "What does he want?"

"A meeting—ten-thirty, on the dock."

A feeling of unease sidled in. "Which dock?"

His mouth was inches from hers when he turned to answer. "The one where Robbie Hollyburn was killed."

THE WATER MADE a rude sloshing sound against the pier. It wasn't the only sound Torbel's alert ears picked out.

Victoria's fingers dug into his forearm. "I heard a footstep," she whispered.

"I know." He made no move to pry her hand free. In truth, while the bite was painful, it also had the effect of warming his blood. God help him, this woman had trouble written all over her beautiful face.

Strands of her dark hair, lifted by the wind, blew into his eyes. He tucked them absently behind her ear and continued to listen.

It came again, the same stealthy squish as before, thirty feet behind them and slightly to the right.

His sharp eyes noted the outline of several large crates. Rice, flour and tea shipped from the Orient. Someone vanished into the shelter of the tallest stack.

"Street wouldn't hide," he reflected more to himself than to Victoria.

"Would he stick a knife in our backs?" she countered softly.

"Mine maybe, not yours. He has no quarrel with you. The crown attorney's office helped get the charge against him reduced, remember?"

She loosened her grip with difficulty, more out of pride, he suspected, than a lessening of fear. "What should we do?"

He shot her a steady look. "You stay here in the open where both he and I can see you. I'll circle around and grab him."

The expression on her face told him precisely what she thought of that idea. She swallowed the retort, however, and nodded. "Just hurry, will you? I feel like an arcade duck."

He summoned a cryptic smile. "You don't look like one. Walk around a bit, like you're waiting for someone."

Without waiting for a reply, Torbel ducked into the shadow of a large shipping barrel. With a speed born of experience, he surveyed the area. When nothing stirred, he stretched his muscles and ran for the crates. If Victoria was doing her part, his approach should go unnoticed.

Ten feet ahead, not quite concealed in a patch of sooty darkness, he spied a shape, huddled near the front of the stack. From a crouch, Torbel launched himself at the figure's back, catching it easily and wrapping a sinewy arm about its throat.

It was a man, and he gurgled helplessly in Torbel's grasp. "Don't—" He clawed at the forearm that held him. "It's—Torbel, it's . . . me."

More gurgles followed, but Torbel was too incensed to heed them. He spun the young man around, grabbing him by the sides of his rough-cut vest and yanking him up. "You bloody idiot. I could have broken your neck. What are you doing down here?"

"W-watching out for you and—and her." Shamefaced, Oswyn pointed at Victoria.

Swearing again, Torbel released him. "It's all right," he called out. "It's Oswyn."

"Thank God." Victoria approached, peering at the youth more closely. "What on earth are you doing out here?"

He didn't meet her eyes. "Watching your backs."

Torbel thought it prudent to change the subject. "Have you seen Lenny Street?"

"Haven't seen anyone eyt."

"Yet," Torbel corrected. "What time is it?"

"Ten forty-five," Victoria said.

"Go back to the agency," Torbel told Oswyn.

Oswyn's eyes challenged him, but only for a moment. "Yeah, all right." He swiped the hair from his thick brow. "I just thought maybe you'd need help is all."

"It was very nice of you," Victoria said from Torbel's side. He slid her a narrowed look but didn't comment.

"Go" was all he said to Oswyn.

The boy turned, shoulders slumped, and started off. He hadn't taken more than twenty steps, however, when one of the large crates above him began to wobble.

"Torbel!" Victoria spotted it the same time.

"Oswyn, move!"

Torbel shouted the warning, but he knew Oswyn wouldn't react fast enough. He'd been an awkward burglar. In five attempts, he'd been caught three times.

"Yea...ahh...!" Releasing a fierce cry, he lunged, tackling Oswyn from behind and rolling them out of harm's way.

When it toppled, the crate missed his leg by less than six inches. It crashed to the ground and splintered, spilling out several hundred pounds of brown rice.

Panting, Torbel lay back and fought to regain his breath.

Victoria reached them before he had a chance to remonstrate with Oswyn. "That would have killed you if it had hit," she declared, going to her knees beside him. Torbel felt her hand on his leg and had to force himself not to jerk away.

"I'm fine," he said brusquely. "Help Oswyn."

Annoyed, she retorted, "I forgot, leaders like to think they're invincible. You Bonapartes are all alike."

She was throwing his own words back at him. Torbel felt his temper rising—and with it something else, a feeling that he knew better than to acknowledge.

"It was my fault...." Oswyn began. He stopped, his dark eyes widening in astonishment. "Torbel, look!"

He didn't have to; the forklift was making enough racket to wake every rummy on the docks. "Go!" He shoved Oswyn aside. In the same motion, he grabbed Victoria by the waist and yanked her in the opposite direction. A split second later, the forklift plowed over the very spot where they'd stood.

From behind the rice pile, Torbel surveyed the machine's amorphous operator. "Bloody— Wait here," he told Victoria. "I'm going to—"

"No." She clamped a surprisingly strong hand on his arm. "Don't you see, Torbel, it's what he wants. He'll get you, then he'll get me and that'll be it. Mission accomplished. Unless he decides to kill Oswyn for good measure. The police would never catch him. How could they with no witnesses?" Her tone grew more imperative. "We'll be dead, and he'll be free—and I'm not ready to die, Torbel. Not for a long time yet."

"Torbel!" Oswyn hailed him hoarsely from beside a sturdy pylon. "He's turning."

Of course he was. He'd had enough time during Victoria's diatribe to turn the forklift twice. She had a point, though, and while he'd been accused of many things in his life, stupidity was not one of them.

"Come on, then." Taking Victoria by the arm, he pressed her firmly sideways. "Oswyn," he barked.

The boy darted across the wet pavement. "We won't make it," he panted.

"We need a diversion," Victoria said.

"We could push a crate onto the forklift," Oswyn suggested.

Torbel sent him an acerbic look. "Or we could just hide behind them. He isn't terribly maneuverable."

"We can't hide all night," Victoria argued reasonably. "Why couldn't we push over a crate? They can't be very stable, or he couldn't have done it earlier."

"He probably had it rigged, Victoria."

"Fine, then what do you suggest? Playing musical stacks until morning?"

Torbel ground his teeth. He disliked stubborn people, especially when that stubbornness came with a brain and a beautiful face.

"Shut up and move," he snapped.

He focused his gaze on the forklift. The operator appeared to be having trouble with the controls. The machine shot forward, jerked, then turned abruptly left. Out of the pool of dockside light, Torbel noted shrewdly. He'd been right in his earlier assessment. This person was no fool.

"What's he doing?" Victoria whispered in his ear.

"Doesn't matter." Torbel located a sanctuary. "Run for the dockman's cottage, and keep out of the light."

Their attacker caught sight of them, as Torbel had anticipated. He veered the vehicle away from the crates and pointed it at the stone-and-timber cottage.

"Go around," Torbel instructed Victoria and Oswyn from behind. "He won't be able to maneuver in there."

He tried, though, and came a good deal closer than Torbel had thought possible. The prongs actually stripped off a layer of timber on the wall.

Oswyn tripped and would have sprawled headfirst into a sodden pylon, but Torbel caught him by the waistband to steady him.

For a West Ender, Victoria seemed quite at home, hopping over seaman's rigging and rubble. For all his disdain of the upstairs life, Torbel had to admire her grit. And if there were numerous other things to admire about her, well, they would just have to wait for a more appropriate time.

The machine crunched to a halt. Over his shoulder, Torbel saw the operator leap out, as nimbly as any acrobat. He also saw a hand dip into the baggy black jacket.

"Duck," he shouted, and shoved the pair in front of him toward the next level of docks.

Three shots rang out in succession. Two embedded themselves in the creaking wood; the third grazed his left shoulder. He stifled a hiss of pain, holding Victoria down when she would have raised her head.

"Stay down," he snarled. "Oswyn." With his head, he motioned upward. Oswyn nodded and began climbing the ladderwork frame.

Three more shots rang out, none of them aimed at Oswyn. But their attacker must have seen him climbing, because he ran back several paces. Releasing a final shot, he dropped his hands and, turning, vanished into the darkness.

Torbel felt Victoria's fingers probing his bloodied shoulder. "He hit you," she exclaimed in dismay.

He gritted his teeth, more to combat her touch than the fiery pain. "It's just a scratch. Oswyn!" He ensnared Victoria's wrist when she would have shifted his jersey. "Don't."

"But you're bleeding."

"I've bled before. Let's get the hell out of here before that prat of a note writer comes back."

He wouldn't, of course, but she couldn't know that.

Damn her, he thought irritably. Why did she have to be the one woman in all of London whose touch had the power to drive him mad? The silky feel of her skin, the flowery scent of her hair, the flashes of fire in her blue eyes—she was a Gypsy, all right, with American pluck and a cool British stare. He should have ordered Keiran to boot her out the storehouse door the moment Fox had called to say she was on her way. Unfortunately, seeing her, it had been too late. He'd been trapped. And if only he knew that, it wouldn't be long before Keiran figured it out, as well.

"Torbel?"

He glanced up to find Oswyn peering at him.

"You coming?"

Aware of Victoria's accusing stare, he relegated the pain in his shoulder to the back of his mind and nudged her firmly forward. "I'll watch your back," he said in a tone that left no room for argument.

She raised her head. "Who'll watch yours, Torbel? Or do you have a lucky aura that bullets can't penetrate?"

"Meaning?" he countered evenly.

Barely four inches separated them. He saw the glimmer of anger—and perhaps a trace of some other emotion—in her eyes. "I don't need you to die for me," she told him.

"No, you don't," he agreed. "What you need is this." And hauling her hard against him, he covered her mouth with his.

Chapter Five

Victoria groped for a mental foothold, any leverage she could use to fight his powerful hold on her. He held her physically; she could feel the iron band of his arms around her waist and shoulders, but she was not a prisoner in that sense. It was her own thoughts and feelings that prevented her from struggling as logic dictated she should.

The stubble on his unshaved jaw felt like sandpaper against her face. He moved his mouth over hers with a pressure that was at once insistent and punishing. He blamed her for this kiss.

Since she couldn't seem to fight him, she made no further attempt to do so. She simply allowed her senses to absorb the taste of him, the feel and the heady masculine scent.

His tongue delved past her lips, exploring her teeth and more. Victoria's head swam. His mouth was hot and wet, demanding, a little rough but not bruising. Through a haze of awareness, she realized that he was punishing himself more than her.

She ran her fingers lightly over his back, amazed and vaguely unsettled by the wiry muscles lurking beneath the smooth expanse of skin. His leanness was entirely deceptive. Torbel's sleek build would undoubtedly give him the strength, speed and agility of a jaguar.

She took a token stab at pushing him away. She hadn't intended for it to work. But as if his head had been yanked up by a giant hand, he tore his mouth from hers and stood breathing heavily for several seconds. His dark blue-green eyes bored into hers, impaling her as surely as his kiss had done. He did not look pleased. In fact, he looked downright grim, and that, more than his hasty withdrawal, wounded Victoria's pride. It also got her moving.

Chin up, shoulders back, she stepped away. But she was trembling, and no directive from her brain could possibly change that. She only prayed that in the gauzy light of the pier, he wouldn't notice.

"You coming, Torbel?" Oswyn poked his head over the side of the high dock. "That loon could come back anytime."

"I know." Gaze steady—though his breathing still was not—Torbel stared her down. His eyes had a glint that Victoria perceived as both dangerous and fascinating. Dangerous because the sensual nature of this man affected her in ways she did not yet fully understand.

What if...? she wondered, then shook herself. No. Absolutely not. She would not let herself become involved with him. Scar or no, sexy mouth notwithstanding, kiss—well, best to forget the kiss. It wouldn't happen again anyway, or she was no judge of the Rag Man.

Although she wanted as little help as possible climbing, she wasn't foolish enough to slap his hands away. The broken framework took thirty tedious seconds to navigate.

At the top, she wriggled free. She needed to get out of range quite badly, away from the sight of his face and his beautiful mouth, which reminded her even more disturbingly of his kiss.

No one spoke during the walk back. The notorious East End of London carried on with life as always. Thieves and pickpockets worked their victims, and, no doubt, worse crimes were being contemplated behind several of the closed doors they passed.

Victoria tried to envision Torbel in the same picture. She saw it with frightening clarity. Street kid turned cop, turned—she didn't know what.

He cared about people, though; he must. He'd saved Oswyn's life tonight. And hers.

"Go on ahead," he instructed Oswyn now. They'd stopped outside the entrance to Zoe's flat. A graphic Irish ballad emanated from the pub, which must be past closing by now. Did Torbel ever go in there and drink himself senseless? she wondered with a covert glance at his profile. Did he let his guard down with anyone? How had he gotten that scar? When had he gotten it? Before or after he worked for Scotland Yard? Had he always been a leader? A loner? Should she kiss him this time? . . .

A tantalizing idea, but the answer had to be an unequivocal no.

Resisting the temptation to touch his shoulder, she indicated his bloodstained jersey. "Do you want me to look at that? I've had first-aid training."

She thought his lips might have quirked. "So has Grimsby. It's not that serious."

Who was Grimsby? She had no intention of leaving until she'd said what needed to be said. "Torbel, I want to . . ." she began, then took a deep breath and said steadily, "Thank you for what you did tonight. You saved my life more than once. I won't forget that." Or the rest of it, either, she reflected silently.

His eyes glittered in the Stepney lamplight. She spied something in his face, desire perhaps. She couldn't tell, and he wasn't prepared to explain. With his good arm, he pushed open the door and nodded into the darkness. "Good night, Victoria," he said with no perceptible expression. "Don't forget to lock up."

"But Zoe—"

"Has keys, and tends to be a night owl."

"Old habits die hard, huh?"

"You could say that." Again that disconcerting gleam in his eyes. "Sleep well, Victoria."

She didn't miss the subtle barb, but neither did she retaliate. Let him think he could frighten her. A former cat burglar was no real problem. A homicidal maniac on a forklift was a different story.

She started across the threshold, then stopped partway and turned her head. "Do you think Lenny Street set us up on the dock tonight?" she asked softly.

Half-lidded, Torbel regarded her. "I doubt it. He's not stupid. He knows I won't die easily. And I'm not above revenge."

Was that supposed to comfort her? "You take a lot for granted, Torbel. Anyone can die easily in the right circumstances. You're not invincible. No one is. A sorcerer might cheat death for a while, but it'll catch up with him at some point. You're not a sorcerer, are you, Torbel?"

She hadn't expected an answer and so was shocked into silence when, his eyes darkening noticeably, he responded, "A lot of people think that's exactly what I am. And Augustus Hollyburn tops the list."

ZOE HAD TO TALK herself across town to Mayfair. The old man shouldn't be up at 2:00 a.m., but anything was possible. If he thought she might darken his doorstep, he would stay awake all night, with Chivers standing guard and possibly even old Scratch absorbed in a game of chess.

She'd have to sneak in. She knew the way, every step.

Careful not to make a sound, she eased open a small rear window and wriggled through the gap. A long hike through the darkness and there it was, the door she sought.

She didn't knock, merely eased it open and slipped inside. An even thicker blanket of darkness spread out around her. Clover must be asleep.

Zoe listened to the even breathing that came from the bed, a massive thing with heavy velvet curtains around it. Clover was so macabre, Zoe thought with a shudder of distaste.

As if her thoughts had thrown the switch, a light flared across the room. Clover's face, a tight-lipped replica of her own, stared at her with a hard measuring look.

"What do you want?"

A clinical question, no surprise—or anger, either, for that matter.

Zoe collected her wits, grinned and strolled closer. "Just wanted to ask you a few questions is all. Is grandfather in bed?"

Clover sat like a statue, rigid and unmoving, hands clasped on the bed covers. "He isn't your grandfather."

Zoe sighed. "Call him what you will. Where is he?"

"Downstairs with Scratch, I imagine. Is that all you wanted to know?"

Her hand moved to flip off the light. Only Zoe's casual "You're behind it, aren't you?" stopped her. And stop she did, with her hand halfway to the lamp. Zoe chuckled. "Yeah, I thought that would get your attention."

"I don't know what you're talking about." Clover's cheeks seemed unnaturally pale. "I'm not behind anything."

"You didn't throw a rock through the storehouse window tonight, or heave a mace at Victoria and Torbel earlier? You haven't threatened their lives, maybe tried to ram a forklift prong through their throats?"

"You're talking gibberish," Clover said coldly.

"Tell that to Oswyn. I gather he was full of the story earlier. It'll be all over the waterfront by morning."

"Who filled you in?"

"A reliable source."

"One of your crooked friends?" Clover jeered. "To answer your question, I haven't been near the waterfront tonight. I got home just after seven, took five aspirins for a blinding head-ache and went straight to bed."

"No witnesses?"

Clover's fists clenched. "I didn't realize I'd need one. Sleep is usually a private thing."

"For you, it is," Zoe said under her breath. The glare from Clover's teal-colored eyes intensified.

They had their grandfather's eyes, Zoe reflected distantly. Hollyburn blue, someone had called them once. Robbie used to say that if looks could kill, Hollyburn eyes would be deadly weapons. But in Zoe's opinion, you needed the icy nature to go with them. She didn't have it. Neither had her mother. Only Clover had inherited from old Goggy the ability to incite vi-sual frostbite.

Speaking of Goggy—she swiveled. Was that a slippered footstep on the hall carpet? He wasn't above creeping around, not if he had an inkling she might be about.

"You're a thief, Zoe," her twin was charging now. "If there's anything untoward going on at that Rag Man's storehouse, either you or he or one of your slithering cohorts is behind it."

Zoe would have responded tartly in kind had she not detected that stealthy footstep again. It must be Goggy. Furtiveness was beneath Chivers, and what would Scratch care if she was here?

She melted into the shadows. Damask draperies covered the window, but it was a large bay, readily unlatched. The moment that door handle turned . . .

The door burst open and crashed against the paneled wall.

"Where is she?" Augustus bellowed.

From her hiding place, Zoe saw Clover jump. "She—she isn't here."

He jabbed a bony finger at her. "Don't lie to me, girl. I can smell her. She carries the odor of mendacity."

"*Cat on a Hot Tin Roof,*" Zoe muttered under her breath.

"What's that?" Old Groggy cupped one ear.

"Nothing, Grandfather." Climbing from the bed, Clover stuck her feet in her slippers. "You should have your cane," she said, starting toward him. "The doctor told you—"

"Damn the doctor. You shouldn't have let her in here. You know she'll try to corrupt you—she always does."

He was shaking, Zoe noted. She could see his bony joints rattling in their sockets. Did he really hate her so much?

"Believe me, Grandfather," Clover said, "I can handle her. She won't corrupt me."

She'd reached his side by now and managed to guide him to a chair. Wouldn't want the old geezer to collapse on her, Zoe thought cynically. He would die, and Clover would weep tears but let him draw his last breath in his own bed. Zoe felt her upper lip curl in disdain at her sister's uncaring nature.

"I'll help you to your room," her twin offered. "Catch your breath, then we'll go."

Augustus made a sputtering sound and batted at her hands. "Stop fussing, girl. I'm not totally decrepit. Neither am I daft. I heard her voice. I know you let her in."

Clover's hands dropped to her sides. Her fingers, Zoe noticed, twitched as if the nerves in them had been stretched taut. "No one lets Zoe in, Grandfather. She comes all on her own."

The old man's lips compressed. "You're all I've got, Clover," he said tightly. "Robbie's gone. Your mother, too. And Blanche, dead these past eight years. My beloved Blanche..." His eyes spewed fire. "It's all that witch Blodwyn's fault. She caused my sorrow, made my life a living hell. And all for one mistake. One night. One hellish night. A witch, that's what she was, a whore, like your sister. Oh, poor, dear Blanche. Maybe it's as well after all that she's gone."

It was all Zoe could do not to choke. Grandma Blanche would have. What a whopper. Beloved? Goggy didn't know the meaning of the word—except where Robbie had been concerned, and even then he hadn't seen the kid properly at all.

"It's that Rag Man," Goggy declared in a righteous tone. "He's brought bad fortune on our family from the moment he set foot in this country. He's a curse—that's what he is, a living, breathing curse, and he's fallen on me." Augustus struggled to his feet. "Mark my words, girl," he grunted. "Stay away from that Rag Man. He's a pox on our family. He's wicked and he has a purpose. He went for Robbie because he knew the boy was vulnerable, but it's me he really wants to get. Has for years."

Zoe frowned. She hadn't heard this before. Who was Blodwyn? And why would Torbel want to "get" old Goggy? Unless, in his days as a high-court judge, the old man had done something to him. Now there, Zoe mused, was an intriguing prospect.

She regarded her grandfather's unforgiving face with its wrinkled skin and eyes like teal bullets. He reminded her of a skeleton with skin stretched over it and a shock of wavy white hair sprouting out around gaunt cheeks. The proper British gentleman on the surface—a snake with legs underneath.

Her sleek muscles bunched. For all this man had done to her, and to Clover, too, for that matter, he deserved to be gotten. And who better to do the honors than the enigmatic and highly dangerous Rag Man.

Smiling, Zoe slid through the window and back into the darkness of the London night.

Chapter Six

Damn, she was going to be late.

Victoria rubbed her damp hair with a towel, pulled on her white silk top and stepped into the navy blue pumps that matched her pin-striped skirt.

This was all Zoe's fault, she decided crankily. Although that wasn't strictly true. Zoe had burst in at 3:00 a.m., brimming with a story that, even sleepy eyed and groggy, Victoria had been unable to resist.

"I don't know what their hatred entails," Zoe had concluded at four-fifteen, "but it sounds older than Robbie's murder. There must have been a real cock-up involved, because old Goggy despises Torbel almost as much as he hates me."

Victoria supposed that Augustus Hollyburn might have had Torbel locked up prior to Robbie's death, but for what crime? Assault? Theft? Cursing their family? She dismissed the last, fanciful thought. The truth, if indeed there was one, would be in the computer records. Assuming she was able to find a cab, she'd do some checking when she reached her office on Bouverie Street.

Sighing, Victoria regarded her reflection in the wall mirror. If she pinned her hair up en route, that would save time.

She tugged on her jacket, located her soft-sided briefcase, glanced at Zoe's closed door, then started out. She emerged into the pub from the narrow, low-ceilinged central staircase. Ratz stood behind the bar, cleaning glasses and humming an English ballad. Ten scarred wooden tables dotted the small room. She estimated at least five times that many chairs.

Ratz nodded at her. She nodded back but kept her eyes trained discreetly on the floor. The polished boards sagged in the middle. Not that she blamed them after more than two hundred years of hard wear, but it made walking in heels a tricky feat at best.

"Torbel know you're going out?" the giant demanded gruffly as she set her hand on the knob.

Victoria swung around. "He'll figure it out."

"You should tell him."

She gave him a perfunctory smile. "Or you could do it for me. I presume you're one of his watchdogs."

"I work for him, right enough, but he never told me to watch you. That was my idea."

Relaxing somewhat, Victoria said, "It's nice of you to be concerned, Ratz, but I'm only going to work. I'll be safe enough there." She recalled Friday night when she'd been followed through the lobby and added an uneasy "In broad daylight anyway." She thought for a moment, then took the plunge. "Uh, Ratz, do you know anything about the night Robbie Hollyburn was killed? Nothing that would place Torbel's neck in a noose, just something that didn't come out."

Ratz squinted through the glass in his hand. "I know the kid had something gnawing on him that night. He came in here and started rabbiting on about how he needed to see Torbel and there was no sign of him at the storehouse."

"Maybe he was eager to join up," Victoria theorized.

"Oh, he was eager, right enough, but he'd been on to Torbel about that for a good month already. This was...different. He was excited. Said he needed to talk to Torbel right away."

"Did you tell this to the police?"

Ratz snorted. "I told Fox, but he has cloth ears when his mind's on other things. Doubt he heard much of what any of us said that day. Doris was hanging about, and she's his— Well, let's say he likes her best."

"So no one ever pursued the matter?"

"Wouldn't have made much difference if they had. The buzzards—er, solicitors—would have gone for Torbel just the same. The kid died—that's a fact."

"Do you think Street did it?"

He shrugged. "None of my business, is it?"

"But you must have an opinion."

Ratz's black eyes were guarded, but he relented and moved a noncommittal shoulder. "Lenny's ma and mine are cousins. That's all I've got to say. Except that Fox and Peacock did a bloody poor job of digging to my mind. They figured it was Torbel and Street, and that was that. No other suspects, they said. They didn't even question the likes of Tito and Boots."

Tito she knew. "Who's Boots?" she asked.

"An odd-jobber. You'd call him a beggar."

"Does he beg?"

"Most days."

"Then he's a beggar. Do Boots and Tito spend a lot of time on the docks?"

"More than some, less than others. They keep their ears to the ground better 'n most."

"Not cloth ears, I hope," Victoria murmured. Louder, she said, "Can you tell me where I might find them?"

"Tito could be anywhere. Boots usually does the route between the butcher shop and the station house."

Victoria tugged on the door. "Thanks, Ratz."

"I still think you should—"

Ron's hushed voice cut in from the far wall. " . . . going to need ten or more of them if we plan to pull this off under Torbel's—" The Scotsman halted abruptly when he spied Victoria. His eyes flicked from her to Ratz and back again. "Pub's closed, isn't it?" he said gruffly.

"I'm staying with Zoe," Victoria reminded him, although she doubted there was any need. He'd gone dark red right down his thick neck. "What were you saying about Torbel?"

A woman she hadn't noticed stepped forward. "We were just gabbling, weren't we, Ratz?"

"Ron's a gabbler," Ratz agreed. He blew a speck of lint from the last glass. "Lazy bugger, too. Takes shortcuts through the shops to get from the storehouse to here. What's up, then, Ivy?'' he asked the petite blond woman who had the look of a pixie. ''You on a case?''

''We're both on a case,'' Ron answered. Nudging his companion, he nodded stiffly at Victoria and made for the door like a bull desperate to escape the paddock.

One look at Ratz's face told Victoria that he was unlikely to explain the bizarre encounter. What had Ron meant? Pull what off under Torbel's nose? Were Ron and Ivy planning some kind of subterfuge? She pictured Torbel's satyric features and decided that Ron couldn't possibly be that stupid. Either that or his life meant nothing to him. As little as she knew of the Rag Man, Victoria had no doubt that he would not take a double cross lying down.

Five seconds after Ron and Ivy left, she bade a preoccupied goodbye to Ratz and stepped onto the sidewalk. Both agents had disappeared.

The day was muggy and close with a high overcast typical of London in late spring. The air smelled of baking, flowers and the sooty aroma of old buildings. The hawkers were out and hard at work, selling their ''caulies and green veg'' to any passerby whose attention they could attract.

Ragamuffin children, playing tag and urging their dogs to beg for scraps, added to the Dickensian feel of the area, but as she gazed around, it occurred to Victoria that there were entirely too many children doing too many things that had nothing to do with school.

A man's hand snagged her arm from behind, halting her in her tracks. ''What do you think you're doing?''

Her heart jumped into her throat, but she managed to force it down and snatch her arm free. ''Trying to find a cab—and wondering why these children aren't in school on a Monday morning.''

Torbel wore a black jersey today, with the sleeves pushed up over his lean, tanned forearms and the three top buttons undone. His brown hair was clean and shiny; the stubble on his chin had not been shaved. He looked predatory and dangerous and altogether too sexy for her to cope with on an empty stomach.

One of those damnable mocking brows rose. "Can't you figure it out?"

"If I could, I wouldn't ask."

"Those particular children belong to the Pottses. Both parents work at the garment factory. They're there from seven till six and can't always be sure their offspring get away on time, or at all for that matter. There'll be a note from the teacher about it." He trapped her wrist before she could flag a passing taxi. "I'm on my way to the local precinct house. I'd like you to come along."

"Is it about last night?"

"Not in the sense you mean. One of my agents, Tristan, was involved in a fight behind the pub."

She thought back. "I didn't hear anything."

"He knocked his opponent out with one punch."

"How does that involve me?" As if she couldn't guess.

That same wicked brow arched again.

She endeavored discreetly to extricate her wrist. "You're crazy, Torbel. I don't defend ex-cat-burglars who brawl behind bars in their spare time."

"Not even one whose opponent was getting rough with his escort? Doris has a bigger black eye than her so-called companion."

She stopped tugging. "That's terrible."

"I know." Giving her no chance to object, he propelled her firmly along the narrow street.

Although she wished he wouldn't walk quite so close, Victoria made no further attempt to break free. It was too crowded in any event, and as she recalled, the police station was only a few blocks away.

Even so, it took an eternity to forge a path along the sidewalk. The corners were the worst. Carts, trolleys and barrows vied for position. Thank heaven she found a vendor selling hot scones. She ordered one smothered in strawberry jam, with a cup of tea and milk on the side. Apart from satisfying her overwhelming hunger, the food also kept her from dwelling too deeply on the man beside her.

She managed only one question between the corner and the precinct house. At that, she sensed Torbel didn't appreciate it. "Why do you and Judge Hollyburn hate each other so much?"

A muscle in his jaw twitched. "Isn't the trial reason enough?"

"Zoe thinks there's more to it, some earlier clash between you."

"Yeah, well, Zoe doesn't know squat when it comes to Augustus and me. Clover knows even less if that's her source."

"That isn't quite—"

"Morning, Torbel. Morning, Ms. Summers." Tito fell into step with them near the precinct house. Sticking his head out, he greeted a man seated on a black case. "Morning, Boots."

Victoria immediately perceived why he was called Boots. The man wore a beautiful pair, made of black leather, with polished gold buckles on the top. The rest of his clothing consisted of a tattered 1920s tuxedo, a top hat with the top punched out and a red ascot tied around his sagging throat. He looked to be about seventy years old. He had a round, smiling face and white hair that fell in wisps to his shoulders.

He said nothing, merely beamed at Tito then more broadly at Torbel.

"Boots isn't much of a talker," Tito confided to Victoria. He twisted off one of the five rings on his left hand. "Got a bauble for you, Boots," he said. "Yours to keep or pawn. Pure gold it is, ten karat."

Not quite pure, but more than Tito could likely afford to purchase. Victoria kept her mouth shut, finished her scone and, licking her fingers, trailed Torbel into the station.

A chimney sweep with a grimy face and cap pulled low over his eyes paused to let her pass.

Sergeant Peacock stood behind the desk, looking formal if somewhat harassed. Officers and civilians buzzed around like flies. In the background, Inspector Fox talked to one of his female officers—a charming smile on his lips.

Seeing him reminded Victoria of something. "Ratz mentioned a woman called Doris that Fox likes. Is she the Doris with the black eye?"

"She likes dangerous men."

Two thoughts sprang to mind. Victoria voiced only the second. "Inspector Fox isn't dangerous, is he?"

"He's killed people in his time."

"Before he joined the force, of course," Tito put in.

Victoria studied the man from a distance. He had straight dark hair, parted in the middle and slicked back, with a neat little mustache to match. She estimated that he was the same height and build as Sergeant Peacock, six-one or so. "How old is he?" she asked Torbel, who now stood disconcertingly behind her shoulder.

"Forty-six."

"Nah, he's fifty if he's a day," Tito declared, then snatched his hand from the air and tucked it behind his back.

Peacock regarded him sternly. "Come here, Tito."

Tito looked around innocently. "I'm with them."

"We had a report of a stolen ring last week," the sergeant said. "A gent's ruby. Show me your right hand, please."

"Damn his eagle eyes," Tito muttered. Reluctantly he shuffled forward.

The sergeant regarded the ring, hesitated, then took it. "M.V. Martin Valder." His graying brows went up. "Would you mind telling me how this came to be in your possession?"

"I—"

"Found it," Torbel supplied smoothly.

Tito's head bobbed. "That's right, I did. In Mersey Lane near the pawnshop. I figured some bloke must have dropped it. I would have turned it in, but I was hungry and it slipped me mind."

Peacock set the ring down, wiping his hands thoroughly on a handkerchief. "Gold gives him a rash," Tito whispered to Victoria.

"Stolen gold gives me more of a rash, Tito. It also gives me problems."

Victoria came to life. "What kind of problems, Sergeant?"

"Legal ones." Pocketing the handkerchief, Peacock inspected his contaminated fingers. "Is this man your client?"

"That depends. Are you going to charge him with possession of stolen merchandise?"

A derisive snort brought her attention to Inspector Fox, who'd joined them. "Might as well try to catch water in a sieve. Confiscate the ring, Sergeant. Bugger off, Tito."

With a grin for Torbel and Victoria, the little man shrank out of sight.

Fox came to stand beside the sergeant, his long fingers splayed on the desk. "What brings you here, Torbel?"

"Tristan Law, sir," Peacock reminded in an undertone.

"Yes, of course. Brawling in public, making an affray."

Privately Victoria thought the inspector's smile was too smooth.

"Defending a woman was how I heard it," Torbel returned. His tone and expression were both unreadable.

A chilly female voice cut in. "You would defend him, wouldn't you, Torbel. You'd lie through your teeth to save any of your smarmy cohorts."

Clover Hollyburn. Victoria tried hard not to stare. For all their differences, the physical resemblance between her and Zoe was staggering, right down to their double-pierced left earlobe.

Inspector Fox straightened. "That will be all, Clover. Torbel has paid his debt to society."

Clover's lip curled, but she obeyed. With a stilted "Yes, sir," she turned and marched down a narrow hall.

Sergeant Peacock smothered a cough behind his hand. "You say you've come to see Tristan Law, Torbel?"

Victoria watched Torbel's discerning eyes as they assessed Clover's receding back. "Has bail been set?"

"I believe—uh, was there something else, sir?"

Inspector Fox had stretched his neck to follow Torbel's gaze. "Dammit, what are you looking at, Torbel? Clover's gone."

"I'm thinking."

"Yes, well, don't do it here. It makes me itch. At any rate, I took Doris's statement, as well as the statements of the two witnesses."

Which was more than he'd apparently done during the Robbie Hollyburn murder investigation. "Can I talk to Tristan Law?" Victoria inquired politely.

"Of course. He's in the lockup if and until someone posts a bond for his release." The inspector smiled. "We put him next to Lenny Street."

Torbel didn't bat an eye, so Victoria asked, "What did Lenny Street do to be arrested?"

"Drunk and disorderly, together with attempted robbery."

The look on Torbel's face caused the inspector to take an involuntary step backward. "Street's no thief, Fox," Torbel growled. "He ran cons."

Sergeant Peacock endeavored to keep the peace. "I assure you, Torbel, Street was apprehended in Lammeth Lane. He had smashed the front window of Bottle's Clock Shoppe."

Inspector Fox sighed. "Street was holding a broken pendulum like a cricket bat, for God's sake. Ask him yourself if you doubt me. He's sleeping it off downstairs."

Victoria shivered at the unpromising set of Torbel's features. His eyes glittered with a warning light. He said nothing, but then he didn't have to. Fox got the message. So did she, and she hardly knew him. He didn't trust the inspector or the Stepney police.

"I'll see Tristan now," she said quickly.

Torbel's gaze remained locked on Oliver Fox. "I'll see Lenny Street."

"And I'll see you in hell, Torbel," a woman's voice hissed from the hallway to their left. Pale and furious, Clover Hollyburn aimed an accusing finger at Torbel's face. "You're going to pay for what you did to Robbie. Grandfather would forfeit his knighthood in order to see justice served, but he won't have to do that. Justice will out, Torbel. Your blood's as red as Robbie's—and just as readily spilled from the back."

AUGUSTUS HOLLYBURN HAD never seen fit to update his mansion to include a proper ventilation system. That is to say, he was cheap. As a result, he sat in his conservatory surrounded by a lush variety of green plants and sweltered in the afternoon heat.

The view from the large windows should have soothed his frayed nerves. The garden of his late wife, Blanche, spread out in a pleasing array of roses, violets and lilacs. The magnolias still showered the lawn, and the pansies might have been a velvet carpet, so thick was the bed that bordered the glass doors.

But he appreciated none of Blanche's efforts today. His old hands trembled as he sorted through papers from the open file on his desk.

Why had fate, or whatever force controlled such things, allowed Robbie to die? And at that bastard Rag Man's hands, no less.

One aged fist struck the blotter. If only he could be in league with the devil for five minutes, Torbel would be as dead as the doornail Charles Dickens had spoken of in *A Christmas Carol.* Deader, in fact. Jacob Marley had returned as a ghost. Torbel deserved no chance at spiritual redemption. Lenny Street, either, for that matter. Both men should rot in hell for the crime they'd committed.

A soft footfall from the doorway alerted him to another presence. He brought his head up, and his baleful eyes focused on the figure standing just inside the threshold.

His fingers went cold on his papers. His neck, however, throbbed, deep red beneath his ascot. "You," he breathed, too enraged to hurl the epithets he would have preferred. "How dare you present yourself to me!"

"Good afternoon to you, too, Grandfather." Zoe strolled brazenly into the conservatory.

She wore plain black pants and a white shirt that might have been mistaken for a police uniform. But Augustus knew Zoe when he saw her. She was a hussy, a witch and a thief, and he would never, never acknowledge her, not as a person and certainly not as his granddaughter.

He'd only felt this way once before that he could remember, the morning he'd woken up in Wales next to a witch. Oh, yes, she'd been a witch, all right, an emissary of the devil, truth be told. Blodwyn, she'd called herself, a flame-haired demon sent to lure him straight into purgatory. Of course, he hadn't known that at the time. Not until . . .

His blood boiled, shattering the memory. All thumbs, he stuffed the papers back into the file and shoved the whole thing into the first drawer he could locate. The pain in his chest started as it always did with a faint twinge, one he almost missed in his mounting rage.

Rubbing the affected area behind his ribs, he spluttered, "Get out!" He rose on unsteady legs. "Get out before I have Chivers throw you out."

"Chivers goes to market on Monday afternoons," Zoe returned in a level tone. "Don't excite yourself. I haven't come here to flaunt my worthless existence in your face. I have a question to put to you. When you answer it to my satisfaction, I'll leave."

The pain intensified. "Blast you," Augustus charged. He groped for the arm of his chair, subsiding into it with as much dignity as his stiff bones would allow.

He absolutely could not look at her, not out of any latent sense of sentimentality or affection, but because doing so would take the pain in his chest to heights that frightened even him. He wasn't done with life yet; he wouldn't be until the Rag Man paid the price for murdering Robbie.

"Ask your question then, and leave," he ordered roughly.

She moved to the front of his desk. Her fists were balled. He closed his eyes briefly, not wanting to view even that much of her.

"Are you behind the attacks on Torbel and Victoria?"

His eyes snapped open. Pain surged through his veins like broken bits of glass. "Damn you, woman! Are you accusing me of skulduggery? You who've thieved for more than half your—" he broke off, unable to continue. Gasping, he lay back in his chair and fought for breath.

He didn't know whether she reacted or not. Likely not, he reflected bitterly, although a glass of water did seem to have materialized on the blotter.

He needed his pills badly, but he'd be damned if he'd show dependency in front of her. Nor would he die at her feet. No, by God, he would fight this thing that weakened him. He would calm his temper, give her the answer she desired and forbid her to set foot in this house again.

Fingers strangling the chair arms, he said stiltedly, "I've had no part in any attacks on anyone."

Blast her, she didn't budge. "You know what I'm talking about, though, don't you?"

"I like to keep up to date where the murder of my grandson is concerned."

"Do you know Victoria?"

He grunted. "Victoria Summers. Twenty-nine years old, American-born lawyer, once the late Lord Hobday's junior assistant, now a solicitor at the firm of Bock, Press and Woodbury. She's been threatened, or so she claims, a number of times, after which she had the spectacularly bad sense to turn to that piece of scum Torbel for assistance. Beyond that, I know nothing about the woman. Now, get out and leave me be."

"Your pills are in the top right desk drawer," Zoe told him. "I can see them from here."

"I don't want my bloody pills—I want you gone!"

"You swear you're not in league with anyone regarding these attacks?"

"I swear," he said through his teeth.

Blindly he hunted for the top right drawer. It took him several seconds to locate the open edge. When he did, he very nearly yanked it off its track.

He needed two of them, he thought, panting. One to stop the pain, the second to keep it at bay.

He shook them out, spilling the bottle in the process. He managed to get them into his mouth and sat breathing heavily for a full sixty seconds.

Thank God, the stabbing behind his ribs eased. He massaged his left arm, sighed and, eyes closed, rested his head against the chair back.

"Goggy, you old adulterer. How are you this fine spring afternoon?"

Scratch? Augustus's eyes popped open. When had Zoe left? He'd heard nothing. He, whose hearing had always been as sharp as a cat's.

Scratch peered at him, his expression solicitous. "I say, you look a bit blue around the edges."

Augustus sat up. "Where did she go?" he demanded. "Did you see Zoe leave?"

Scratch shook his elegant head. "Sorry, no. Should I have? It's been years since I've seen, er, Zoe. I came by to finish last night's game. We packed it in rather abruptly." His golden eyes sparkled. "On my turn, as I recall."

Augustus grunted. "Why not? As *I* recall, I was winning."

"Game's not over yet," Scratch reminded in amusement. "There are still several moves to go."

Yes, there were, Augustus agreed, spitefully silent. But the moves he wanted to see played out had nothing to do with a wooden board and little bronze men.

"I'll win," he assured Scratch. He permitted the other man to help him up. On his feet, he swayed for a moment, then growled, albeit with a completely different subject in mind, "I'll dance on that bastard's grave, Scratch, if it's the last thing I do." He eyed his friend critically. "You sure you didn't see her?"

"Not a sign," Scratch promised. He placed a firm hand under Augustus's elbow. "You won't last the summer at this rate," he remonstrated. "Why don't you come with me to—?"

"No!" Adamant, Augustus jerked free. The movement unbalanced him. He stumbled into the desk but remained upright. "I have to see this through. The Rag Man killed my grandson. He'll burn for that. And I fully intend to light the flame."

Chapter Seven

"She got Tristan off, you know." Keiran and Torbel walked companionably toward the dockyard. "I'd have thought you'd be pleased."

Torbel fought a snarl—and a sharp pang that shot straight to his loins. "She lives a tidy little life in the West End of London, Keiran. The Stepney jails shocked her. She should go back where she belongs and hire an upscale detective to protect her. What time is it?"

"Three-ten, and you're snapping."

"The hell I am. I'm pissed off at Street for being too hung over this morning to talk. If the prat doesn't show today, I'll break his neck."

Keiran chuckled. "He'll show. Hey, Boots, how's it going?"

Boots's wrinkled face broke into a smile. "Lots of lolly, Keiran."

Not normally prone to conversation, Boots had been known to gabble at length to Keiran. Torbel paused.

"Pretty, dark-haired lady you was with this morning, Torbel," Boots remarked. "Looked like a Gypsy. Heard someone's out to kill her, and you, too. Not Lenny, though, no sir, not him."

Torbel studied the man's suddenly serious face, then crouched down. "What do you know, Boots?" he asked in a somber voice.

Boots tapped his temple. "People say I'm top, but I got eyes and ears like you an' all. Me mind works differently, but I know what's what. Lenny, he got a note just like your pretty lady."

"What did Street's note say, Boots?"

Boots's ring, his ill-gotten gift from Tito, flashed in a shaft of late-afternoon sun. "Not sure, but it rhymed. Find Lenny. He's prowling the docks now. I can see him in me head. I see lots in me head these days, Torbel. Sweep it clean, that's what me dreams told me last night. Sweep all the soot away."

Keiran stuffed a pound note in his top hat. "Sounds like your head needs a good cleaning, Boots."

The old man chuckled. "Lots of cobwebs in there, right enough. It'll be like that for you someday, Torbel. You got the magic in your blood. Powerful combination, that, Welsh and Irish. Your mam was—" The statement ended at the look Torbel cast from under his lashes. Boots shrugged, then grinned again. "Sweep it clean, Torbel. Sweep all the soot away." With that, he stood, picked up his black case and tottered off toward the storehouse.

"He's getting worse," Torbel noted in his wake.

"Maybe," Keiran agreed. "He's eighty-two."

"I believe it. He was old when I was born."

Keiran slanted him a humorous look. "I didn't know you had Welsh blood. Thought that temper of yours was pure Irish spit."

"It's pure enough." Torbel started off. The dockyard loomed under the arch of the train bridge. A murky atmosphere prevailed on this part of the waterfront. The Thames flowed green and slow, and everything was covered in grime. A group of street performers practicing their sleight of hand provided the only visible splash of color.

"Watch this, Torbel," a boy with spiked silver hair called out. He whipped three cups around on the stone street. "Where's the ball, then?"

Torbel grinned. "On your left, Needles."

"Damn. How'd you know?"

"He saw it in his mind," Keiran teased.

"Shut up," Torbel ordered without rancor. "Has anyone seen Lenny Street?"

Needles, so nicknamed because of his pointy hair, nodded. "He went dockside ten minutes ago with a brown paper bag in his jacket."

Torbel swore, thinking back. Hungover in the Stepney jail today, Street had mumbled a disjointed tale of a threat he'd received early last night. What that threat entailed hadn't been clear—and never would be if Torbel didn't catch his former associate before he drank himself senseless.

"Torbel?"

Her voice more than the sound of his name brought his head around with a surprised jerk. His features darkened ominously. "What," he demanded of a faintly breathless Victoria, "are you doing here?"

"I saw you from my cab—taxi. I wanted to tell you about Tristan. Hello, Keiran. I got the charges—"

"Dropped. I heard."

"From whom? Tristan's been with me all day."

"News travels fast down here."

"Western Union should be so fast." She swiped at a strand of silky hair that had tumbled across her cheek. "You're welcome anyway."

"Your thanks will come in the form of a check," Torbel told her, feeling out of sorts and uncustomarily edgy. "I don't ask favors of clients."

"Well, this client doesn't want a check," she retorted. "My da didn't raise any Scroogey old sinners. Now, what's happening with our case?"

Torbel's eyes, and only his eyes, came up. "Our case?"

She faced him, chin up, shoulders back, a challenging stance he gave her credit for pulling off. His mother had warned him as a child to use his stare with discretion. Turquoise ice had a power all its own—or so she'd insisted. Torbel had never been a believer in mysticism.

He did, however, have a powerful stare, one that had intimidated more than its share of individuals, Keiran and Augustus Hollyburn excluded. Apparently Victoria Summers had joined that select group.

Damn the woman for getting to him like this, though, for making the blood boil up hot and fast in his veins, for calling up visions of his mother and Ireland and Wales. Later memories of his grandparents in London had no bite, but the first eleven years of his life were a different story.

"I'm going to meet Lenny Street," he drawled at length, too aware of her for a fierce verbal spar. "Trust me, he's not apt to say much in front of a stranger."

"If he's in anything resembling this morning's state of health, he's not apt to say much at all. You think he's behind this, don't you? Do you also think he killed Robbie Hollyburn?"

"No and no." Torbel tapped his wrist at Keiran.

"Three-fifty," Keiran obliged. "Street'll be halfway to ratted by now. We'll find him faster if we split up."

Torbel gnashed his teeth. He wasn't about to send Victoria off with Keiran, and all three of them standing there in the shadowy heat of the railway arch knew it.

"All right," he allowed reluctantly. "Let's go." He exchanged a look with Keiran that spoke of taking care, then cupped Victoria's elbow firmly in his palm and nudged.

Her skin felt like hot silk against his callused fingers. A jolt of awareness so strong it made his breath stutter speared through him. Her hair smelled of roses and some other wildflower he remembered from Ireland. She'd removed her pin-striped jacket and now wore only a sleeveless white silk top with her slim-fitting skirt and high heels.

Her hair was a riot of raven dark curls around her face and shoulders. He fought a sigh. Hair like that surrounding features like hers, so clear and delicately sculpted, should be a crime. It made men do crazy things—like allowing her to accompany them back to the docks, he thought dryly. God must be punishing him for a wicked life.

"Hey, Torbel, you after Street?" A heavyset man in a cap and coal-smudged trousers flapped a hand at a collection of stone buildings near the worst part of the waterfront. "He's in Myrtle's."

What the hell was he doing in there? Torbel's irritation must have transmitted itself to Victoria, for she glanced at him.

"You look like a thundercloud. What's Myrtle's?"

A brothel was what it was, loosely disguised as a dockside pub. He couldn't take Victoria there. On the other hand, leaving her here would be even more dangerous. He debated with himself, then said shortly, "Put your jacket on."

"But it's too..." Her eyes narrowed. "Why? What is Myrtle's?"

"Likely what you think."

She sent him a look of distrust and annoyance and pulled on her jacket. "Men," she said with feeling.

He was sorely tempted to kiss her, but that would be a serious mistake right now. Let her be angry. Better for both of them that her guard remain intact. Myrtle's had seen its share of violence, and his feelings for her were too volatile by half.

The building had a beetle brow and doors that creaked as if they'd been hinged in the Middle Ages. Inside was a smoky den of sailors and dockworkers, women in skimpy outfits and a piano player dressed in rumpled, turn-of-the-century clothes: a striped shirt, black vest, cuffs and collar. On his head sat a black derby, gnawed and dented in more than a few places.

Victoria ventured a sardonic "The stage is for stripping, I presume."

Torbel regarded the dusty blue velvet curtains and shrugged. "It's nondiscriminatory. Oswyn worked here once."

"Oswyn's just a boy. He couldn't possibly have..." But of course he could have, and she knew it. Her denial trailed off. "That's sick."

Keeping a tight grip on her arm—and a tight leash on his mounting desire, Torbel guided her through the sea of sweating bodies toward a booth next to the stage. "He wasn't a rent-boy, Victoria. Don't be so judgmental."

"A cat burglar who works strip joints on the side doesn't have to be judged. His actions speak for themselves—and I'm not a prude."

"I never said you were." Torbel spotted Lenny, hunched over a glass of ale with a paper bag beside him. "Stop squirming. Pretend you're with me, and no one will bother you."

Lenny's eyes, bleary from drink, raked Victoria from head to toe. A smile lit his scruffy face. "Wah-hey, pretty lawyer lady. Have a seat, and we'll compare notes." He dangled his glass over the table. "Go away, Torbel. Me and the lady got things to discuss. Things in common, we got."

He was drunk and getting drunker by the minute. Torbel made no move to leave. "Show me the note, Lenny."

"Can't be showed," the man slurred, and flicked at a pile of ashes on the table. "Burned it."

Torbel was on him in an instant, dropping Victoria's arm and forcing Street up against the side of the booth. "You stupid idiot. Why?"

He heard Victoria's hissed "Torbel! People are staring."

Once aroused, however, his temper was difficult to assuage. And desire for Victoria had only heightened it. Ignoring her, he focused on the man huddled against the wall. "What'd the note say, Street? Tell me what it said and where and when you got it."

Street's flinty eyes held the distant light of rage. But he answered in a grudging mumble. "I found it on the table at Gooseberries last night."

"What time?"

"Going on seven o'clock."

Near the time they'd left for Victoria's flat. "What did it say?" Lenny's head bobbed, forcing Torbel to shake him. "Wake up, Street. Tell me what the note said."

"Don't remember," Lenny said fuzzily. "'Bang, you're dead' or something."

"Did it rhyme?" Victoria asked. Torbel spared her a sideways glance. She was kneeling on the wooden bench opposite Lenny. "'Twinkle, twinkle, little star'—that sort of thing?"

Street blinked in vague recognition. "Not that—the other one. 'Star bright, star light.'"

"Yes, go on," Victoria urged.

Torbel shook him again to keep him conscious. "Think, Street. You have a photographic memory, for Christ's sake."

Street's head lolled, but he cracked a canny eye at Torbel. "I do know, actually," he slurred proudly. Torbel released him as Lenny's face screwed up in concentration. "'Bang, bang, bang,'" he began. "No, it was 'Bang, stab . . .' I better write it down."

Victoria hunted through her purse for a paper and pen. Lenny took them and began to scrawl tiny, illegible words.

"How much for an hour?" a voice boomed out.

Torbel closed resigned eyes. It was bound to happen, he supposed.

The man slobbering over Victoria had a beer belly and jowls like a Saint Bernard. "She's not . . ." Torbel began, and would have said "a prostitute," had Victoria not inserted a swift "available."

The man emitted a disbelieving snort. "Who're you with? Not Street, that's for sure. And not Torbel, 'cause he don't do it with Myrtle's ladies. Got his own at Gooseberries, eh, Torbel?"

Did he know this git? Since he couldn't summon a name, Torbel said simply, "Sod off," and reached for Victoria's hand. He could have been gentler when he hauled her out of the booth and tucked her in beside him, but too soft and even a git would catch on.

Whether this one caught on or not, Torbel never knew. Nor did he see the meaty fist coming at him from the side. He heard a grunt, then the man's knuckles planted themselves in his cheek. Around him, the pub tilted precariously. The last thing he recalled was Victoria shouting his name and the man's tooth glinting gold in the flickering bar light.

"YOU SON OF A . . ." Victoria's accusation ended on a startled "Ooomph" as the man, using his elbow, knocked her roughly out of the way.

"I'll get to you later," he promised.

She landed in someone's arms, a slender man covered with soot. "Sorry," she mumbled to the chimney sweep into whom she'd stumbled. He merely thrust her upright and pushed his way through the crowd to the door. "Same to you, pal," she muttered at his departing back.

It took her several nerve-racking moments to locate Torbel on the floor, for the simple reason that he was no longer *on* the ground. The creep with the blackberry eyes and saggy jowls was sprawled like a felled giant in his place.

"Let's go." She was seized by a hand and spun around before she could object. But Torbel's touch in all things was unique and inimitable. "Lenny," he barked in the direction of the booth.

The fight gained momentum behind them; Victoria heard a chair crash over a table, followed by the sound of breaking glass. How, she wondered in amazement, could the piano man keep playing through such a ruckus? He didn't pause, just kept pounding out his off-key reel.

"Did I start this?" She looked back in amazement. "Hey, that's my foot," she said crossly as Lenny Street banged into her.

"Watch it," Torbel snapped.

"Something pricked me," Street defended.

Victoria caught the sickly sweet odor of rotting flowers. To her shock, a theatrically made-up woman flew past, landing hard in a sailor's lap. In the most bawdy pub of her da's acquaintance, she'd never witnessed a brawl. It was fascinating, if not entirely pleasant.

Lenny scribbled as he staggered into the night. "'Bang or stab,'" he mumbled, too intoxicated to be afraid. "'Don't look now, Street'..."

He finished with a proud flourish, held the paper out, then promptly collapsed onto a half-closed rain barrel.

"It's a threat, you know," he said in a blurred voice. "I'm gonna d-die."

He flexed stiff fingers in consternation. Cigarette smoke wafted from Myrtle's, along with numerous shrieks and crashes.

"I..." A look of sudden alarm swept over his saturnine face. His mouth moved like a fish. "Torbel," he gasped, "I—I can't...breathe. I—I..." His hands went up to circle his throat.

"Street?" Torbel looked over. "What is it? What's wrong?"

"He's hyperventilating." Victoria shook the man's thin arm. "Calm down, Lenny. There's no one here. It's only a note."

"Can't..." He stood, thrashing his arms as he fought for air. "Torbel—help me!"

Torbel caught him as he pitched forward. With Victoria's help, he laid Lenny down on the cracked pavement. Victoria loosened his collar to no apparent avail. If anything, Lenny's breathing grew increasingly ragged.

"What is it?" Fear shot through her. "Does he have a bad heart?"

Torbel's features were grim. He pumped Street's chest with the heels of his hand. "It isn't his heart, Victoria. Call an ambulance."

She scrambled to her feet. She would have returned to Myrtle's, but he motioned her away. "There's a call box at the end of the pier. Get the police while you're at it."

"I— Okay." Did she have money? She scrabbled through her purse as she ran, abandoning her shoes halfway to the booth.

Ambulance first, then police.

The sergeant at the local precinct house told her to stay put, an officer would be dispatched at once.

When she returned to Torbel, winded and hot, he was crouched beside Lenny Street's supine form, staring blank faced. "He's dead."

Deflated, Victoria sank to her knees. "I don't understand. Dead how? He wasn't shot. He isn't bleeding, so he wasn't stabbed." Very slowly logic began to creep in. "He couldn't breathe." She questioned Torbel with her eyes. "Poison?"

"Probably. Did you call the precinct house?"

"They're sending someone." She hesitated, then asked quietly, "What kind of poison? Fast, slow? In his beer? What?"

"I don't know." Torbel regarded the paper at Lenny's side, the one on which he'd scrawled the threat. His brow furrowed as he read:

Starlight, star bright,
No star for you tonight.
Bang and stab in back or head.
Don't look now, Street,
Bang, you're dead!

MUCH TO DO. The sweep hastened through a press of bodies to his underground lair. A quick wash and change, check the new mirror for details and away.

The heat lacked no punch for the absence of the sun. A high haze continued to blanket London and the Thames. The sweep unpocketed the dart gun and peered into a cluttered alley. Ten rubbish bins . . . No, better still, the junkyard.

Careful now, mustn't be observed. Toss the gun. No prints to identify, no darts or poison. Not that the gun was likely to be found, but stranger things had happened. Look at Victoria Summers. She'd fallen right on top of the thing at Myrtle's. It could have gone off easily, discharged straight into her backside. But up she'd jumped unharmed, and the sweep had been forced to beat a hasty retreat.

Time for a new disguise, a more visible, less noticeable one. Now, there was a dichotomy. More visible, less noticeable. And there was that other matter, as well. The bomb. It must be procured tonight and all the bits and pieces checked. Too bad an innocent life would be sacrificed, but justice must be served. A noble end to an ignoble existence.

The former sweep eased back into the usual routine. All would be well very soon. But, oh, how gratifying it would have been to see Lenny Street die. That pleasure must not be missed with Victoria and Torbel. Perhaps the event should be videotaped. Old Augustus would view such a tape with relish.

So, thought the one-time sweep with a vengeful chuckle, would the perpetrator.

Chapter Eight

Poison. Lenny Street had been shot with a poisoned dart. That's what had pricked him when he'd stomped on her foot at Myrtle's.

Inside Zoe's Baker Street flat above Gooseberries, Victoria sat with the lights out, hugging an overstuffed cushion and struggling with the morbid sense of guilt that threatened to consume her. This whole nightmare had started with her. Now a man was dead.

Try as she might to lock the picture away, it kept returning: a distant reel, flies droning against the pub windows, the smell of river water and old wood, Torbel trying to pound life into Lenny's constricted chest. . . .

Torbel . . .

She hugged the cushion closer, focusing on the uneven collection of London chimneys and rooftops. He'd taken his old comrade's death with seeming equanimity, but that lack of expression on his face had been a sham. He cared. Not as deeply as if it had been Keiran lying there at his feet, but he cared. And so did she.

One thing she knew: Torbel would never admit it. That stony exterior of his hid—she didn't know what yet. But it was no heart of ice.

Damn! She closed her eyes to the patchwork London night. Why hadn't she done something this afternoon? Put her arms around Torbel and kissed him. Why hadn't he turned to her?

"Because we're both pigheaded idiots, that's why," she said out loud.

The walls didn't respond, and Zoe wasn't home. As far as Victoria could tell, she hadn't been home since early afternoon, which was when the note she'd scribbled said she'd left to follow a lead on her current case.

A chill feathered along Victoria's spine at the thought of notes and cases. Lenny Street's note had had all the earmarks of insanity about it: a childish rhyme, altered in the most gruesome fashion. Plus, according to Boots, who'd glimpsed the original, the words had been comprised of large, poorly cut letters. Whoever the perpetrator was, his or her mind must be deteriorating. Victoria's threats had been neatly cut and pasted.

Resting her forehead against the cushion, she tried for a less disruptive train of thought. Her mind kept calling up images of the Rag Man. With his dark, satyric features and penetrating eyes, he was undeniably the most compelling man she'd ever met, and that included the thieves, con artists and murderers she'd once helped Lord Hobday to convict.

So, knowing that, why did she keep dwelling on him? Sexy and appealing he might be, but she wanted no part of him, or shouldn't if she was smart.

Determined, Victoria fastened her mind on Prudie and the Florida bayou where she'd spent so many happy years. She missed Prudie. She missed America and Taco Bell and pizzas with panache. But if she left London now, she'd miss her da. She might also come to miss Torbel, but, of course, any feelings in that area must not be allowed to develop. A child would have understood that from the start.

"Any child but me," she mumbled into the cushion.

He knew virtually nothing about her or she about him. It was galling. He thought she came from a wealthy background; she'd bet on it. He probably believed she loved her job, loved her flat, her car and her dog. Well, she loved Rosie, all right, but as for the other things—she just didn't know anymore. Maybe she never really had.

The sound of the door creaking open intruded on her thoughts and brought her head up swiftly.

"Zoe?"

It looked like Zoe; however, the woman on the threshold clad in black pants and a tight black cotton T-shirt froze at the sight of her. She carried a flashlight and hadn't bothered to switch on the apartment lights. Her sharp intake of breath spoke as eloquently as words.

Victoria came to her feet. "Clover," she said, uncertain how to handle this.

"I knocked," the woman said stiffly. Definitely Clover's rigorously controlled voice. But had it not been for that, Clover Hollyburn could have passed for Zoe in a minute. She was even dressed like a cat burglar. Come to think of it . . .

Victoria's eyes landed with open suspicion on the flashlight. "What are you doing here?"

"I did knock," Clover repeated. She sounded like a robot, no emotion, no change of expression.

Keeping her distance, Victoria crossed to the wall and flipped the light switch. Clover blinked at the glare, started to edge away, then thought better of it and lifted her chin. "I thought you were out with Torbel."

"He had something to do." Victoria studied Clover's face feature by feature. The makeup was different, but they had the same small beauty spot on their right cheeks. The similarity was so strong as to be almost eerie. "Obviously you didn't expect to find anyone," she continued, "so why did you come if not to see Zoe?"

Clover's jaw tightened. "I knocked," she said for the third time.

Victoria's temper rose. "And I didn't answer. Most people would have turned around and left, but you came in. Why?"

"That's none of your business."

"I think it is since I'm staying here."

"It's between Zoe and me, then. We're twins, after all. Maybe I just wanted to be here when she got home."

Victoria arched a skeptical brow. "For a sisterly chat?"

"Why not?"

"Well, for one thing, you're carrying a flashlight and wearing gloves. For another, the door was locked. You had to pick that lock in order to get in. I don't know your habits, Clover, but that seems a bit extreme to me just for the sake of having a few words with your estranged sister."

"Who said we were estranged?"

"Zoe implied as much."

Clover balled her free fist. "Zoe and Grandfather are at odds. I happen to value our relationship more than that. Now, if it's all the same to you, I'll go."

"Shall I tell Zoe you stopped by?"

Clover whirled. Her lips were thin and white; her eyes flashed blue fire. "Tell her any damned thing you please, Victoria Summers. You've allied yourself with the man who murdered my brother. All of you in the crown attorney's office were on his side from day one. So don't come the saint with me, lady. You jumped on the devil's bandwagon. You'd better be prepared for one hell of a ride."

Victoria stared in disbelief. She'd never seen such hatred. "You're crazy," she said softly. She realized her mistake instantly. Never call a spade a spade when dealing with sorely strained emotions.

She could almost see the wire in Clover's brain snap. Emitting a snarl, the woman came for her, shoving her hard with both gloved hands, then pouncing on her like a mad tiger.

Thank heaven for the years she'd spent with her da, because there was no way to avoid the attack except to throw her arm across her face and thrust her knee up hard into Clover's stomach.

Clover made a choked noise and fell to the side. Victoria scrambled away, first on hands and knees, then, using the table for support, on foot. She yanked open the door, rushed through—and crashed full bore into a black wall.

Her first thought was that it was a wet wall, her second that it was moving and therefore not a wall at all. She jerked her head back and, when her eyes focused, wasn't sure whether to hit him or hug him. She settled for a glare followed by an apprehensive glance over her shoulder. "What are you doing here?"

The faint bark that emerged from under his jersey answered her question and brought a smile to her lips. "Rosie!" she exclaimed, forgetting for the moment the woman behind her.

A little mop-top head poked out to peer around in wonder. With more gentleness than Victoria thought he possessed, Torbel extricated the tiny Yorkshire terrier and handed her over.

"Is that Clover?" he asked, sounding displeased. "What's she doing here?"

"Ask her." Victoria let Rosie lick her face. "All I got was some gibberish about wanting to see her sister."

"Bull."

It was as good a response as any, but it incited Clover's rage all over again—although seeing the object of her hatred probably hadn't done much to defuse it. She faced him resentfully, breathing hard and glowering.

"I don't have to explain myself to you or your new client," she growled. "This is between Zoe and me."

"Did you attack Victoria just now?"

"Stick to your own business, Torbel. You've more than enough of it these days." She fixed Victoria with a furious stare. "Did my sister say when she'd be back?"

"I haven't seen her all day," Victoria answered. She couldn't resist adding a barbed "I could have told you that earlier if you'd bothered to ask."

"I knocked," Clover said through her teeth.

Odd, Victoria thought, how some people could rationalize any crime they chose to commit.

"Go home, Clover," Torbel said without inflection. "And tell your grandfather, if he's involved in this mess, to back off. His age won't stop me from squeezing the life out of him the day I find his hand in any of it."

Clover trembled with suppressed fury. "How dare you," she declared in a raw voice. "You, a murderer, accusing my grandfather of conspiracy. He has class, Torbel. He wouldn't sink to your level for a minute, not for a million pounds and a knighthood guaranteed."

"No, he'd leave that chore to you, wouldn't he, his faithful dogsbody. You'd sacrifice Zoe, yourself, your official oath, everything and anything to get me, wouldn't you? To hell with the legal system, you're a bloody one-woman crusade, a vigilante with a single aim in life—to see me dead." He began to advance on her, his manner slow and intimidating. "Did you send the notes to Victoria or Street? Did you kill Lenny today on the docks? Were you in Myrtle's when the fight broke out? Or maybe you instigated it by suggesting that git of a man make an offer for Victoria."

Her lithe body coiled like a spring, Clover snapped, "The word's been out on that incident for hours, Torbel. You took your client into Myrtle's. What did you expect? Did you think your high and mighty legal lady could just sashay in and out without having her delicate sensibilities disrupted?" Her eyes glittered in the overhead light. "Now, if you two will excuse me, I'm on early watch tomorrow."

"I'll give your regards to Zoe," Victoria remarked as Clover brushed past.

A muffled hiss was the only answer she received. Five seconds later, the rear stairwell door clicked shut and Clover was gone.

Victoria sighed into the silky fur of Rosie's head, then arched a meaningful brow. "She broke in, Torbel. That bulge in her pocket was probably lock picks."

He went to the window, holding back the curtain with two fingers and gazing out. "She's a cop with a former cat burglar for a sister. She knows plenty about breaking and entering."

"So do I, but I wouldn't go around using the knowledge."

He slid her a steady look. "Come again, Victoria?"

She backpedaled hastily. "Breaking into a place like this would be child's play, Torbel." She deposited Rosie into an easy chair. "I didn't mean to imply that I knew how...."

"The hell you didn't."

His words were softly spoken, but Victoria recognized a potential explosion when she heard one. He started menacingly toward her, yet for the life of her she couldn't back away.

"What are you?" he demanded in that same low voice.

"I'm a lawyer," she replied with false composure. "Not born to this life exactly, but not pampered, either. My mother's a poet-painter. She lives in a cabin with no bathroom and few other conveniences. I lived with her for a while when I was very young, but my Aunt Prudie, who's really my great-aunt, thought my mother's life-style was too Spartan for a child. So she took me to Florida. Prudie has a house in the bayou. I can catch and gut fish and make a terrific stew out of them—if that's of any interest to you, which I'm sure it isn't.

"My da's English, Yorkshire born and bred. He lives in London now. He's a hawker with a barrow that he uses to sell everything from cabbages to corn flour. He has a one-room flat in Whitechapel, not the better part, but it isn't a council flat. He pays full rent, helps his friends when he can and bought Rosie from a Southampton breeder for my birthday last fall. He also sent money to help pay my tuition at law school in New England. He has scruples and morals, and if you make one nasty or sarcastic remark about either he or Prudie, I swear, Torbel, I'll use the fireplace poker to give you a matching scar on your other cheek."

Her hands had planted themselves on her hips during her tirade. Her voice had firmed up, as well, ending now in a direct challenge. Just let him disparage the two people she loved most in the world. That would stop any attraction she felt for him dead in its tracks.

To her surprise, and perhaps relief—she was reluctant to analyze the second feeling—he halted less than a foot in front of her. She thought for one heart-stopping moment that he was going to kiss her. Instead, he stared into her eyes, his own dark and unfathomable. She saw the scar on his cheek at close range and felt a now-familiar flutter in her stomach. The heat and humidity pressed in with suffocating potential. Dark, dangerous and sexy. She might have been a fly trapped in the Rag Man's web.

His presence filled not merely the room but the entire apartment. Victoria experienced a moment of breathlessness, but fought it. This was no time for attraction. He hadn't responded to her challenge yet.

Lifting a hand, he cupped her cheek. The callused texture of his skin against hers felt strangely erotic. His eyes, deep blue flecked with green, continued to hold hers. Would he deride her da and Prudie as others in her profession had done so subtly in the past?

She waited, not breathing as he ran his fingers along her cheek and jaw. The kiss that he unexpectedly dropped on her startled lips demanded nothing in return. In fact, it was over before she even realized he'd moved.

"Your da and Prudie sound like good people" was all he said. "You're a very lucky woman."

Then he was gone, and all Victoria could do was stare after him with a blend of bemusement and suspicion. She hadn't thanked him for bringing Rosie here tonight. She'd have to do that tomorrow. Because she certainly wasn't about to follow him into the street, not feeling the way she did at this moment. Rosie aside, she still didn't trust him an inch. More important, she didn't trust herself.

And that, she reflected with a deep, consuming shiver, might just be the most frightening discovery of all.

ZOE STUMBLED IN near dawn, yawning and distracted. The sound of the door closing roused Victoria from a fitful sleep.

Zoe's clothes were smudged and smelled of burned matches. "I had a tussle with a group of teens lighting fireworks," she explained, then headed off toward the bedroom, coffee and a piece of raisin toast in hand.

When Victoria mentioned Clover's strange visit, she'd offered no comment. The news agitated her, though; Victoria could see that by the way her slender shoulder muscles bunched beneath her shirt.

She liked Zoe and wanted to help, but there was little she could do until Zoe told her the exact nature of the problem between herself and Clover. So she fell back into bed for three hours, then got up for good, showered, dressed and went out to buy some proper food for Rosie.

London in late spring contained its own brand of magic and charm, most of it rooted in centuries of history. The early-morning markets drew her like a magnet. Soon she was laden with parcels and bags.

Boots hailed her from his post outside the bake shop. He had half a baguette in one hand and a spoon covered with raspberry jam in the other. "I heard it again in me dreams last night, pretty lady," he said gravely.

She didn't understand. "Heard what, Mr., er, Boots?"

"'Sweep the soot away,' it said. 'Sweep it clean.'" He peered at her face from every angle. "You look Gypsy. You got Gypsy blood in you? No? The Welsh, then?"

"I don't think so," Victoria said politely. Despite his close scrutiny, something about the old man appealed to her. Maybe he reminded her of her da thirty years from now. Or maybe he resembled a character in a book. Dr. Watson, or Mr. Doyce from *Little Dorrit*. At any rate, she found herself digging through her wallet while he talked.

"Torbel, he's got the Welsh, you know. Oh, yes, the Welsh and the Irish. You can never tell about a mix like that. Gets it from his mam. She was a beauty, that one. Came to London for a time in the late fifties. A vision she was, and a visionary."

Her curiosity piqued, Victoria set her parcels down. She had to kneel, because Boots had settled onto his case to eat his baguette. "So Torbel's mother was a fortune-teller, a clairvoyant?"

"She saw things in her head, aye. But that wasn't all she could do when up against it. I saw her once make a man start to choke who was pushing around his wife and sister. The man was an M.P. He tried to have her charged with assault. He got laughed off the block in the end, but she did it to him, no mistake about it, and he knew it. His wife left him after that, and he never got reelected, so it was a good ending all around. But only a few would believe if you told them the story."

"Does Torbel believe?"

"He says no, but I think he knows what's what." The old man's eyes sparkled. "Maybe he's afraid, eh, lass?"

"Of what? His mother?"

"Nah. She's dead more than twenty years now. Afraid of himself, of what his own mind could do, put to the test."

"But that's…" She started to say "silly," caught herself and changed it to "nothing to worry about, surely. If he had any clairvoyant ability, it would have manifested itself before now."

The sparkle deepened. "How do you know it ain't?"

How indeed? Instinct perhaps. Or maybe because, of the psychics she'd met through Prudie and mother, not one of them had possessed a scrap of ESP. They couldn't even read tea leaves or tarot cards with any degree of success. Still, she wanted to hear anything about Torbel that Boots was willing to share.

"Why did he leave Scotland Yard, Boots?"

"Therein lies one of the great mysteries of our age," a new but familiar voice put in. Sergeant Peacock touched his cap. "Good morning, Ms. Summers, Boots." Victoria saw the old man slip the money she'd given him into his shirt. "So, you're curious about Torbel, eh?" The sergeant smiled, a cordial, albeit less than open smile. "I'm afraid the only person who can answer questions of that sort is Torbel himself. And speaking of questions, I'm told he's been asking several of his own this morning."

"About Lenny Street?" Victoria inquired from her knees. Boots, she noticed, had clammed right up. He was currently tucking his stash of smaller treasures into his shirt, away from Peacock's keen eyes.

"That and any strangers who might have been seen lurking about lately. Inspector Fox is, shall we say, less than impressed."

"Why?"

"Because it isn't Torbel's province to interfere."

"You're contradicting yourself, Sergeant. You sent me to Torbel—now you don't want him to help me?"

The sergeant clasped his hands behind his back, his military stance halfway between attention and at ease. "Lenny Street's death falls under our jurisdiction," he stated. "It has nothing to do with your problem."

"No? Then how do you explain his note?"

"I don't. First of all, it was written in his own handwriting."

"The original wasn't."

"As far as we are aware, the note in Street's possession at the time of death was the original."

"Then you're unaware. Tell him, Boots." Victoria turned to the old man.

Boots shook his head. "Already told Inspector Fox. He said I was top and sent me on me way. Just like old Goggy, that one. But I'll go with the sergeant to the station if he wants."

Sergeant Peacock nodded. "If we need you, we'll send Clover to fetch you, Boots. Can I walk you to the Rag Man's storehouse, Ms. Summers?"

"No, thanks, I'm going to talk to Boots for a while longer."

"As you wish." He dipped his head. "Watch out for pickpockets. This neighborhood remains infamous despite the best efforts of our department."

"Pompous prig," Boots declared when he was gone. "Still, he's better than Fox and all. Now, there's a fitting name if ever I heard one. Cunning as any fox you'll meet is our inspector. Not like how he looks, all polished and primped like a toff. Can't trust the toffs, miss. They're the trickiest of all." His old eyes clouded. "Robbie knew that. Figured it out on his own, he did. Can't trust a toff as far as you can throw them." His gaze sharpened on hers. "Can't trust a fox what owes his soul to a toff even more."

Chapter Nine

"Inspector Fox is a crook!" Victoria declared. She looked around the storehouse. "Where's Torbel?"

Keiran pushed off from the desk where he'd been going through a pile of notes and grinned at her. "Out, and I know."

Victoria paused in the midst of extracting a file from her briefcase. It was 8:00 a.m. Wednesday morning, muggy, overcast and threatening rain. She'd been up half the night with a borrowed laptop computer, and for Keiran to tell her that he already knew what had taken her a great deal of time and even more luck to unearth was not what she wanted to hear. "How did you find out?"

"We like to keep track of who's pulling the strings at the local station. What did you dig up?"

Was there any point to this? Victoria sighed. "Large gambling debts, mysteriously paid in the eleventh hour, then neatly glossed over as being part of an undercover investigation. Several assaults, buried in red tape and also glossed over. Several more alcohol-related charges, too cloudy to interpret properly."

"And all charges ultimately dismissed," Keiran concluded. "Anything else?"

"Three thefts."

"Really? We only know about two in Durham."

"There was a third in Manchester twenty-five years ago. He robbed a pub at closing time." She flicked through the file.

"The official report is sketchy, but in the end it was put down to an undercover preventive-measures investigation."

"Same as the first two." Keiran shrugged a broad shoulder. "The powers that be said he was conducting an investigation into safety and awareness in the community. I say that's a load of old cobblers. I'd also say that Fox has an angel on his shoulder."

"More like friends in high places," Ron grumbled, passing through with a large box. "Torbel's back if you want him," he told Victoria. He didn't look at her, though. And he wasn't about to let her see what he was carrying in the box.

"Whatever." Keiran addressed Ron's first remark. "Fox isn't the only person with connections. Police, politicians, just plain rich people—you get off and get ahead a lot easier if you've got someone above you with the clout keeping you squeaky-clean while they're pulling you up your chosen ladder."

Sliding the file back in her case, Victoria asked, "So who's Fox's 'someone with clout'?"

Keiran grinned. He really was a very handsome man, not classically so, but good-looking just the same. And not a fraction of the shadowy mystery that Torbel was, either, she'd bet.

"Some say it's the chief inspector himself. Others think there's a royal connection."

"Sounds like Jack the Ripper."

"Not quite that bad, but he's no paragon of virtue."

"Is he bad enough to have killed a man?"

"If you mean Robbie, I wouldn't have said so. Street, either, for that matter. Fox has never been overly bloodthirsty."

"Neither has Peacock," Ron put in gruffly on his way back through the central area. "But he can kill. Spent a fair bit of time in the navy. Word is he could pick off the enemy at two hundreds yards in heavy fog."

"Stories like that tend to be exaggerated over time," Keiran countered easily. "Morning, Torbel. Any luck?"

"Not much." Victoria caught the mocking edge in his voice when he added, "No forays to Bouverie Street today?"

Of course, her cutoffs and oversize white T-shirt would give that away. "I thought it might be more productive to do some investigating on my own," she retorted sweetly. God, he looked good today, freshly showered and in clean jeans, an off-white jersey and boots. His brown hair was all unruly curls; his eyes gleamed wickedly in the sullen morning light.

The air felt sticky and close. Victoria sensed a thunderstorm approaching, but so far there'd been nothing. Hardly a puff of wind stirred the air. She smelled bread baking, oranges and soap—the latter no doubt from Torbel's skin. She needed to get out of here quickly, she thought in mild desperation.

"Victoria did a recce through Fox's confidential files," Keiran was saying. "It seems we missed a few details."

"We know how he cartwheeled over Peacock and others like him to get to the top spot," Ron noted sourly.

Victoria was uncomfortably aware of Torbel's eyes on her as he returned, "Top spot down here is no coup."

She found her tongue. "That would depend on your background, Torbel. For someone like Fox, this might be considered quite a coup."

"Or a stepping stone to bigger and better things," Keiran added.

"Yes, and to hell with how many toes he has to step on to get there." Victoria frowned. "I wonder if Sergeant Peacock resents being passed over for promotion in favor of Inspector Fox."

Torbel poured himself a cup of coffee from an urn on one of the cluttered tables and brought it steaming to his mouth. "I doubt if he'd be too happy about it, but he isn't likely to drop Fox at two hundred yards in the fog out of spite, either."

Keiran chuckled. "You heard that, did you? You're the one who wants suspects, Torbel. We're just trying to provide a few viable ones."

Victoria's mouth watered for the coffee she'd missed that morning. "Suspects for what?" she asked. "Robbie Hollyburn's death, the poisoning of Lenny Street or the attack on Torbel and me?"

"Take your pick," Torbel said dryly. "Information's hard to come by on any of them right now. No one's seen or heard a thing as far as I can tell. Except Boots, and I haven't bumped into him yet this morning."

Victoria's spirits sank. If Torbel couldn't eke out information down here, she doubted anyone could. Hopefully Boots wouldn't turn out to be their only source. He might be a lovable old codger, but he was also caught up in Welsh-Irish magic and premonitory dreams.

He'd told her things about the Rag Man, though, fascinating tidbits, which she'd promised to keep secret and would never have been able to worm out of Torbel. Not yet anyway. He was too private a man for that.

He had a university education, but no major in criminology. What he knew of criminals and crime fighting, he'd picked up on the streets—mostly in London, but also apparently in Ireland and Wales as a child.

Also his grandfather on his mother's side was still alive. He lived in County Clare. His grandmother was dead, but she'd been Welsh-American, born and raised in New York City. It was, Victoria decided, a very small world.

However, his reasons for leaving Scotland Yard were, as Sergeant Peacock suggested, one of life's great mysteries. Boots had no idea. Neither did Tito, whom she'd quite literally bumped into later that afternoon.

She hadn't bumped into Zoe until this morning. Unfortunately, with all the information about Inspector Fox running through her head, she'd forgotten to ask about Torbel.

"What about it, Victoria?" Torbel's question broke into her thoughts.

"I—" She searched for the thread of their conversation but found nothing. "I'm sorry," she said truthfully. "I didn't hear you."

Was it amusement that danced through Torbel's eyes? He handed her a cup of coffee. "Here, this'll wake you up. Do you know where Boots might be today?"

"I'm not sure." She sipped the coffee and shuddered. It tasted like hot turpentine. "He mentioned trying his luck at the pub. I think he meant Gooseberries."

Torbel gave Keiran a meaningful look.

"Gooseberries it is," Keiran agreed, heading for the door.

The phone jangled and Ron answered it. "Yeah, he's here," he said at length. The distasteful expression on his face reminded Victoria of the look Prudie got when she ate turnip greens. "It's Peacock."

Not especially interested, Victoria explored the storehouse work area while Torbel talked. Zoe's poster of Sherlock Holmes in *The Scarlet Claw* brought a delicious chill to her skin. The ghostly apparition wandering the moor, like the hellhound of the Baskervilles, had turned out to be a fake—the local postman playing a role within a role and covered with phosphorous paint to make him glow.

She didn't believe in spooks or spirits or telepathy. Actually she wasn't sure what she believed in these days. Even her career had lost its luster.

From behind a painted screen, she slid Torbel a considering look. Was it possible . . . ? No, she didn't dare think that.

Three people entered the storehouse but appeared not to notice her. They congregated in the corner farthest from Torbel. Ron joined them, let his eyes dart about, then, satisfied, began to draw something on a scrap of paper.

"Here's how we'll get the necessaries in," he said in a low voice. "Ivy, you handle the masks. Oswyn, you stand watch in the lane. The stuff we need is starting to arrive, so keep your eyes open. Lucky for us, Torbel's wrapped up in this vendetta thing."

Ivy shook her head. "If he finds out about this, he'll kill us."

Ron made a Scottish sound of dismissal. "Never. Torbel's sharp but he's preoccupied right now. Still, we have to keep our eyes and ears open. He spots one thing out of place, and we can kiss this whole caper goodbye . . . What was that?"

It wasn't Victoria; she hadn't moved a muscle. But the sound had come from some place close by. Swinging her head around, she spied the source—Torbel's little black cat, Smudge. She was walking across a stack of files like feline royalty.

"Victoria!"

Her heart stopped for a full three seconds. She spun as Torbel's fingers gripped her arm. Just as forcefully, four pairs of eyes bored into her through the silk screen. The agents dispersed instantly, all but Ron, who came to glare at her, his fists clenching and unclenching.

"Come on," Torbel said, then he frowned. "What's the matter, have you gone deaf? I said Peacock wants to meet us."

"What? Good—I mean, why?" She forced herself to turn her back on Ron. Surely he wouldn't stab her in front of Torbel. "Does he know something?"

"He says he does."

"About Street?"

"Robbie Hollyburn."

"But what . . . ? Never mind. Go on."

"That's it. He wants us to meet him at the Totter's Lane junkyard in half an hour."

"Should I come with you for protection?" Ron continued to glower at Victoria. The unreadable sideways look Torbel cast him had the Scotsman shrugging. "I guess not. You need me for anything, then?"

"I want you and Oswyn to watch Judge Hollyburn's place. Let me know who comes and goes."

"But I've got—"

"Things to do?" Torbel countered levelly.

Again Ron shrugged. "They can wait. Why doesn't Peacock come here if he's got news? Safer at the storehouse than at the Totter's Lane Junkyard."

"Not so many ears to hear." Torbel's grim tone made Victoria's blood run cold. Because it implied that the Rag Man's agency was no more a haven than her Tower Bridge flat. And that being the case, where, in all of London's notorious nooks and crannies, would she and Torbel be safe?

Her answer took the form of a rhyme, the last two rhyming lines of the note that had crashed through the kitchen window Sunday night.

To those who long have lived the lie,
Time now for justice... Time to die!

"GRANDFATHER?"

Her subdued voice sounded like a bomb blast. Augustus fumbled with the files and papers he'd almost dropped on the floor. "What is it, girl?" he snapped, thrusting them quickly into his magazine rack.

Clover entered the parlor on cat feet. She crossed to the fireplace and gave the coals a poke. "Nothing important. I saw Chivers climbing the stairs at six o'clock this morning carrying a letter. You didn't come in for breakfast. I thought it might have been bad news."

"No." He fought to control his voice. "Not bad news. Just a letter Chivers overlooked yesterday. He found it on the carpet inside the front door. I—" His shaggy brows came together in sudden suspicion. "What's that you're wearing, girl? Black? Why black?"

She calmly fanned the embers of the fire, necessary for his old bones even in this heat. "I'm undercover today."

"As what?" he demanded, shuffling over to study her. He'd know for sure if he could see her face. Zoe's eyes were different, not in color or size, but in something he couldn't define. He wouldn't put it past her to sneak in here, bold as brass.

Clover looked at him without hesitation, and he breathed a sigh of relief. Only for a moment, though, then the tension returned. Words bobbed and danced in his head like firecrackers. He didn't want to analyze their meaning, didn't want to know anything before the fact. How could he make that clear without seeming to disapprove or discourage?

"I heard Inspector Fox is coming to dinner," Clover said quietly.

His head jerked back. "What of it?"

"You needn't bite my head off, Grandfather. I wondered if you needed me to be here."

"No." He regarded her warily. "Why do you ask?"

"I have... something to do."

Did he want to know what? A sharp twinge in his chest made the decision for him. "Whatever you wish." He waved a dismissing hand. It amazed him that, after so many years of sharp pains and pills, he managed to go on living. Maybe it was his consuming hatred of the Rag Man. "Oli— The inspector wants to see me, not I him." He seated himself carefully. "Dinner was simply the most expedient means to that end."

Clover rose, shifting her weight from foot to foot and fidgeting with her hands. He despised fidgeters. "You, uh, won't talk about me at all, will you?" she asked haltingly.

"Of course not. Why should we?" His eyes flashed in a spurt of anger. "If we discuss anyone, it'll be that bastard Rag Man."

She finally stopped wringing her hands. "He'll get his, Grandfather. We both know that."

"No, we don't!" He stomped a slippered foot. "We don't *know* anything, either of us. Do you hear me? We don't know a thing. Say it. We don't . . ."

"We don't know anything," she said, obliging him in a perfectly reasonable tone. "But we hope."

Augustus opened his mouth to protest, then slowly closed it. Hoping was acceptable. Yes, they could hope—no law broken by that. Hope, wish and even pray for the Rag Man to pay. . . .

Bloody hell! He turned away. Now he was doing it, making up ridiculous rhymes.

He glanced at the magazine rack and the piece of white paper sticking out of it. His skin prickled. These particular rhymes weren't ridiculous, and he knew it, whether he cared to acknowledge that unpleasant truth or not. Lenny Street was dead; that was a fact. But now there was this new threat that spoke of bangs and poison and other things he preferred not to recall.

His eyes shifted briefly to Clover, then rose to the ceiling, to Sophie's room. Should he do the unthinkable and search . . . ? No, dammit, he should not! He would not. He knew nothing and wanted to know less. Leave it be.

If she had secrets, leave them be, too. After all, he had secrets of his own, didn't he? Blodwyn being the big one. Seductive, flame-haired Blodwyn, who'd done everything in her power to witch him. Who'd come to him months later, proudly but with tears burning behind her green eyes. She'd wanted him to know, to care, to accept and change.

The devil, he'd stormed at her; that's what she'd been, what she remained today in hell. What a vixen to have caused so much damage in his life.

He brought his thoughts back harshly to Sophie, then to Clover before him. Fox was coming over tonight. He would have dinner with the man, be polite and unrevealing. Listen, answer questions and offer trite opinions. No need to probe. Let all skeletons remain in their closets. Let justice prevail. Let those responsible for Robbie's death be punished at last.

He waited until Clover left the parlor, then went over and retrieved the note. He did not read it again, but folded it twice and shuffled back to the fire. He positioned it carefully on the burning coals, fully aware of the pain that gripped him. Only when the last of the note was reduced to ashes did he begin to rub his chest.

It was gone, and he knew nothing. The lack of knowledge brought a wicked smile to his lips.

THE JUNKYARD WAS too quiet for 9:00 a.m. on a weekday, too inactive, devoid of people, trucks and even children, who loved to play among the rubble. Torbel's sharp ears picked out the sounds of traffic and car horns and a tower clock chiming in the distance. The sky had a black, angry cast to it; the air scarcely moved. He was hot and edgy and more tense than he ought to have been.

The latter was thanks in large part to the woman at his side, he reflected with a veiled glance at her enchanting Gypsy profile. He must be crazy bringing her here after the two previous incidents. But although Peacock had sounded hushed and nervous, it was, after all, broad daylight.

Daylight, yes, but fraught with shadows all the same. And questions, piling up unanswered, that had the power to frighten him. Frighten and anger.

The combination was explosive, not dangerous in the way his mother had believed and Boots still did, but in the sense that he had a temper, one that he knew from experience he must not allow himself to lose.

A shudder he seldom experienced worked its way through his body. To combat it, he let his gaze sweep the shadowy areas of the yard.

"There he is." Victoria pointed through a stack of old tables and benches to the lane beyond the open gate. "He's in his car." She paused. "Should we go to him or let him come to us?"

"We'll go to him." Torbel took her hand. "There are too many hiding places in here."

She pressed herself disconcertingly closer. "Places that could hide a shooter, you mean?"

He felt her breasts against his arm and had to grit his teeth against the sudden rush of heat and desire in his lower body. "Something along those lines."

"That's not very reassuring, Torbel."

It didn't inspire her to step away from him, either, which could be good or bad, depending on which way he viewed it. Under the present circumstances, it was a problem, one that was wreaking havoc with his mind and body.

They emerged through the wooden gate. "I think," Victoria began, then stopped and turned her head. "Do you hear an engine?"

"A car," Torbel told her.

She strained for a better view, past the piles of junk near the outer fence. "I don't see any— Oh, my God!" The last words emerged in a horrified whisper. Her nails bit into his fingers. "Torbel!"

He had no time to respond, no time to do anything except shoulder Victoria roughly aside and dive in the same general direction.

The car shot around a curve in the lane with a roar and a squeal of tires that made Torbel think of a Cobra he'd seen on a trip to New York. It had been used as a getaway vehicle after a jewelry-store robbery, and only the driver's stupidity had prevented the criminals' escape. He'd shot the thing straight into a brick wall.

This driver made no similar mistake as he sped toward them. Torbel saw a glint of black metal and positioned himself to protect Victoria. The passenger window must have been down, because no glass shattered as the person inside aimed and fired. Torbel had been grazed the first night down at the dock, scarcely worth the bandage that Zoe had insisted be stuck on him. This time, however, the bullet lodged. It might even have passed through; he couldn't tell, so fierce was the sudden bolt of pain.

"Torbel—"

"Stay down!" he ordered, tight-lipped.

The car raced on. Dark blue, he noted, squinting, a Mazda RX-7. Sporty, fast and powerful. The plates were a blur, but then so was his vision at the moment. The car flew along the lane, past piles of chairs, car parts and half of an old piano. In his police car, Peacock might have had time to react, but little more than that. In the same vein, the tiny object launched from the window might have been an empty cigarette pack. But no empty package could have brought about the explosion that suddenly rent the sooty London air.

Bits of glass and metal blew out in all directions. A deafening roar sounded in his ears. Torbel held Victoria against him until the debris had settled, then eased his head up.

Where Sergeant Peacock's car had sat seconds before, now there was only an enormous ball of flames. Even the rickety junkyard fence was involved.

Victoria's hair brushed his cheek, a tantalizing reminder that he was still lying partly on top of her. "Sergeant . . ." she said in a voice barely audible above the sudden clamor of feet and shouting voices.

"What happened?" someone yelled. A group of construction workers looked around wildly, spotted Torbel and gestured at the burning car. "Was there anyone inside?"

Torbel gave a grim nod, climbing to his feet and pulling Victoria with him. He felt her probing the bullet hole in his arm but paid no attention to it. "A cop," he said. "Sergeant Robert Peacock of the Stepney Precinct."

One of the men perched on a mound of wooden crates regarded the flames. "Well, he's dead now, right enough. Looks like a bomb to me."

Torbel used the pain to concentrate. Nevertheless, he felt the blood that dripped down his arm to the ground. It looked like a bomb because that's precisely what it had been. His eyes darkened. But had it been meant for Peacock or for them?

ROBBIE HOLLYBURN'S grammar-school scribbler lay open to the fifth page. The eyes that devoured it visualized Robbie's little hand printing out the words: "Jack and Jill went up the hill..."

The rest of the rhyme turned fuzzy and gray. No matter. The message had been duly delivered. Victoria would find it, and she'd go straight to Torbel.

A picture formed of a car and its occupant being consumed by flames. A shame in a way that Peacock had to go. The bomb would have been better used for Torbel and Victoria. But the sergeant had been sacrificed for a noble cause. And if the life taken in order for that cause to be realized had been more or less innocent, it had also been unimportant in the scheme of things. Robbie's death must be avenged. Only he really mattered.

How would old Goggy react to the whole truth? Did he have an inkling already? Did he know but not want to acknowledge it? Some people had the capacity for complete denial. Was he one of them?

Time would tell on that score. Goggy was incidental anyway. Punishment must be meted out.

The lid rose on the sea chest. Time to don a new disguise. The chimney sweep was history. Gloved hands scrabbled through the chest. There it was, the new persona. It would parade about right under their noses, and they'd never know it. Who said the Rag Man was too perceptive to be fooled? He had no idea who was behind this. He wouldn't, either—until the time came for him and Victoria to die....

Chapter Ten

"Have Jack and Jill,
Now had their fill,
Of lies and truths untold?
For bombs and things
With poison stings,
Will kill this lie most bold.

Torbel and Vickie, hear the bang,
Of death before you go.
Your crowns will break,
Make no mistake,
Your blood by me shall flow."

The message had been left on Zoe's answering machine. The voice was disguised, a macabre, distorted blend of rhyming words and laughter.

Torbel, who'd brought Victoria back here after endless hours at the station house in the wake of the explosion, rubbed his forehead as he prowled the floor. "Nursery rhymes," he muttered. "How the hell do you make sense of that?"

"You don't," Victoria said simply. "Why won't you let me have a look at your arm? I don't think the police doctor—"

"He's competent," Torbel cut her off.

He sounded tired. She might just slip past his guard this time.

"I'm not suggesting he isn't," she replied with a calm shrug, difficult to pull off in the wake of Peacock's death and what she'd just heard on Zoe's answering machine. "But he looked a little harried to me. I took an extensive course in first aid at the university."

The look he sent her was a combination of amusement and aggravation. "Your middle name must be 'obstinate.' All right, fine, have your look. But think while you're about it. Did you see any part of the person in the Mazda?"

He perched on the arm of Zoe's overstuffed chair, and gently Victoria began removing the bloodied gauze. "I saw an arm covered in black and a hand wearing a glove. The hand threw something out of the window, and the next thing I knew, Peacock's car was a mass of flames. I already told the police the part of the license plate I saw."

She wondered vaguely how long she could keep up this facade of serenity. Her teeth were chattering—and it wasn't entirely due to the close call they'd had this morning at the junkyard or the threatening message they'd listened to moments before. Some primitive, erotic force began gnawing on her senses whenever she got within a certain range of the Rag Man.

What was worse, she knew he sensed her discomfiture and likely the reasons behind it. If only she could be more certain of her life's goals. How much easier it would—or should in theory—be to assert her will and close her mind to the danger he posed. Yet how did someone, even a person with definite goals, close her heart to feelings too powerful to be denied?

The question had no answer, and Torbel's proximity made searching for one impossible. Heavy rain had started to fall around 7:00 p.m. They'd missed dinner, Victoria recalled as she removed the last of the gauze. Lunch, too, and even tea. She should have been half-starved, and she was, but not for food.

The dampness of the channel storm weighed heavily upon her. Talk, that's what she needed to take her mind off Torbel's smooth skin and nasty-looking wound.

"Why do they call you the Rag Man?" she asked, opening a bottle of hydrogen peroxide.

His gaze was steady on hers. "Because my mother sorted clothes in a charity store when I was a kid. They called places like that rag shops. I was the rag lady's son, the rag boy. The rag boy grew up into the Rag Man.''

"Did you, uh, know your mother well?"

A cynical smile played on the corners of his mouth. ''Well enough.''

Feeling bolder, Victoria persisted. ''Boots said she was—''

"A visionary?" Torbel arched a shrewd brow.

"I was going to say psychic." The skin around the bullet hole felt hot. Or did the heat emanate from her? "I don't believe in witches, not outside the realm of *Snow White* anyway."

"Neither do I, and the answer's no. End of conversation."

Undaunted, Victoria tried again. "Why did you leave Scotland Yard?"

She hadn't anticipated his reaction. The fingers of his good hand caught hers in a not-quite-painful grip. His eyes were an icy shade of green blue, his expression cold and unrelenting. "That isn't for anyone to know. Do you hear me, Victoria? It's my business, so don't start digging around on your computer. My past has nothing to do with the present."

She banked the lump of fear that climbed into her throat at the intensity of his response. "Are you sure?"

"Yes," he said tightly, and although she wasn't entirely convinced, she let the subject slide.

"The bullet went right through," she murmured, focusing her full attention on his arm. "What caliber was it?"

"A .45. Common enough to be virtually untraceable."

"You could have been killed, Torbel. A few more inches, and the bullet would have caught you in the chest."

She was trembling as she applied a new bandage and cursed herself for it. He wouldn't understand female emotions. Boots said he had deep feelings, but what did Boots know of the Rag Man's heart?

Her gaze flicked briefly to Torbel's face. She was unnerved to discover him watching her. The scar on his cheek held a particular fascination for her.

Her hand came up. "How did you get this?" she asked so tentatively that she barely heard the question herself. But Torbel did. He jerked away from the fingers that stroked the uneven mark.

"Don't, Victoria," he warned, yanking his sleeve roughly down. "I'm not Prince Charming in disguise."

The dampness and heat in the air made it difficult to breathe. She'd only turned on the necessary lights, just enough to create a strong forties feeling in the flat. Basil and Nigel shone in the soft glow of lamplight. She thought she heard a swing tune in the distance, maybe from Gooseberries. Rosie was curled up contentedly on the sofa, Zoe was nowhere to be found, darkness had settled beyond the lead-paned windows—and Victoria wanted Torbel to kiss her. Just a kiss, and then...

She felt herself swaying toward him, a purely involuntary motion. Careful, her brain warned, but right then she wasn't listening to her brain. She knew he hesitated, knew he wanted to resist what was growing between them. She felt him halt, then sigh and give in.

His lips caught hers gently, experimentally. She savored the taste of him, the brush of his thumb across her jaw. All her senses seemed to wobble as his tongue slid coaxingly over her teeth. She hadn't expected him to be gentle.

The force of her emotions startled her as Torbel's kisses drugged her mind. She was further startled when she heard his murmured "You want the fairy tale, Victoria." He raised his head, and she saw the faint light of regret in his eyes. "I can't give it to you."

Because she felt half a fool already—and perhaps partly because he wasn't entirely wrong—she pushed away from him. No Prince Charming, he'd said. She wanted fairy tales, he'd said. Maybe there was a grain of truth in those statements, but she was no idealistic female. Her da had taught her better than that.

Fragments of temper began to assert themselves. It didn't lessen her desire for him, but it allayed the weakness in her limbs.

Removing her hand from his cheek, she walked to the window. "You have a jaded sense of women, Torbel," she said over her shoulder. "No one expects fairy tales anymore. Still, it wouldn't hurt you to..." The rest of her statement died in her

throat as she turned to face him. To her surprise, he was
standing directly behind her—and there was a great deal more
than cynicism visible in his eyes.

"Two men are dead, Victoria," he said in a low voice.
"Three if you count Robbie. Some psychotic nut is out to
murder us—we have no idea who it is—and now you want to
goad me."

"I'm not goading you, Torbel." She was challenging him,
though in a subtle sort of way. "I feel badly about what's happened, including Robbie's death, but I can't change any of it,
and I can't see us running around blindly searching for clues
tonight."

"No?" he said softly. "Then what do you suggest we do?"

On edge from before and still feeling tiny pricks of temper,
Victoria took the initiative. "This," she said. And placing her
hands on either side of his face, she pulled his mouth onto hers.

THIS WAS A MISTAKE, an enormous error in judgment, and
Torbel wasn't doing a single thing to fight it. Moreover, once
his astonishment at her impulsive action had faded, he found
himself responding to her, this time with an emotional urgency that almost outweighed the demands of his body.

Sliding his hand around the back of her head, he brought her
up hard against him. The first time he'd been in control. Now
that she'd caught him off guard, he no longer maintained that
edge. He wanted to explore the contours of her mouth one by
one, slowly enough to memorize them all.

The oddity of his behavior struck him even before her fingers slid up and under the front of his jersey. Normally he
didn't like to kiss. A leftover from his youth, when girls' kisses
had ranged from sickeningly demure to outright ravenous. Not
out of love or any semblance of the word, either. During his
teenage years, at least, the female of the species had not been
what he'd expected. On the other hand, he might have been
meeting the wrong females. People from rough neighbor-
hoods, no matter which sex, tended to be brash.

Victoria was not brash. But she was bold and her boldness
was a quality he could admire even as he felt himself harden-

ing against her. She was an enigma, this one, streetwise in some ways, innocent in others, the daughter of a Yorkshire marketeer and a mother about whom she tended not to speak.

He encouraged her with his mouth when she would have drawn away. Maybe she thought he'd be angry with her for starting this. It certainly wasn't from lack of wanting him. Her nipples were hard against his chest, her breathing as uneven as his, the skin of her neck damp to his touch.

With his thumbs, he caressed the sensitive column of her throat. If she feared him, she gave no sign. In fact, the only sound she made was a soft little moan that could have been a blend of frustration and desire.

His breathing grew ragged, a thing that seldom happened. It wasn't wise to let it happen now. On top of everything else, their professional worlds were too disparate to be united. To say nothing of the differences in their personal lives.

It was Victoria who ended the kiss. Truthfully Torbel doubted if he could have done it. She pulled her mouth away but made no move to step back.

A frown marred her smooth forehead. "I don't understand you, Torbel. You act like you don't want me, and yet you kiss me like you do."

Although he could have explained the seeming discrepancy, he chose not to. Let her think the worst. Better for both of them in the end.

"You're a beautiful woman," he said as unemotionally as he was able. "And I've always been partial to brunettes."

Her temper flared. Now she did step back. "What kind of a remark is that?"

He shook his head, regretful but resolute. "Let it go, Victoria. I'm tired, and so are you. We've been through hell today, and we're no closer to a solution now than we were in the beginning."

"'Misfortune makes strange bedfellows,' is that what you're saying?"

"No, but that's how you'll see it until that temper of yours subsides."

"I don't have a temper."

"The hell you don't." He resisted an urge to smooth the tangle of dark hair from her flushed cheeks and settled instead for running an irritable hand through his own. "Let's both try to stay calm, shall we? There's a killer wandering around out there, and I have no intention of letting him catch me off guard."

"What makes you so sure it's a him?" Victoria challenged. "Anyone can throw a bomb, operate a forklift and compose a few freaky notes."

"Meaning?" he demanded, pausing beside a framed poster of *Dr. Jekyll and Mr. Hyde.*

"Nothing really, except that we haven't even got it narrowed down to a specific gender." Her enmity faded to annoyance. "We don't know anything, not who or how or even why."

He fingered the scar on his cheek. "We know why," he said, then drew his hand away, impatient with himself. "It's tied up with Robbie's death. I'd say it was Augustus Hollyburn if he didn't want that knighthood so badly."

"Maybe he thinks he can kill us and still get it. Murderers seldom believe they'll be caught."

Torbel shook his head, aware that his body still burned for her. "It's too risky."

"He could have hired someone anonymously."

"He could have done that. He's a crafty old bugger."

"And don't forget, Sergeant Peacock mentioned Robbie's mother when you talked to him. Maybe he had information that Augustus didn't want passed on."

"About Sophie." Torbel considered a notion he'd been over several times that day already.

"Still," Victoria mused, "why would a woman who's been dead for twenty-three years be of any interest to us?"

Even preoccupied, Torbel heard the door open and Zoe straggle in. "I could have swum home and not gotten any wetter," she declared, kicking off her sodden black boots. "What a downpour. Hi, Rosie." She rumpled the dog's small, furry head, then addressed Torbel and Victoria. "You two look like thunderclouds." Her eyes sparkled. "Anything wrong?"

Torbel resisted an urge to snarl at her. "We were talking about your mother. Peacock was going to tell us something about her today."

Zoe paused in the process of wringing out her thick red hair. The sparkle in her eyes died. "Yes, I heard about that. All they found were a few bones, a gold ring and cuff links and a piece of scorched leather that used to be his wallet. I feel badly for some reason. I never liked Peacock much, but I wouldn't have wished death on him."

"Did Clover like him?" Victoria asked.

"I doubt if she cared one way or the other. I'm not sure she liked anyone—except Grandfather, of course. Hers is a case of severe repression intensified by old Goggy's unique brand of domination." She shivered, then brushed the lapse aside. "What's this about Peacock having information about my mother?"

Torbel eyed the bottle of gin on the end table but made no move toward it. "Peacock must have had something, or he wouldn't have called."

"I guess. Do you think it has any bearing on what's been happening to you two?" Her gaze shifted to the blinking answering machine. "Who's the message for, by the way?"

"Me," Victoria told her truthfully.

"Oh, well, in that case...what was I saying? Something about Sophie, wasn't it? She's been dead for twenty-three years now. How could she possibly tie in to what you're going through? If it'll help, though, I might be able to arrange it so you can poke through her things. Her room hasn't been touched since the day she died. I mean that literally."

A puzzled shadow invaded Victoria's face. "Why was Robbie's last name Hollyburn? What happened to his—your—father?"

"Duffy? He took off twenty years ago. He was a third or fourth cousin on Grandfather's side, the perfect mate in Goggy's eyes for his only daughter. Duffy was a Hollyburn by birth, the last of his scandalous line. He moved out the same week Sophie died, and took off for parts unknown a few years later. We haven't heard from him since."

"You've never been curious to find him?" Victoria asked.

Torbel staved off a cynical laugh. How little she knew of troubled family relationships, although to be fair, the Hollyburns were worse than most in that regard. Infidelity ran rampant in their ranks, and Duffy'd been no exception. He'd left a trail of mournful hearts from London to Glasgow, which, as Torbel and Augustus both knew, was where he currently resided.

Zoe tugged off her black raincoat and tossed it onto a wooden chair. "Why should I be curious?" she said unconcernedly. "I hardly knew the man. He wasn't even there when I was born. But to get back on topic, I might be able to sneak you into Goggy's fortress. Whatever you do, though, don't let him catch you."

Removing her gloves with her teeth, she sighed and flexed her fingers. "You know, Torbel, it'd be easier for me to go back to burgling than it is to follow twisted idiots about the city." She spun the gin bottle around, shook the contents and regarded the label. "I wonder if Ratz has any tonic. How's tomorrow sound for the break-in?"

"After dark," Torbel returned with a narrowed sideways glance at Victoria. If Zoe noticed his disheveled state, she made no further mention of it. With a grin for Torbel, she took the gin bottle in one hand and Victoria's arm in the other and started for the door. "Come on, Ms. Bouverie Street solicitor, let's you and me have a nightcap. I have a feeling you could use one."

So could he, Torbel reflected in their wake. But he wasn't about to have one with Victoria, not feeling the way he currently did.

He contemplated the soggy London night, then went over to the answering machine and removed the taped message. He should take this to the police. They were far more interested in this case now that one of their own was involved.

He stared at the cassette for a full thirty seconds, not seeing it so much as a host of other things. Images of the past, and present. Of Victoria, touching him, kissing him, wanting to know him . . .

But was he ready to confide in her, or anyone, for that matter?

The question plagued him all the way down to the street. Rain pelted the cobbled lane beyond the eaves where he stood in comparative shelter. All of London spread out before him. Historic, regal London. And lurking within the city, a madman, or woman, with secrets as yet undiscovered. Including his, Torbel thought bleakly.

Mindless of the rain, he started for the water's edge and home. The answers were out there somewhere, and he was going to find them. As surely as he'd clawed his way out of the rag jungle, he would unmask this killer. For Robbie's sake, as well as his own. But mostly, he thought, with a sense of inevitability that brought a sigh to his lips, for Victoria's.

"THIS IS CRAZY," Victoria charged Torbel the following evening. "What if Judge Hollyburn's watching? Or his butler. Zoe says he's got eyes everywhere."

Crouching, Torbel surveyed the rear of the Hollyburn mansion, a Manderlay-type silhouette illuminated only by two meager pools of light on the ground floor. "You would be a mean old thing, wouldn't you?" he murmured, presumably to the absent judge. To Victoria, he said, "It's Chivers's night off."

"He lives here, Torbel. What if he comes back early?"

"Zoe says he won't."

"Zoe hasn't lived in this house for years," she argued. "And don't forget, Clover's shift ended at six."

A hint of a smile played on the corners of his mouth. "You'd make a lousy cat burglar, Victoria." Eyes fastened on the darkened house, he nudged her forward. "Head for the pantry window. Lower right. And don't you forget, Zoe's guarding the front entrance in my Pathfinder. She'll beep me if anyone shows up unexpectedly."

Victoria was not appeased, but she swallowed the rest of her objections. It had been her idea to accompany him; she had no right to complain. Besides, it was her life on the line here, too.

It must be the remnants of a hangover making her so cranky and critical.

Zoe had taken her to Gooseberries last night, ostensibly for one glass of gin and dinner. Three Bombay gins and two lime-and-lagers later, both women had forgotten all about food. Victoria did remember Inspector Fox coming in just before closing. He'd taken her aside and asked her about Sergeant Peacock's phone call to Torbel that morning.

"Did Peacock mention any papers?" he'd demanded harshly, which was not, Victoria knew, his usual style.

She'd pulled free of his iron grip. "I have no idea what Sergeant Peacock mentioned. I didn't speak to him."

"You spoke to Torbel." Fox resembled a much more dangerous animal in the dim pub light. "Did he say anything about papers belonging to—? Well, never mind about that. Some valuable documents have gone missing, and in light of his phone call to Torbel, we—that is I—have reason to believe that Sergeant Peacock may have taken them."

"If they were with the sergeant, they burned with him in the fire."

His eyes glittered unpleasantly. "Only if he was carrying them on his person."

Thankfully Ratz intervened at that point. Victoria had no idea what he said, but the inspector had left, red faced and indignant.

Zoe hadn't been in sight at that point, and Ratz hadn't been privy to the conversation. Victoria considered going to Torbel with her strange tale, but she had no idea where he lived, and neither did anyone else. Except maybe Keiran, and he didn't frequent pubs, even those owned by the Rag Man.

So she'd been forced to wait. Unfortunately, by morning the last thing on her mind had been the weird behavior of Inspector Oliver Fox. It was all she could do to find her sunglasses and face the bright, high overcast of day without groaning.

She'd recovered somewhat by afternoon tea, which was when she'd finally located Torbel—or he'd found her.

"Zoe's going to help me get into Augustus Hollyburn's house," he'd said with the faintest quirk of amusement for her pale cheeks and shadowed eyes. "Can you cope with standing watch out front?"

"While you and Zoe break in?"

"Zoe won't go in. She claims that Augustus can sense her presence."

Familial telepathy. Victoria had heard of it, but didn't think she believed in it entirely. Since Zoe obviously did, however, she could stand watch. Victoria would break in with the Rag Man.

To her surprise, Torbel had offered no objections. He'd simply told her to be ready at 11:00 p.m., because he wouldn't wait if she wasn't.

She'd been on time. So had he, and now here they were, creeping across a broad expanse of lawn and flower gardens toward the pantry window.

Torbel carried a beeper on his belt. The two burning lights came from hallways. None of the main rooms was lit, and not a sound except for insects and owls broke the stillness of the warm night air.

Torbel jimmied the pantry window like a pro—which he very well might be, Victoria thought with an apprehensive glance over her shoulder. She still knew next to nothing about his past.

"Victoria."

His impatient whisper came from the far side of the window. Switching off her flashlight, she tucked it into her black backpack—a gift from Zoe—and hoisted herself up and over.

He nodded at the far wall. "Zoe said there was a rear staircase. Sophie's room is at the top and five doors to the left."

Victoria rearranged her pack. "What about Judge Hollyburn's room?"

"Two doors farther on. We'll have to be quiet."

"I don't suppose he's hard of hearing," she ventured as they climbed a set of creaking stairs.

"No. Stay to the left and hug the wall."

She'd rather hug him, but now was hardly the time, even if he did look incredibly good in his black jeans and cotton shirt.

Torbel's flashlight pointed the way. Once they'd navigated the squeaky stairs, he turned off the beam and, holding her still with a hand pressed to her stomach, let his eyes adjust.

"Count five doors," he instructed after a moment.

Victoria did, then stood guard again while he plied a second lock. She thought she detected a tiny creak and looked around hastily; however, no red-faced Augustus Hollyburn burst through his door, ripe for a confrontation.

The butler was out of the house, she reminded herself. The cook slept downstairs, but she'd been snoring away like a lawnmower and wasn't likely to hear them.

"Got it." Torbel was on his feet and through the door before Victoria completed her surveillance of the corridor. He located a lamp, switched it on and closed the door behind him.

Victoria halted just across the threshold, staring at the sheet-draped furniture and cobwebs hanging so thick and numerous she couldn't see through them to the other side. Everything—the carpet, the sheets, the wallpaper, the shelves—every article in Sophie's old bedroom was covered with layer upon layer of dust.

With her gloved hand, she broke one of the larger cobwebs and peered through it to the nightstand where a clock and calendar sat, stopped in time. "Seven thirty-two," she murmured. "July 17, 1973. God, Torbel, it's the 'Twilight Zone' to a T."

"That *T* will stand for *trouble* if you don't get a move on," he retorted. "Check the closet. I'll do the dresser."

She had to make her way through a sea of dusty gray cobwebs to get there. "Why do I get the dirty job?" she muttered. "What exactly are we looking for, Torbel?"

"Anything pertinent."

"That narrows it down." Vexed by his reticent attitude, she flung open the door—and barely managed to stifle the scream that leapt into her throat when a large, dark object toppled out and landed on her. She jumped back and would have kept on going if she hadn't come up hard against Torbel.

"What?" he demanded, obviously not seeing it.

"I don't know." She pointed. "Something black."

Setting her aside, he went down onto one knee and probed the...whatever it was. Victoria didn't want to look; however, curiosity impelled her to keep one eye on the thing. She kept her fingers wrapped around Torbel's shirt collar. If it sprang, she'd...

"It's a skeleton."

A knot formed in her chest. "In the closet?" She shuddered. "What a gruesome woman."

"It's plastic." Torbel pushed aside the black body bag. "She must have been in pre-med at one time."

"Maybe." Victoria allowed herself a final shiver of distaste. "From what I've heard of this family, though, she could have been twisted enough to have been keeping it as some sort of memento."

"They're adulterers, not bone freaks." His head came up suddenly. "Did you hear something?"

Only her own bones knocking together. "No."

He waited for three tension-filled seconds, then swore and grabbed her hand. "The door," he muttered.

"But the closet's—"

Clamping a hand firmly over her mouth, he squeezed himself in behind her and doused the lights.

To her left, the door creaked slowly open. The point of a rifle appeared. Then an old, suspicious voice—the personification of death itself to Victoria's mind—rasped an eerie "Who's there?"

Chapter Eleven

Victoria couldn't have moved if she'd wanted to. Torbel's grip was that strong, and in the dark, the rifle barrel bore the aspect of a cannon.

"Who is it?" the old man demanded again. His voice was raspy and hard. Unflinchingly so.

Dickens's Flintwinch, Victoria thought, then stiffened as the rifle jerked. She felt the muscles of Torbel's body digging into her, but pressed herself tighter against him even so.

"I know you're here, girl," the man snapped. "I can smell you. Come out where I can see you."

She heard Torbel's quick expletive, then felt herself being moved aside.

"Put the rifle down, old man," he said grimly, stepping out. "Unless you think murdering an unarmed intruder will aid your chances for a knighthood."

With a bony elbow, Augustus Hollyburn poked at the wall switch. "You," he breathed. His whole body trembled with rage. "You brought her with you, didn't you?" The rifle swung wildly in Victoria's direction. Only Torbel's quickness made it possible for him to grab the barrel and yank it back.

The old judge offered little resistance. "Is that you back there, girl?" he demanded in a savage hiss.

Shoulders squared, Victoria detached herself from the shadow. "If you mean Zoe, the answer is no."

He blinked at her. "Who in blazes are you?"

Forgettable, obviously. "Victoria Summers," she told him, her eyes on his shaky trigger finger. "We met two years ago."

"In Hobday's office." Now his voice shook, as well. "You helped that criminal get this murderer off."

"No one got off," Victoria reminded him as calmly as possible. "There wasn't enough evidence to support—"

"Hang the evidence." One slippered foot hit the carpet with a thud. "My grandson was murdered." Icy blue-green eyes bored into Torbel's face. "My flesh and blood, my only legitimate male progeny, gone. You killed him. You and that piece of scum, Lenny Street."

"But that makes no sense," Victoria said. "What reason would Torbel have had for killing your grandson?"

"Because Robbie changed his mind about joining up with his band of crooks, that's why."

Torbel's eyes held steady on the old man's. "And you think I'd kill someone over that?"

The ends of Augustus's white hair quivered. He continued to clutch the rifle as his right hand came up to massage his thin chest. "He knew things about your so-called agency, didn't he, Torbel? Things you weren't about to let him take away that night. So when he told you he wanted no part of your miserable operation, you ordered Street to stab him in the back."

Torbel sounded resigned. "Whatever, old man. You'll take your belief to the grave no matter what I say."

Augustus's eyes blazed. "Say why you're here," he barked. "What are you—both—" his glare included Victoria "—doing in my house, in my daughter's room?"

"They're looking for something that will tell them what Peacock was going to reveal before he was killed."

Zoe . . . Victoria brought her head around.

She stood on the threshold, more defensive than insolent despite her cool tone. "Peacock knew or discovered something, didn't he, Grandfather? Maybe you know what it was, maybe you don't, but whatever the case, I think it's high time the truth came out."

His face mottled with rage, Augustus blustered, "You're one to speak of truth. Your very existence is a disgrace to me, to all of us."

"'All of us' being you and Clover. There's no one else left now, is there?" To Victoria and Torbel, she explained. "I saw his bedroom light go on, then the light in the hall. I could see where he was heading, so I thought I'd come and help you out."

The rifle wobbled. "You can help yourselves out, the lot of you, before I call Inspector Fox."

Torbel's eyes never left the old man's face. "Why Fox?" he challenged quietly. "He has no jurisdiction here."

"What's the difference? Inspector Craddock, then."

"The difference," Torbel replied, "is that your first thought was to call Fox. Why? Because he owes you favors?"

"Don't be ridiculous. He owes me nothing."

"He owes someone," Victoria inserted. "A number of charges against him were dropped for no apparent reason. Who better to affect such matters than a high-court judge."

"Are you accusing me of a criminal act, girl? Do you have that much audacity? You, who broke into my home with this—" he flung a furious hand at Torbel "—this...person?"

Having two other people there bolstered her courage, despite the waving gun. "Yes," she said. "I am, and I do."

"Answer the question, Augustus," Torbel said levelly. "Did you have a hand in getting the charges against Fox dropped?"

"That's none of your bloody business," Augustus snapped.

"He did," Zoe exclaimed softly. She sounded surprised and unbelieving. "You really did, you two-faced old thing. Why on earth did you do it?"

The old man merely glowered at her.

"Do you know his family?" she pressed. "His father, maybe?" Her tone soured. "Or is it his mother you know? You always did like women, didn't you? Poor Grandma Blanche. I've no doubt you humiliated her more than a few times over the years. What names do I remember? Gladys, Miranda, Blodwyn, Fiona, Rachel. And there were more, weren't there? Many more than I ever heard about. And you had the nerve to pick on Duffy for cheating on Sophie. She was no saint, and you know it. It's in the blood, Augustus. Lying, cheating hypocrites, that's what you—what we—are. What a legacy to leave. Maybe it's just as well that Robbie died. Before he could be turned into another you."

Augustus's expression grew so ugly that it made Victoria wince. "Get out," he snarled, and would have shouldered the rifle if Torbel hadn't stopped him. He made a crabby sound of defeat. "All of you. Get out now, and don't come back."

"Not until we find out what it was that Peacock was going to tell us," Torbel said with no visible trace of emotion.

The old man's lips quivered with poorly suppressed anger. "I don't know," he said stiffly. "I hardly knew the man."

"You knew the man," Zoe scoffed. "So did Sophie. She also knew Fox and Craddock, if I'm not mistaken, for years before she died. Be honest, Augustus. Cops and solicitors were Sophie's favorite boy toys, and she just loved to play."

"Shut up!" White-faced, Augustus could barely choke the command out.

Sadly Zoe shook her head. "What a pathetic family."

Recovering somewhat, Augustus began to hobble away, using the rifle as a cane. "I'm going to call Fox—Craddock. You have five minutes to disappear."

Zoe stabbed an accusing finger in his wake. "If the devil had children, he'd be one of them. Did you find anything?"

"Only a skeleton in the closet," Victoria told her.

"One of many, it seems," Torbel added, reaching for the light switch. "Come on, let's get out of here before we're arrested."

"All that, and we didn't find a thing," Victoria sighed.

"Yes, we did." Torbel ushered her into the corridor behind Zoe. "We found out that Sophie knew both Peacock and Fox for years before her death, and that old Goggy's done a number of favors for Fox."

"That's not much of a cache, Torbel."

"No, but this might be." Removing a small leather-bound book from his waistband, he thrust it between her fingers.

Victoria frowned. "It looks like a diary."

"It is," Torbel said with an expressive arch of his brows. "Sophie Hollyburn's diary."

As FAR AS VICTORIA could determine, Sophie had been involved with half the London police force, a number of lawyers and a handful of doctors. She'd also been a whimsical woman, because details in her diary were sketchy at best.

She pored over the first half of the book in Zoe's flat. The entries were made the way a person would think, jumping from subject to subject with no connecting sentences. After five hours of struggling to make sense of the thing, she closed the cover and stuck it under the sofa cushion. Maybe Torbel would have better luck when he got here.

If he got here, she amended, stretching her arms over her head and glancing at her watch. A frown crossed her lips when she saw that it was after 4:00 p.m. He should have arrived an hour ago.

With a frustrated grunt, she reached for the phone. She'd promised Mr. Woodbury that she would check in at teatime. She would have preferred to do it personally; however, when she'd explained her current problems to the firm's partners, Mr. Bock had insisted that she remain safely hidden away in Stepney. No point endangering herself needlessly, he'd said, but what he'd really meant was that he didn't want her endangering him.

Pompous old buzzard. He only cared about himself. Rather like Judge Hollyburn, she thought with tolerant contempt. Old Augustus tossed the word *justice* around as if he'd invented it. If *hypocrisy* were a middle name, it would be his. What she hadn't deduced for herself in that area, she'd discovered from reading Sophie's muddled diary.

Not that Sophie'd been any better as far as marital fidelity went, but she'd taken pains to be discreet. According to her, her father had been positively brazen about his affairs.

Oddly to Victoria's mind, Sophie had spared scarcely a word for her girls. She recalled a few references to Robbie—"a chip off the old block" was what Sophie had called him—but Zoe,

Clover and their long-dead brother Joey hadn't rated a single word.

After checking in with Mr. Woodbury, Victoria decided to take a walk. Her da would be selling like crazy on a perfect market day like this. She would drop by and see him in Whitechapel.

Ron and Ivy were huddled in a booth at Gooseberries when she passed through in her oldest pair of cutoffs and a dusty rose tank top. They had spread out a large sheet of paper on the table between them. Ron was making marks on it. The moment he spotted her, he gathered up the paper and stuffed it onto the seat beside him. His eyes, wary and untrusting, trailed her across the room and through the door.

Had he killed Lenny Street? Victoria wondered. Her blood chilled at the prospect. Did he want Torbel dead, as well, so that he could take over the agency?

No, that didn't make sense, or if it did, Ron's plan had no connection to the death threats she and Torbel had been receiving. The Scotsman had no reason to want her dead. Unless, of course, he had some tie to Robbie that she didn't know about. That would give him a reason.

The streets bustled with activity. The air was warm and smelled of all things wonderful in the heart of the old city.

London had charm, she had to admit, even the poorer areas like this one. Her Tower Bridge flat was lovely, but it didn't have the color or character of Zoe's rooms. That wasn't the real problem, though. Her whole life lately lacked color. Visiting her da always improved her spirits, but his livelihood was his barrow. Hers lay in the realm of the legal system.

"I love being a lawyer," she stated out loud. "I do." Several heads turned, but Victoria ignored the curious stares. She wanted ... something. She wasn't sure what, but she had an uneasy feeling it involved the Rag Man. And that thought, more than any of the others, brought a shiver of trepidation to her skin.

She needed to get her mind onto a less disturbing topic. Robbie Hollyburn's trial, for instance. What did she remember of it? She summoned up plenty of tidbits but had no chance to voice them until she located her father in the Puddleby Market.

"I've been back, Da. I read the transcripts of the trial. Apparently Augustus Hollyburn's gardener testified that Robbie was in a hurry the night he died. He said Robbie ran over one of the lilac bushes in his rush to get to the docks."

Her da eyed her shrewdly. "Anxious to join up with your Rag Man, was he?"

"Not according to Augustus...and he's not my Rag Man. The judge insists that Robbie was planning to tell Torbel he'd changed his mind. That's nothing new, though. Now that I think about it, I'm sure I saw the same statement made by Augustus in the transcript of the trial. Still, Da, Torbel wouldn't have killed Robbie over that. It might have been different if Robbie'd pulled a knife on him, but even then I can't see Torbel stabbing anyone in the back. He's got too much pride. Or honor. There must be another answer, something we missed back then and are still missing now."

Her da rearranged heads of red cabbage. "The person after you doesn't seem to think so."

"He's crazy, Da...Or she."

"You're not sure?"

"Not yet. All we ever see are gloved hands and shapeless bodies. And the message on the answering machine was deliberately distorted."

"Who do you think it is, then?"

"I honestly don't know. Clover Hollyburn's a cold fish, but she's not making any attempt to hide her animosity. You'd think whoever was after us would do a better job of acting." She paused. "Da, do you know a man called Boots?"

"No." His eyes sparkled. "Another new friend of yours?"

"Well...yes, I'd say so. But I can't find him. I asked around, and so did Torbel. No one's seen him since the day before yesterday. What's even more peculiar, there was an old woman in his spot today outside Gooseberries. I know the spot doesn't actually belong to Boots, but I've never seen anyone else there. And she wasn't a friendly woman, either. When I asked her about Boots, she mumbled something rude and clumped off in her big brown shoes. I wonder if Torbel . . . ?" She shook the idea away. "No, he'd have told me if he'd found him."

"Does this Boots know your Rag Man well?"

"I think so. And stop calling him my Rag Man, Da. He's not my type."

Her da snorted. "Rubbish, lass. He sounds exactly your type. Those wishy-washy legal twits you've dated in the past are just so much putty. You need something harder to handle."

Surprised and a little stung by an opinion he'd never expressed before, Victoria ventured a quiet "Are you saying that I'm domineering?"

"Assertive," her da corrected, still shifting his wares. The twinkle returned to his eyes. "You got your ma in you, all right. She would have her way when we were together. But except for that, and her black hair and her pretty blue eyes, you got a lot more of me in you than you do her. Those eyes of yours cut, though, lass. Good for your work—not always good when it comes to dealing with regular people."

"You haven't seen Torbel's eyes," she murmured, feeling oddly on edge. Why was the skin on the back of her neck prickling? "He could melt a glacier at fifty yards. What are you looking at, Da?"

"Nothing." He smiled broadly at her. "He's got a sharp stare, eh?"

"Deadly."

"I reckon he uses it to advantage." His smile widened. "Does it work on you?"

"Of course not." When his gaze flicked past her again, she frowned, twisting her head around. "What is it, Da? What's back—?" She closed her eyes at the sight of his lean body and long curling hair. "Damn," she whispered fervently. No wonder her skin had been tingling.

At least he wasn't grinning like her father. He wasn't smiling at all. In fact, she'd have called his expression downright forbidding if it hadn't been for the spark of irritation deep in his eyes.

Unaccustomed to feeling awkward, she managed a hurried, "Da, this is Torbel. Torbel, my da."

"Alfred Summers." Her father stuck out a hand covered with a half-fingered marketer's glove. "It's a pleasure to meet you."

"And you, Mr. Summers."

The usual banter ensued, with her da insisting that Torbel call him Alfred and asking him about his agency.

"Why are you here?" Victoria finally broke in. She'd be damned if she'd let those blue-green eyes of his put her on the defensive.

His dark brows rose in something akin to a challenge. "You were supposed to wait for me at Zoe's flat."

"I did wait. You said teatime. That hour came and went, so I did the same."

"Glib, ain't she?" her da said with a wink. "Gets her tongue from me an' all."

Torbel's gaze remained on her face. "I wondered about that."

"Did you follow me here?" Victoria asked, not liking the idea. She hadn't noticed a thing, and she'd been watching.

"At a distance. It wasn't difficult. You kept to the main streets."

"With a homicidal lunatic after me, I'd be crazy to walk down dark alleys, wouldn't I?"

She hadn't meant to say that. Her father's face went from amused to appalled. "You got a lunatic on your tail?"

"No, Da, not really—"

"Yes, really," Torbel interrupted.

Her da wrapped his fingers around a carrot and squeezed. "What's he done?"

"Not much," Victoria lied.

"He killed a cop," Torbel contradicted. "There's no point, Victoria. It's all over the papers. He'll find out about it sooner or later."

Before she could protest further, her da scuttled off and snatched up a neighbor's newspaper. Nose buried in the small print, he read, "Stepney Police Officer, Sergeant Robert Peacock, Dies In Junkyard Explosion." His head bobbed up. "How do you know this is the same loony what's after you?"

Victoria shot Torbel a nasty glare. "It's a long story, Da. Sergeant Peacock said he had some information for us about Robbie Hollyburn's mother. When we got there—well, the rest is right in front of you. That's it. That's all we know. Lenny Street is dead, and so is Sergeant Peacock. Boots is missing, Judge Hollyburn's out for blood, though whether literally or not we're not sure. Zoe's been disowned, Clover's a mystery and Inspector Fox is a—a . . ."

"Prat," Torbel supplied. "One whose police record was cleaned up by Augustus Hollyburn."

"And who knew Sophie Hollyburn when she was alive," Victoria said. She did not add Ron's name to the list for the simple reason that she had no proof he was doing anything untoward, only a suspicion, and she wasn't about to spread tales based on something as nebulous as that.

"Sounds like you got yourselves a fine mess," her da observed sagely. He zoned in on a surprisingly good photo. "Is that your Peacock? He looks a dead tired man to me, big brown eyes an' all. What's that on his jaw? A birthmark shaped like a kidney bean? Reminds me of the cows I used to milk in Yorkshire." One finger stabbed the newspaper column. "It says here that the bombing was a drive-by in a stolen sports car. No fingerprints on the vehicle."

"Really?" Victoria took the paper from him. "I didn't hear that. When did they find the car?"

"This morning," Torbel told her. He glanced past her shoulder as he spoke. "That's why I was so late. I've been down at the station house ever since."

Victoria studied his unrevealing features. Why on earth was she so drawn to this man? Why, even now, in front of her da and all the other market vendors, did she long to pull his mouth and hands onto her.

She took a deep breath instead and asked, "What are you looking at, Torbel?"

"Someone in black lurking around the fruit barrow. He's gone now." A meaningful brow arched in her direction. "Or she."

Victoria managed not to react. Her da had enough to worry about. "Maybe we should go," she murmured, rubbing a suddenly damp palm on her bare leg. Leaning over, she kissed Alfred's weathered cheek. "I'll come and see you again soon, Da."

"Very soon," he insisted. She noticed that his hands were trembling now as he rearranged his cabbages.

"I promise." She kissed him again. "It'll be fine," she whispered. "Torbel's good. We'll figure it out."

"I'll hold you to that, lass. I don't like the idea of loony car bombers chasing my daughter about London."

As Torbel's fingers curled about her upper arm, she let her gaze stray to the flower stall. "Neither do I, Da," she replied with a mounting sense of dread. "Neither do I."

"One, two, a note for you.
Three, four, open the door.
Five, six, pick up sticks.
Seven, eight, lay them straight.
Nine, ten, you lose, I win...."

Augustus heard Clover's voice through the closed parlor door. Pick up sticks? His old face hardened as he barged inside.

He'd taken her unawares. Her face mirrored her surprise at the intrusion. Twin spots of color appeared on her normally pale cheeks.

She balled the paper swiftly in her lap. "Grandfather," she exclaimed to cover the crinkling sound. "I thought you and Scratch were having lunch today."

"He stood me up. Had another matter to attend to." He stabbed an accusing finger at the wad of paper. "What's that?"

"It—it was on the floor inside the mail slot."

"Chivers collects the mail. He's been double-checking lately. Why didn't he find it?"

"This one had no postmark. It must have been hand delivered. It's nothing really, Grandfather. A childish prank.

Harmless. We get these all the time at the station. Jack the Rip—''

"I don't give a flying fig about a century-old nutball. Let me see that note. When did you—?" He faltered but thrust the thought away. "When did you find it?" He emphasized the word "find" and watched for her reaction. She gave him nothing except the wadded paper.

"Five minutes ago. Your name was on the envelope. No address. It's chicken scratch on ordinary writing paper. Standard issue." Her eyes came to rest on his face, ingenuous eyes if not entirely innocent in Augustus's opinion. "What's it doing here, Grandfather? What does it mean?"

He gave an inelegant snort. "Don't hand me that, girl. You're a member of the London police force—though why you should choose an assignment in Stepney is beyond my comprehension."

"You know why," she returned in a low voice.

"It doesn't matter what I know or don't know," he snapped. "What matters is this note. I want to know who wrote it."

She looked him straight in the eye and said placidly, "I should imagine the person who's trying to kill Torbel and Victoria Summers."

He turned away, sickened to hear the words spoken, yet oddly delighted inside. It was the pleasure he strove to conceal.

He skimmed the note, another altered nursery rhyme. Why rhymes?

He pondered that question consciously but knew his subconscious was working on a far more frightening question. Who was behind all of this?

The answer, too, lay buried deep inside him. One of two people, it said. More likely one than the other, but he would still say one or two for the moment.

His eyes fell on a picture of Robbie on the mantel. Dark, soulful eyes, slender features, tiny scar under his left cheek. Where had that come from? Augustus couldn't remember. Or maybe he didn't want to...

His chest began to hurt. He'd pay the devil good money to finish this nightmare for him. Mete out justice without revealing an unpleasant detail that must surely be fact—even if his brain chose to deny it.

But he would deny it. He must. This horrible thing was not possible.

But he knew. Deep down, he thought he knew who it must be. For all his faults, and as much as Augustus despised him, Torbel was too smart to be deceived for long. He'd figure it out. If he knew what Augustus did of the nature of the family, he'd have figured it out long ago.

Stuffing the note in his waistcoat, he faced his silent granddaughter. She resembled a solemn angel sitting there on that ottoman in her creamy caftan. But there were no angels in the Hollyburn ranks. Except maybe Robbie, who'd been too young and idealistic to understand.

"Have my, er, missing documents been located yet?" he asked in a cautious tone.

"No, but I have a plan."

Pain like a lightning bolt shot through his chest. "Not infiltration, I hope."

Her chin came up. "Can you think of a better way? You say it's imperative those documents be retrieved. Maybe Peacock got hold of them, maybe he didn't. Maybe they burned with him, maybe they didn't. Or maybe someone else has them, and she's planning to show them to Torbel."

Augustus's breathing grew thready. He mustn't die. Not yet. Not until justice was served.

"Do what you have to," he gasped with a cranky flap of his hand. "Just get those papers back."

An eerie little smile crossed her lips. "'Three, four, open the door.... Nine, ten, you lose, I win....'" she quoted from the note in his pocket. "Who knows, Grandfather. Maybe I won't have to do much at all."

Chapter Twelve

"Excuse me—ouch!" Victoria snatched her foot out from under a worn clodhopper.

The man wearing it merely scowled at her. He would have stomped off, but Victoria tried again to waylay him. "Excuse me, have you seen someone called Boots? He used to come to this spot a lot."

The man cast her a mistrustful look and muttered an unintelligible response.

Victoria sighed. No one she'd talked to had seen Boots for days. And now this scruffy old man in a red bowler hat had joined a brown-shoed woman poaching on his territory.

The man was no friendlier than his female counterpart. All he did was march away when she asked him about Boots. And neither the man nor the woman really looked her in the eye.

She was considering returning to Zoe's flat and going through more of Sophie's diary when Tito emerged from a nearby alley to hail her.

"You're harder to find than a pocket of lolly," he panted, fanning himself with his cap. "I got a note for you from Torbel. One of his people gave it to me half an hour ago."

Victoria read the message out loud. "'Meet me in the storehouse—fourth floor, west side. I think I've found something.' Typical," she said, stuffing the paper in her backpack. "No time mentioned. No hint of what he found."

"That'd be his Scotland Yard training, miss," Tito told her. "They do stuff like that. Real cloak-and-dagger. Torbel said nothing's ever straightforward at the Yard. Those what work there always talk in code. Have to watch their backs, too, I'm told.''

"Sort of shakes your faith in the legal system, doesn't it?"

Tito grinned. "Wouldn't know, miss. I never had any faith to start with. You spotted Boots yet?"

"No, just two old grouches usurping his spots."

"Ah, he'll turn up. Boots goes off sometimes."

"For four days?"

"For three last year. He'll be back."

Tito left with a cheery wave, and Victoria started for the storehouse. High heat and humidity combined with the bank of black clouds overhead to lend a macabre aspect to the area. The usual crowd of people swarmed the streets, but they were abnormally subdued. Hushed, as if they knew the storm was about to break but didn't want to be the cause of it.

A group of men in suits scurried by, a pack of oily little entrepreneurs. Victoria had seen them before. Their office building stood across from the storehouse. She wondered what Torbel thought of them. Probably not a whole lot, she decided in amusement.

She cut through Potter's Lane to the agency. One of many small side doors allowed her to enter unseen. The last thing she felt like doing with so many other things on her mind was bumping into Ron and company.

The rear and central staircases merged on the second floor. She passed three agents on the way up, but they were absorbed in files and didn't notice her.

"Fourth floor, west side," she read again.

Winded from the heat, she climbed on, ever more reliant on the handrail to pull herself along. She felt as though she'd been on her feet for seven days instead of seven hours. Why on earth, she wondered, with an aggravated look upward, had Torbel chosen this place for a rendezvous?

Because he didn't want an audience? So he could seduce her in private?

The second was a tantalizing prospect, but not very likely. She'd hardly seen him since he'd followed her to the Puddleby

Market two days ago. She'd seen precious little more of her roommate, she reflected wearily.

"Zoe has a touch of feline in her, all right," an easygoing Keiran had told her yesterday. "She comes and goes at will. As long as she does her work, Torbel doesn't mind what hours she keeps. He's stricter with Ron and some of the others, but they need rules."

Interesting, Victoria mused. Had those rules become too confining for Ron? She stepped across the fourth-floor threshold. Was he thinking about moving up at the agency?

She shivered, partly at the grimness of her thoughts and partly because a full inch of dust covered the floor and clung to the centuries-old fixtures before her. The tarnished candle sconces adorning the wall had to be the originals. Obviously this part of the storehouse was no longer in use.

Rows of footprints, indistinct after numerous comings and goings, led from the door all the way down the jagged passageway. To the west end, she presumed.

She proceeded cautiously, mindful of the dark patches that concealed dangerous piles of old brick and mortar. The walls appeared more or less intact, but several of the windows were broken. Also a number of heavy timbers had found their way in here. They lay at odd angles, together with chunks of yellowed plaster on both sides of the corridor.

"Torbel?" she called, then jumped as her hand passed through a large spiderweb. "Are you here?"

She received no answer, nothing but a weird howl of wind swirling about the eaves. If it hadn't been for the footprints, recently made by someone wearing larger shoes than her, she would have turned back.

"Torbel?" she said again in a firmer voice.

She heard a sound at the far end of the passage on the other side of the only intact door.

Stopping in front of it, she tried the knob. Despite years of neglect and a latch so rusty that several flakes dropped onto her sneakers, the thing turned.

Her courage bolstered, she pushed hard, using her shoulder and much of her body weight. Why she hadn't expected it to open easily she couldn't have said. Possibly because the latch had taken a certain strength to shift. Not so the door. It swung back on oiled hinges so readily that it might have been yanked open from the other side.

Except that that was impossible, her startled brain realized, because there was no other side. There was only air and a sheer, four-story drop into the alley.

Victoria fought frantically to regain her balance. Whether she would have done it or not, she never knew. She was still combating her forward momentum when a pair of hands planted themselves squarely in the small of her back.

Her fingers scrabbled for, and thankfully caught, the knob. The door swung open wide, taking her with it. She watched in numb horror as the floor disappeared beneath her. And everything from Dickens's storehouse to cluttered alleyway became a terrifying blur.

"TRUST A FEMALE," Torbel stated angrily. He tossed the scrap of paper in his hand onto Keiran's makeshift desk and swore volubly. "She sent me a note telling me to meet her in Blackheath of all places. Said her da had his cart there today."

"And he didn't?" Keiran inquired from the floor, where he'd been tinkering with a raft of sound equipment.

"No, he bloody did not. And Victoria never showed. I swear, Keiran, when I get hold of her I'm going to—"

"Torbel!" A breathless Oswyn burst through the side door. "She's there!" He pointed upward, panting hard. "I was in the knacker's yard—I mean, Tom Froggett's butcher shop—and I saw her hanging by her fingers."

Torbel frowned. "Who?"

"Victoria!"

He reacted instantly, grabbing the boy by his shirtfront and hauling him upright. "Where, Oswyn? Where did you see her?"

"Up there, on the west side. Top floor. She's—she's holding on to the doorknob. Swinging from it."

"Jesus," Keiran breathed.

Torbel dropped Oswyn and started for the staircase at a dead run. "Find a rope and get into the alley," he ordered over his shoulder.

He took the stairs three at a time, envisioning all the while Victoria losing her grip and plunging to her death in the alley.

No, not death. She wasn't going to die. He wouldn't let that happen. But someone sure as hell would.

They'd never used the fourth floor or gotten around to fixing it up. It was a rubbish heap in its own right—and somebody intent on harm had known it. Because it was no accident that Victoria was in this predicament; Torbel would stake his life on that.

He swore under his breath when he spied the open door at the far end of the corridor. She was clinging to the worn knob, but God only knew how long that rusted bit of metal would support her.

He reached the threshold at the same moment as she caught sight of him.

"Torbel," she cried, struggling to pull herself higher.

The hinges gave a frightening creak. Torbel's stomach gave a matching lurch. "Don't move," he warned her. "Keep as still as you can."

He zeroed in on the hinges. They were going, he realized. He'd never get to her before they gave out.

"I can't hold on," she whispered desperately.

"Just a few more seconds," he promised. He looked around, his mind racing. He could see Keiran and Oswyn in the alley below. Keiran had a rope, but there was no time to jury-rig a pulley.

One hand almost lost its grip. "Torbel . . ." she gasped.

"Stop squirming," he yelled. He hadn't meant to snap at her, but it was the best thing he could have done.

She twisted her head around just far enough to hiss at him. "As easy as that, huh? Stop squirming—ahh."

He reached out a hand as she almost lost her hold completely. His eyes scoured the alley. Piles of refuse lay everywhere, the largest pressed against the building across from the storehouse. Cardboard mostly, he reflected without a great deal of optimism, but who knew what might lurk beneath it. And yet, what other hope did she have? He could see her fingers slipping on the knob, and the hinges were pulling out farther with every passing second.

"Listen to me, Victoria," he called to her. "We're both going across the alley to that pile of rubbish. When I grab you, let go, duck your head and make yourself go limp. Do you understand?"

"I . . . yes."

He could hear her arm muscles screaming in agony. Closing his eyes, he backed up, took a deep breath and, using all his strength, lunged.

The cry he let out was nothing more than a release of adrenaline. His attack cry, Keiran called it. He only hoped this attack would be successful.

The instant his arms circled her, she released her hold on the knob. Hot air rushed past them on all sides. God help them both if his aim was off.

The rubbish pile came up to meet them, a sea of corrugated boxes, green plastic bags and old newspaper. Torbel had to wrench his body around in midair to avoid landing on her. But he realized he'd misjudged the time required to complete the turn when his sore arm impacted with the cardboard—and something much more solid directly beneath it.

Victoria must have experienced the same jolt, for he heard her grunt of surprise and pain right before she slipped from his arms.

He was alive, though, and alert enough to set his teeth against the pain that shot upward into his shoulder. Victoria must be alive, too, because he'd cushioned a large portion of her fall with his body.

Disregarding the blood that seeped through his jersey, he groped for her among the bags. "Victoria!"

She emitted a weak groan. "It's like being hit by a train," she mumbled, then roused herself and added a stronger "Torbel! Are you all right? Where are you?"

Buried, it seemed. Either that or he'd gone blind. Freeing his sore arm, he rolled over, shoving the layers of cardboard aside and wincing at the white-hot arrows that tore through his entire body. He saw Keiran's face beside him and felt his steadying hand. As much as he appreciated his friend's gesture, however, he shook the help off. "Where's Victoria?"

"Oswyn's there. She's got a small bump on her temple. You're the one who's a mess, my friend."

He wasn't really, but he probably looked it. He'd been in worse shape many times during his days at Scotland Yard.

A red haze colored his mind when he thought back to how those days had ended and why—and at whose autocratic hands.

"Torbel?"

"Yeah, I'm fine." He banked the unpleasant thought, far in the past now, and crawled out of the rubbish, his eyes immediately locating Victoria. She knelt to one side with Oswyn, rubbing her temple.

A large drop of water hit his head, then another and another.

"Here it comes," Keiran said, motioning to Oswyn. "Get her inside."

But Torbel stopped the boy. "Leave her. You and Keiran go ahead. Batten down if you have to. This storm's gonna blow. Keep working on that tape, Keiran. I want to know whose voice it was."

"I'll do my best, but I don't think it was electronically distorted. Whoever left the message at Zoe's knows something about fixing sound."

"Do your best." Torbel's expression hardened as his gaze flicked upward to the swinging door. "I want this bastard identified. Now. Because whoever he is, I swear to God I'm going to kill him."

"THIS IS WHERE YOU LIVE?" Victoria was both shocked and delighted, despite a sore head and a lingering sense of fear that even Torbel's reassuring presence couldn't erase.

A faint smile pulled on his lips. "It has its good and bad points."

More good than bad in Victoria's opinion. She hadn't known what to expect; however, a collection of hardcover books crammed into an entire wall of oak shelves would not have been her first guess.

The living-room furniture was equally charming, over-stuffed and comfortable, in varying shades of rust, blue and brown. There was a rolltop desk, open and brimming with files, a round table with chairs sitting in front of the dormer window and beyond that a wooden deck with a wonderful over-view of Dockland. The kitchen was serviceable yet homey, the bedroom...well, she'd only glimpsed that, but she expected the windows would share the same dockside view as the living room. It was a fifth-floor walk-up in a crowded city quadran-gle called Just-So-Square—and she'd trade her Tower Bridge apartment for it in a minute.

What surprised her even more than the flat itself was the fact that Torbel had brought her here. They'd have stayed a great deal drier by returning to the storehouse with Keiran and Os-wyn. True, it had eased her rattled nerves to stroll past painted windows and hear the prattle of Cockney shoppers searching for a bargain, but she'd been soaked by the time they reached the square, and Torbel's arm was bleeding quite badly.

He allowed her to deal with that problem now, though not, she noted, within the confines of the bathroom. He brought the bandages, tape and ointment to the table, then watched with seeming abstraction while she patched him up.

"You'll want a warm bath, I imagine," he said when she was finished.

That was one of the things she wanted, all right. Unfortu-nately she wouldn't get the first by being too hasty, and she hesitated to ask for the second after that gin-and-tonic episode with Zoe at Gooseberries, so she opted for the third. Setting a hand on his good arm, she forced him to look at her. "He's getting bolder, isn't he?" *Or she,* she added silently. "That note was a trick, Torbel, and I fell for it. I shouldn't have but I did. So did Tito."

"So did I," Torbel said darkly. "It's a game, Victoria, a deadly bloody game, and we're caught in the middle of it. I've got Keiran dissecting the message that was left on Zoe's an-swering machine, but so far he's come up empty."

"You don't think the police . . . ?" At his tolerant look, her voice trailed off. "I guess not. Not in light of Fox's nonexistent record, Sophie's diary, Judge Hollyburn's attitude, Peacock's death and—" she shuddered "—Clover's entire manner."

The phone rang before Torbel could respond. Reaching over her to the desk, he flicked a switch. Ron's Scottish brogue cut through the lash of rain and wind outside.

"I found an envelope," he announced bluntly. "Someone pushed it under the kitchen door. I don't know who or when."

Rubbing her arms, Victoria stood and began to pace. She didn't want to hear this. So many more intriguing pastimes were possible in Torbel's flat. She'd rather not be privy to any more ghoulish notes.

Torbel massaged his closed eyes with the thumb and forefinger of his left hand. "Read it," he said, his voice deceptively benign.

Ron obeyed, ending with an eerie " 'Nine, ten, you lose, I win.' "

Victoria's blood felt like ice water; she wasn't sure why. Obviously she'd survived the attack to which this latest note-rhyme referred. Pick up sticks, though? Lay them straight? She could see herself and Torbel being laid out straight in coffins, broken bone by broken bone.

"Is that all?" Torbel demanded when Ron stopped.

"Keiran says to tell you the tape was deliberately fixed and beyond him, whatever that means."

"It means," Torbel said flatly, "that we're being led around by the nose. Tell him to forget the tape, Ron, and concentrate on finding Boots."

"Right, aye." Ron paused. "You, uh, coming back here tonight, then?"

Was that the faintest quirk of irony on Torbel's lips? It was gone before Victoria could be certain. "I doubt it," he drawled. "But you never know, I might do. Concentrate on your work, Ron, and don't worry about me."

Ron made a disgruntled sound. "See you whenever, then."

"Whenever," Torbel agreed, ending the conversation.

Victoria eyed him suspiciously from the windowsill. "You did that on purpose, didn't you?"

His eyes came up. If looks could kill, those eyes would be a lethal weapon. "I do most things on purpose, Victoria."

"Don't you trust him?"

"We've been over this before," he said heavily. "Why the sudden lack of faith in Ron? Or do all people with criminal records receive this treatment?"

"That's not fair," she retorted, instantly defensive. "How many times have you found yourself hanging by your fingernails over what you're sure is going to be a stony grave? Not very often, I bet. All right, so I suspect Ron. I also suspect Clover and Inspector Fox, and they're cops. I'm not a pampered princess, Torbel. You've met my da—you know that. But I'm not used to going through doors and finding nothing except air on the other side, either. And the nursery rhymes I was told weren't full of dire predictions about death and suffering and avengers sent by some higher—or lower—force to see that justice is served. You and I both know full well that our deaths won't bring that end about any more than hope alone will end this horrible nightmare. We have to stop this crazy person, Torbel, and we have to do it before we really do walk through a door and straight into our graves."

She paused for breath at that point and to push the heavy mass of dark curls from her flushed face. The rain had sent the humidity level soaring to new heights. His flat felt like a Turkish steam bath. She was hot and irritable and scared and, after hearing that note, in no mood to be baited.

She realized belatedly that he'd stood and shoved back his chair. His eyes, those deadly, beautiful blue-green eyes, were locked on her face. She'd gone too far—and yet she knew she really hadn't. She'd only stated the obvious.

So why was she suddenly trembling inside? Why was her spine tingling where it pressed against the window frame, her breath suspended hotly in her chest?

Rain ran in rivulets down the glass. She heard thunder rolling over the Thames and saw a flash of lightning in the black night sky.

When had full darkness descended? And why did it feel so close, so threatening to her heart?

He reached her in two strides. Once there, he seemed infinitely closer than the night. She saw the lines that fanned out from the corners of his eyes and recalled obscurely that he was thirty-seven. Not old by any means, but well lived. Or perhaps not so well, she thought, a small sensation of panic climbing into her throat. What did she know about the Rag Man?

"Is that fear I see in your eyes, Victoria?" he challenged silkily. She would have said sensuously, had it not been for the ruthless cast to his face and the scar that stood out in bold relief against his skin.

She lifted her chin and lied. "No."

"What, then? Uncertainty? Mistrust?"

"Call it circumspection," she retorted coolly. "I'm leery of human puzzles, Torbel, and you're the biggest puzzle I've ever met."

Her fingers had wrapped themselves around the painted sill, as if by clinging to that she could hold on to the last vestiges of her sanity.

He'd become a fever in her blood. She didn't know how or when, but she knew she wanted to make love to him. Wanted to, and would have her way if it killed her.

She held his unrelenting stare. It seemed to pierce right through her. Could desire kill, she wondered, or would it, in her case, merely deal the final, fatal blow to all her childhood ideals?

A shiver she couldn't hide worked its way across her heated skin. Carefully, because she had no idea how he would react, she reached out and touched his face, tracing the line of the scar that curved under his right cheekbone.

His hand shot up instantly to grip her fingers. "You don't want to do this, Victoria," he said in a low voice.

Her fingers curled in his iron grip, but her gaze remained calm on his face. "How do you know what I want?"

"I don't. But I do know you don't know me."

"Tell me, then."

"You won't like what you hear."

"I'll chance it."

Using his grip for leverage, he drew her forward until she could feel his arousal digging into her softer flesh. With his mouth mere inches from hers, he said quietly, "You don't know what you're getting into. You can't know. The truth of my life isn't on computer."

Her heart pounded against her ribs. Her breath came in short, rapid spurts. Still, she had her pride. "You brought me here, Torbel," she reminded him. "I can't believe it was just to talk."

"I make mistakes, too, Victoria. I shouldn't have brought you here. On the other hand, you shouldn't have come. Shaken or not, you had sufficient good sense left to say no."

Her delicate eyebrows rose. "Yes," she agreed. "I did. And yet I'm here, aren't I?"

A telltale muscle in his jaw twitched. The heat and humidity seemed to have doubled in the tiny flat. More thunder rumbled through the London sky. Rain tapped at the windows, like wet needles striking the glass. Victoria swayed but stopped short of actually falling into him. She'd made her choice; she wouldn't let him accuse her of using her feminine wiles on top of that.

He sighed at her stubborn silence. "You really are pigheaded, aren't you?" he said, his free hand moving reluctantly to stroke the hair from her warm face. "You almost died an hour ago, and now you want sex."

She froze. "Is that how you see it, Torbel? Sex between consenting adults?"

He regarded her with a steady expression. "It's how I have to see it. Trust me, you wouldn't be happy afterward."

Annoyed, she twisted her hand free. "Isn't that for me to decide? Since when did sex become such a clinical topic of discussion anyway? You have no sense of romance, do you? I mean, it isn't as if—"

He cut her off with a resigned "Victoria..."

"What?"

"Shut up."

And before she could respond, he lowered his head, placed his mouth over hers and proceeded to kiss her as she'd never been kissed before.

Chapter Thirteen

He could be pushed so far and no further. And a black-haired Gypsy with accusations spilling from her lips and sparks of anger flying from her electric blue eyes was more than any healthy, sexually aroused man could take.

He'd planned to put her off with his kiss, but he realized instantly, and with a vague sense of inevitability, that it wouldn't work out that way. How could it when he loved her? Not that he was prepared to admit that to her—he was barely able to admit it to himself—but love it was, and would remain for as long as he lived.

Such had always been the depth of his emotions. When he hated, he hated. When he loved, he loved all the way.

His mouth moved hungrily over hers, his tongue circling, tasting, exploring the delicate contours. She reminded him of a violet. Beautiful, finely built and fragile. Which was to say she appeared fragile, yet in reality possessed the strength of ten women.

The small sound she made in her throat caused his insides to constrict. He acknowledged the insistent throbbing in his lower limbs and pulled her closer, until his arousal dug into the soft skin of her lower belly.

Her fingers twined themselves in his hair. She kissed him back eagerly now, her initial surprise and wariness vanishing as one by one his defenses fell away.

He wouldn't be able to wait long, his instincts told him. He wanted Victoria as he'd never wanted another woman.

She was tugging his shirt from the waistband of his jeans and sliding her hands beneath it. Tantalizing, tentative hands that stretched his self-control to the breaking point.

Hauling her closer, he tucked her more firmly against him, teasing her with his mouth, breathing in the warm, exotic scent of her skin and hair.

The bedroom loomed to his left, a place of darkness and intrigue. For some reason, there was an element of mystery attached to the idea of making love to her. Mystery . . . and fear.

"Victoria." He tried again to find an excuse, a reason to prevent this thing from happening.

But she merely shook her head and let her hands stray lower. He felt a groan rise in his throat and knew with a hazy, distant certainty that he was lost. Well and truly lost for the first time in his life.

He wondered obscurely what old Goggy would make of that. . . .

VICTORIA'S ENTIRE BODY ached for him. She wanted to crawl under his skin, to be so close to him that no one and nothing could separate them.

Rain pelted the roof and walls. The heat inside her soared. She kissed his face, his eyes, his nose, his mouth and finally, daringly, the scar that ran from brow to cheekbone.

For once he offered no objection, just caressed her back and shoulders as she took the initiative. When her questing fingers found the hot, throbbing length of him, he caught back a tight breath, and she smiled even as a shiver of desire swept through her.

She allowed herself to become bolder, kissing him first on the mouth, then on the throat, then lower still on his shoulders and chest.

The tremor that gripped him also infected her. Her skin felt on fire. She was so aware of him that it actually hurt to breathe.

At long last, she reached that most needful spot on his body. His fingers slid through her hair, and in the back of her mind she heard his murmur of encouragement.

Her skin felt damp yet strangely seared. It was a delicious sensation, almost as heady as the one that enveloped her when she put her mouth on him.

He reacted instantly, convulsively, his hips arching toward her. "Help me," he moaned, and then more softly, "Victoria..."

His hands, strong and sure, reached for her. She didn't want to leave, but she allowed him to ease her upward.

Her mind was a hazy jumble of awareness, of things both heard and felt, of the rain and thunder outside and waves of heat and light inside her head.

She experienced a momentary floating sensation, then felt herself sinking through a soft cotton cloud. As if waking from a dream, she realized that they were no longer in the living room, but lying on his bed. A bed of clouds, it seemed to her fuzzy mind, like the one Mary Poppins must have slept on, because she lived in the clouds, didn't she? A witch nanny sent to help bring families together.

Boots had called Torbel's mother a witch of sorts. If that was true, what was Torbel?

A man, she decided, closing her eyes in pleasure as his roving mouth slid over her breast to her nipple.

He suckled the hardened tip, gently yet with enough taunting force to make her neck arch on the pillow.

Piece by piece, her already loosened clothing disappeared. First her tank top, then her bra, then her shorts and lacy briefs. When the last item had fluttered off to shadowy oblivion she ran her hands across his shirt and pulled it slowly over his head. She was groping for his belt when another, fiercer sensation gripped her.

He was kissing her ear. She hadn't known that ears could be erogenous zones, but evidently they were. It was all her fumbling fingers could do to deal with his fly.

When she finally did, he kicked his jeans impatiently away. It seemed he was kissing her everywhere now. What he didn't kiss with his mouth, he stroked with his hands. Victoria felt herself drifting upward, through a white-hot haze of awareness, heading for—she didn't know what. She'd never had a real climax before, hadn't been sure what to expect if and when she ever did.

It was no longer in question. And *when* seemed imminent, exquisitely, painfully so.

Her hair was wet, her head thrashing back and forth on the pillow. She pulled him closer and, through a murky haze, heard again his quick, indrawn breath.

Now, she pleaded with him silently. *Do it now.*

He did, as swiftly and surely as if she'd spoken the words out loud. Maybe she had. She only knew that he was as hungry for her as she was for him.

He entered her in a single, fiery thrust that had her fingernails digging into his shoulders and a gasp spilling from her lips.

"Don't stop," she whispered when he hesitated.

She saw his eyes glittering in the shadows, heard the rain hammering the roof and felt oddly suspended in time. "Are you sure?" His voice was low and husky, his breathing harsh as he searched for an answer in her face.

She gave him one, reaching up and pulling his mouth onto hers, then sliding her hands to his buttocks and urging him deeper inside her.

He began the rhythm, that timeless male-female ritual, at a decorous pace. But Victoria wanted no part of decorum. She wanted to be in that place where she knew she'd never been. She wanted him to fill her with heat and energy and love. She wanted the Rag Man. Completely. Now.

His movements became faster. Her heart raced, the blood pounding hot and frenzied in her veins. Her head swam, alive with sensations she scarcely recognized. The fever that seized her must have transmitted itself to him. The strain and pleasure were plainly written on his face. His hair was wet with perspiration; his half-lidded eyes shimmered in the dim light of the city.

The docks of London hovered before her, wet and mysterious, an age-old city playing backdrop to an even older dance.

For one brief moment, it seemed that her heightened senses hung in the balance. She felt nothing and everything. She forgot to breathe.

Then, just when she thought she would burst, he moved again, exploding inside her with an intensity that brought a cry of exultation to her lips.

It was beautiful, beyond anything she'd ever dreamed. She wanted to hold the moment, to make it last forever. Yet even as that thought flitted through her mind, she knew it wasn't to be. Nothing in life was forever, least of all a moment as exquisite as the one she'd just experienced. She felt herself sliding downward, a slow, inexorable descent into the embers of their lovemaking.

He collapsed on top of her, exhausted. He would have rolled away if she hadn't caught and held him tight against her.

She knew he spoke, but his murmured words were indistinguishable above the rain and the subsiding drumbeat of her heart.

Boots said Torbel had the magic in his veins. Ancestral magic, she assumed. Whatever he meant, she understood one thing quite clearly. He had the magic for her.

A tremor of remembered fear ran through her. She loved him. If it was the last thing she ever did, she was going to make him understand that. She only hoped she would have enough time to accomplish her task. Before the homicidal maniac after them closed in for the kill.

THERE WAS NO POINT at all standing out here in the rain, no way to see into Torbel's flat and spy on their lovemaking.

Because that's what they were doing, wan't it? A good scare and bam, straight into his bed. She was a slut, as well as an accessory to murder. She should be dead. They should be picking up her bones even now, stacking them on the nearest rubbish heap with the rest of the waste.

Torbel, too, but he was harder to nab. Maybe he did have the magic at that. People spoke of it down here, whispered it actually because they knew he had a temper and no one wanted to see it unleashed. Only Boots had the nerve to mention it out loud, but then, who ever listened to Boots?

Listen to me, thought the disguised beggar with a spiteful mental thrust. *Torbel is a murderer. Torbel and Victoria.*

But there was no one about on this rainy night to hear—and nothing to do while those two diddled away the hours upstairs. Nothing except wait and watch and think up a newer, surer way to get them both.

The beggar crouched under the closed bakeshop eaves and dreamed of a threat fulfilled. A bloodred threat fulfilled. Old Goggy had better be pleased.

"ROSIE!"

Victoria sat up with a start. In her desire for Torbel, she'd forgotten about her dog. What a monster she was.

The apartment stood in darkness, a steamy, wet den of angled shapes and shadows. The rain had stopped. Only the residue dripped from the eaves. The storm must have moved north while she slept.

While they slept, she amended, laying a careful hand on the neck of the man beside her. He slept as he lived, without fuss or bother. His breathing was deep and even, his lithe body ready to spring should the need arise. Through a cloud of thought and emotion, Victoria found herself wondering yet again what had prompted him to leave Scotland Yard.

She longed to wake him up, to make love to him all over again—although they'd done it three times already, twice in here and once in the shower, and it wasn't even midnight. Her conscience, however, dictated that she take care of Rosie, then worry about satisfying her own needs.

Slipping from the bed, she moved silently across the hardwood floor to the living room, pulling Torbel's red jersey over her head as she went. It hung down to midthigh, and she had to shove back the sleeves to use the telephone, but it smelled clean and sexy like him, which was why she'd chosen to wear it.

The answering machine picked up her call on the sixth ring. "Zoe?" she said into the receiver. "Are you there? Zoe, it's

Victoria. If you're there, pick up the phone. It's about Rosie.'' She waited, but no one came on the line. "Damn." Sighing, she depressed the button. "Now what?"

She thought for a moment then dialed again.

"Gooseberries, Ratz. We're closed—"

"Ratz, it's Victoria," she broke in. "I need a favor."

"If it's about Boots, no one's seen him. I've been asking all night. No one knows who those two are lurking around his usual hangouts, either. His name might be Dippy or Dudley or something. Don't know about the woman."

Victoria made a mental note of the names. "Look, Ratz," she said. "I'm not...Well, let's just say I'm out, and Zoe's not home, and I forgot about Rosie. She had food and water when I left this morning, but I need someone to check on her."

Ratz chuckled. "You got a real night owl for a roommate, Victoria. Good tenant, though. I hardly ever see her. Don't worry, Keiran dropped by at closing. He's still here. He'll look in on your pooch."

"Thanks, Ratz. Oh, and could you ask Keiran...?" She heard a faint click and paused. "Ratz? Are you there? Ratz?"

No answer. She considered redialing, then decided not to bother. As long as Rosie was all right, the rest could wait.

Torbel showed no signs of waking up, so Victoria opened a bottle of Coke, pulled Sophie's diary from her backpack, which Keiran had thoughtfully rescued from the rubbish heap earlier, and curled up in the chair beside the bookshelves.

She skimmed the entries made in the diary the year prior to Robbie's birth. One, scribbled with more apparent haste than its predecessors, caught her eye.

April 3

He should have been born with wings, Diary, dragon, not angel. He talks of fairness, of playing by the rules, but he means his own personal rules and his weird concept of fairness. What a two-faced liar he is....

The following entries spoke of traveling north to visit old

friends. It wasn't until she returned to London that Sophie mentioned "him" again.

April 16
I think I hate him, Diary, I really do. If there's a woman under sixty in all of the British Isles that he hasn't at least propositioned, I'd be very surprised. And he has the nerve to tell me that he senses an indiscretion on my part. I cling to the word "senses," for I am confident that he cannot know....

Victoria scanned farther, curious to know what Augustus apparently did not.

April 23
My poor, dearest love, Diary, he looks like a powdery ghost. And all old Goggy can do is chortle and tell him he shouldn't have trod in poison ivy. The man has the perception of a clay turtle. Poison ivy indeed. The only thing old Goggy's allergic to is feeling. And yet there are times when he can be altogether too discerning. Yes, he can surely be a cunning old fox, but his cunning is no match for my darling love's. My love says that with caution we will not be caught. I hope I can believe him....

Victoria searched the next few pages for names, but discovered none. Obviously Sophie wanted to believe that her diary would remain private, just as she realized there was a good chance it would not. She continued.

May 17
I do wish Father would leave me alone, stick to his own "affairs," as it were. Why does he have to butt in to every part of my life? Mr. Fix-it, Mother Blanche sarcastically calls him. One wave of his magic judge's wand and, poof, crimes vanish. Exit a lawbreaker, enter a police officer. I shudder to think what kind of dirty deal brought that switch about. I'm convinced Father knows the truth, and

that's why he fixed things, but my even foxier friend assures me that old Goggy is well off the scent. I am pleased in one way, but not in another. Difficult always to soothe ruffled feathers. I wish I could know what my love really thinks of Father's misguided interference. . . .

"Interference," Victoria repeated, pausing to stare out over the sodden rooftops leading down to the river. Mr. Fix-it, the crime fixer. Whose crimes had he caused to disappear? Oliver Fox's? There was no surprise in that revelation; they'd already guessed as much about Fox and Judge Hollyburn, but why should Sophie refer to the matter in her diary?

The word "affair" sprang to mind, although Victoria had a difficult time conjuring up the image. She wouldn't have taken Oliver Fox on a dare. Then again, Sophie'd been her own woman, with her own peculiar taste in men.

Victoria was flipping through the later pages when the overhead light flickered. A moment later, it went out completely.

Frowning, she stuck the diary into her backpack and made her way to the window. It was late; many people were in bed. However, lights continued to burn in the neighboring buildings, and the storm was long gone.

A prickly sensation crawled over her skin. Lights everywhere but here. No storm. Something felt very wrong.

Backing up, she started for the bedroom and Torbel. She stubbed her toe en route and had to stifle a cry of pain. The bedroom doorway had the look of a cavern entrance until she turned the corner. Then the city lights guided her to the bed.

"Torbel." She reached down to shake him, but wound up shaking a quilt. Perplexed, she leaned closer, "Torbel?"

"Here."

He startled her so badly she almost jumped onto the bed. Fist pressed to her racing heart, she demanded, "Why are you sneaking around?"

"I'm getting dressed. Here, put on your shorts. I heard a noise."

The room was bathed in sooty shadows. She saw his profile, a grim silhouette that did nothing to bolster her confidence. Something was definitely not right.

He zipped his fly quickly, his eyes scanning the huddled shops in the lane below. "When did the lights go out?"

He must have tried the bedside lamp. "About two minutes ago. I was coming to wake you up. Damn, where are they?" She'd dragged on her shorts but couldn't locate her sneakers. "Is someone out there?"

"No. That's what worries me."

Had she left them by the door? She began crawling in that direction—then swallowed a scream as something dark and human covered her and sent her hurtling sideways into the wall.

Chapter Fourteen

"Stay down," Torbel ordered.

Her head swam. It took several seconds for her to realize that he'd tackled her and they were now on the floor behind the door.

As the shock of impact wore off, she heard a tiny click that sounded suspiciously like a lock being picked.

"Someone's here," Torbel said in a low voice. "He must have cut the power lines. We'll have to climb once we get out the window."

Climb onto a narrow ledge, five floors above the ground? Victoria's palms went clammy; her heart slammed into her ribs. "I can't, Torbel," she protested. "It's too high."

"You have to. I'll be right behind you, and it's a solid ledge."

"But..."

The door to his flat creaked open. A stealthy footfall sounded on the wooden floor.

Victoria controlled the knot of panic in her stomach. She had to do it. She'd die—they'd both die—if she didn't.

With Torbel close behind her, she forced her trembling legs to carry her to the window. Breath held, she crawled out.

A shadow fell across the bedroom threshold. A quick glance backward revealed quite clearly the outline of a gun.

"Torbel," she whispered urgently. Precariously balanced on the ledge, she tugged on the shoulder of his red shirt to hurry him.

As if galvanized, the intruder whipped the gun up and fired. Luckily he missed. Or she. Victoria couldn't make out a definite shape beneath the baggy layers of clothing. They looked like beggar's clothes, though, from the brief glimpse she caught.

Torbel pushed her against the outer wall with his wrist, then hoisted himself over the sill. Another shot flew past, zinging off the frame and causing him to jerk sideways.

He nodded to her right. "That way."

She followed his eyes to a metal ladder some twenty feet away. She'd never make that without falling.

Yes, she would, she told herself. She had to.

Her legs trembled. It was a long way, and there was no time to inch along. She moved as quickly as possible, clinging like a limpet to the old bricks, on a gritty stone ledge that, although strong enough to support them, had a wet, powdery substance on the surface, which made maneuvering in bare feet tricky at best.

"I'd make a lousy goat," she mumbled as she went.

"You're doing fine," Torbel prompted from behind. "Keep going."

A bullet whizzed past her ear. "Where—?" she began, but Torbel cut her off.

"Hanging out the window."

She was within stretching distance of the ladder. Her fingers clawed for and caught the rim. Close behind her, Torbel swore as a fourth shot almost nicked her hand.

"Up or down?" Victoria's arms and legs felt like rubber.

He winced at a shot that just missed his shoulder. "Up."

"What's he—? Oh, damn!" A fearful backward glance revealed that the shooter was moving along the ledge, seemingly unimpeded by his baggy clothes.

Victoria forced herself to climb. One, two, three rungs. She tipped her head back. Ten to go, at least. It looked like ten thousand.

Questions whirled through her brain. What if Torbel got hit? What if the ladder broke? Who was this crazy killer? Connected to Robbie Hollyburn, how? Where was Boots? What had Sergeant Peacock wanted to tell them? Was Torbel all right? Did he care about her? Did he love her? . . .

She lost her grip, but he steadied her, reaching up and placing her slippery hand back on the metal rung. "We're almost there," he promised. "Five more steps."

Their attacker fired again. How many bullets did he have? How many did he need, she reflected darkly?

Her fingers grasped the final rung. Adrenaline pumping, she hauled herself up and onto the roof.

It would be cinders, she thought, wincing at the prickly surface underfoot. Sharp, wet and sticky in bare feet.

Torbel appeared beside her. "This way." Grabbing her hand, he took off, across a narrow gap and onto a roof made of rough shingles.

He pushed, prompted and once even bullied her through the rooftop maze of lower Stepney, past crooked chimneys, along impossible ledges and finally over a stone archway.

Shots flew past at odd intervals, presumably whenever their attacker caught a glimpse of them.

Finally Victoria collapsed against a stone chimney. "I . . . can't . . . I have . . . to stop," she gasped.

Torbel didn't argue. Pulling her low, he let his gaze sift through the shadows. "We're almost at the storehouse. Gooseberries is on our right."

Victoria was sorely tempted to slither down the nearest ladder and into Zoe's flat. "Did we lose him?" she asked instead.

"No." She felt his eyes on her face, his thumb absently massaging her upper arm. "Can you run now?"

"I think so."

"Then let's—" He stood, then halted abruptly, a look of horror and fury invading his dark features. A man had just appeared on the side of the roof. "Keiran!" Torbel shouted as a shot echoed through the darkness. He lunged, a feral growl on his lips. Five more shots followed in rapid succession.

Checking his forward momentum, he spun to face her. "Don't move," he ordered in such a fierce tone that she felt herself nodding automatically.

"Keiran?" she whispered. She'd seen him, too, but only for a moment. "Is he . . . ?"

The expression on Torbel's face said it all. His features hardened to stone. "I don't know. He came over the edge of the roof, then dropped. Stay right here, Victoria. You'll be safe if you stay here."

She believed him, shouldn't have but did.

Seconds passed like hours while she huddled next to the chimney. She heard nothing, saw nothing in the darkness. She was alone and too terrified to move.

When sixty seconds ticked by and Torbel still did not return, she risked a peek around the charred bricks to the place where Keiran had fallen.

Two shots ricocheted off the bricks beside her. Without warning, a pair of hands clamped themselves to her shoulders and snatched her backward. Only the memory of his touch kept the scream from emerging.

"I said stay put," Torbel hissed in her ear. "Whoever he is, he's not ready to give up."

Her heart rate slowed somewhat as her initial panic subsided. "Where's Keiran?"

"Next roof. He's been hit."

The words came out like tiny whips, sharp and biting. Vengeful. Victoria shuddered. "Is he . . . hurt?"

"I couldn't tell."

"Then we have to— Torbel, look!" She clutched at his shirt, pointing. "That's the person over there. His arm's caught on something."

"Not for long." Torbel's eyes glittered with a predatory light. "Get to Keiran. If he needs help, there's another ladder. Find Ratz. He'll be at the pub."

Arguing was pointless; she knew that, so she simply nodded. And in that nod lay an unspoken warning: be careful. Then he was gone, and it was her turn to exercise caution.

Keeping the chimney between herself and Keiran, she offered a brief prayer and, bending low, ran for the adjoining roof.

When no shots blasted past, she risked a look behind her. But a dozen other chimneys blocked her view.

Torbel would be all right, she promised herself. He was a cat, wary and smart, and he had nine lives, to boot. He could handle a psychopath with a gun.

She fought the chill that rippled along her backbone and set her sights on Keiran. He wasn't moving.

The three-foot gap between roofs was a piece of cake after the obstacle course she and Torbel had just run. She jumped across and went down on her knees at Keiran's side.

His chest rose slightly. "Keiran?" she whispered. "Can you hear me?"

His hazel eyes cracked open, but they were bleary and unfocused. Blood flowed from a spot on his right shoulder. She breathed a shaky sigh of relief. Better the right side than the left.

"Keiran, listen to me. I'm going to find Ratz. Don't try to move. Torbel's gone after the person who shot you."

A ghost of a smile played on Keiran's lips. "Knife..." he whispered. "Missed him..."

Victoria recalled the image of their attacker, caught on...something. Pinned by Keiran's knife, now seemed the answer.

"Don't move," she said again, simultaneously pushing the hair from his forehead and sweeping her own away. "I'll be right back."

Standing, she twisted her head around. Where was the ladder Torbel had mentioned? She spied it twenty yards ahead and ran.

Her knees were shaking again by the time she hopped off the last rung. As predicted, Ratz was still in the pub, disinclined to respond to her pounding fists, but he finally relented and gave the door a belligerent yank.

The next hour passed in a blur of activity. Victoria was so tired she could have slept for a week on any spot where she happened to drop. But getting Keiran to the ground posed a number of problems, and his refusal to have anything to do with a hospital only made matters worse.

Cross and primed for a fight, Torbel reappeared to tell her that the shooter had escaped before he could reach him. His concern for Keiran took precedence, however, and in the end it was his decision that his friend be taken home instead of to a hospital or clinic.

The doctor, a thin, overworked woman in her thirties, argued the matter briefly, then gave in with a dry "You're a real pain, Torbel. I have to report this to the police, of course, but I've dug the bullet out and given him a shot to prevent infection. Watch him closely tonight. If the bleeding starts again, call me at once, and then it will be the hospital, like it or not."

Torbel didn't like it, but he agreed to her terms without comment.

It was approaching 4:00 a.m. by the time the furor died down. Victoria retrieved Rosie from Zoe's flat, noted the closed bedroom door but decided not to knock. Let her sleep if she was in there. No need for all of them to be zombies tomorrow, especially when nothing more could be done for Keiran.

Not surprisingly, Torbel had his own ideas on that subject. From Keiran's bedroom window, between storehouse and pub, he regarded the slumbering city. A tower clock chimed in the distance, its ancient bell resonating through the predawn air.

"We were shot at, and Keiran was hit. He could be dead." His eyes fastened on hers across the room. "You could be dead." His jaw hardened into a determined line she'd come to know well. "I'm going to find him, Victoria. And when I do, I'm going to kill him."

Rosie jingled to the window, climbed onto the chair and yipped at him.

"She likes you," Victoria murmured as Torbel's preoccupied fingers fluffed the Yorkshire's silky fur. "It says something when animals like you."

He regarded the dog but spoke quietly to her. "Will you stay with Keiran while I go out?"

Her muscles tensed. "If you kill him—the person—Torbel, you'll be the one on trial for murder."

"I know the law, Victoria."

She stood, fists balled. "But you don't care?"

The bitterness of her challenge was not lost on him. Somberly he said, "I care, Victoria. That's why I'm going out."

Frustration welled inside her. However, instinct told her that showing it would be wrong. Possibly because she was wrong to reproach him. Pride kept her chin up and her eyes calm when she replied, "Do what you have to, Torbel. I'll stay with Keiran."

It said something, she supposed, that he trusted her to watch his best friend. Closest male friend, she corrected, stubbornly resolved.

Taking one of Keiran's black cotton jackets, Torbel pulled it on. On his way to the door, he stopped and set his hands on her upper arms. "Trust me" was all he said. He hesitated, drew her forward, hesitated again, then kissed her.

It wasn't long, but she felt an element of desperation in his touch. He had to do this. Maybe one day she would understand why.

She fingered her lips in wonder. Maybe she understood already.

VICTORIA CAME AND WENT. The rain came and went, then came again. An eerie gray dawn light filled the flat. Typically London. Only fog hovering over the Thames was missing. And Sherlock's brilliant powers of deduction.

If it hadn't been for a loud clatter of trash cans in the alley below, Zoe wouldn't have awakened. She would have missed completely the furtive sounds of intrusion, the cautious scrape of wood as someone searched the desk drawers.

Aided by the stealth of her former profession, she stole from her bed and across the carpeted floor. Even swathed in shadows, she recognized her twin instantly.

"What are you doing here?" she demanded in a strident voice.

Clover stiffened, then slowly turned to face her. "I thought you'd be out."

Zoe cleared the roughness of sleep from her throat. "What are you looking for? Goggy's so-called documents again? First you break in, then Fox badgers Victoria about them, now you're back in person. What's so special about a bunch of papers? Are they some sort of unofficial confession on old Goggy's part? 'Crimes and Misdemeanors I Have Condoned.' Or is 'whitewashed' the politically correct term?''

Clover's voice was as strained as her demeanor. "He found the documents. He'd simply misplaced them. I have no idea what information they contained."

Zoe studied her deadpan twin. Clover was here, if not for Goggy's "lost" documents, then for another reason.

From childhood, Zoe had been considered the tougher of the pair. She'd seen Goggy's faults and Sophie's, too, for that matter. Infidelity ran rampant in both of them. But unlike her, Clover had never really been able to accept the truth of their indiscretions. Either that or she hadn't wanted to.

Ostrich, Zoe thought, advancing on her. And a transparent one at that. Books the size of diaries lay atop the desk. Only those—no papers, notepads or magazines. She'd come in search of Sophie's diary.

"It isn't here," she said, closing in.

Clover gave her credit for perceptiveness if little else. "Where, then? With the solicitor who condoned—" she emphasized the word nastily "—Robbie's murder?"

Zoe sighed, halting. "You won't give up, will you? You or Goggy. Victoria had no active part in the trial. As for Robbie, yes, he was murdered, but Torbel didn't do it, and neither did Lenny Street. And no matter what Grandfather says, I for one do not believe that Robbie changed his mind about joining up. He was too excited that night, too anxious to find Torbel. Personally, if I had bad news to pass on to the Rag Man, I wouldn't be bursting at the seams to do it. He's not murderous, but he's got a streak of something in him that he takes great pains not to let out."

"Oh, really. And what would that be if not murderous intent?"

"I have no idea. Something in his background. Maybe in his genes."

Clover scoffed. "You mean that Irish-Welsh magic stuff he supposedly inherited from his mother? It's bollocks."

"Possibly. But certain traits are hereditary, aren't they, Clover? Meanness, spite, infidelity—all the gifts we received from dear old Goggy. Poor Grandma Blanche's gentler qualities must have died a swift death in the genetic pool. The only one of us who wasn't totally screwed up was Robbie, and he's gone. There's just you and me left to pass on the honorable family blood, pure on both sides all the way back to dear Oliver Cromwell. How lucky can you get?" Her tone was sour, her knuckles white where they gripped the top of the chair. "I hate him, Clover, and all I can say is that I hope, when the end comes for him, he gets what he deserves."

"He deserves—"

"To fry in the deepest part of hell," Zoe snapped. The anger and resentment she'd held in for years now rushed to the fore. "He's a bastard, and God alone knows how many of the same name he's spawned over the years. Sophie was—"

"Stop bringing her into this."

"Why?" Zoe made a jerky gesture of impatience. "Don't you see? She was no different than him. How do you know that we—that any of us—are really Duffy's children?"

"We all have the same blood type," Clover said through gritted teeth. "Duffy's type."

"Type O, the most common of all. But that's not the point. I want you to see, to really understand, what a monster Grandfather is. He cleaned up Fox's record—you know he did. Why? Old Goggy doesn't do favors out of the goodness of his heart. So why help Fox? Unless, of course, Fox—" She paused, a shadow passing over her face. "Unless," she repeated less forcefully, "Grandfather knows something about him—some secret we've never been privy to."

Clover's cheeks resembled chalk. "How dare you attack Grandfather in his absence." Zoe couldn't tell if her rasping tone was born of fear or fury. She wasn't sure she cared. Her own train of thought disturbed her to the point where all she wanted was for her sister to disappear.

"Go away, Clover," she said dully. "Go home and spin your mean little plots in old Goggy's parlor. You'll pay for your vindictiveness in the end. You, him, and me, too, I should think—wayward in my own fashion and unrepentant to the end."

"A thief," Clover said scathingly.

"Once upon a time," Zoe agreed. "I wouldn't throw stones right now if I were you, not standing there with your hands in my desk drawers. If Sophie gave away any secrets in her diary, then it's time they were aired. By the way, has anyone bothered to investigate Sergeant Peacock's death any further?"

Clover's stance was rigid. "I'm not on the case."

"Maybe you're working on Boots's disappearance, then?"

Clover's face turned scarlet.

"Not that either, eh? No sense of duty to an old man, or even loyalty to your co-workers. Poor old Boots and Robert Alistair Peacock—that's his full name, in case you never bothered to learn it. One's as dead as a doornail, the other seems to have vanished into thin air, and all you care about is Mother's stupid diary."

Clover appeared ready to burst. But a red light flashing on her belt pager had her snatching up the phone instead. "Do you mind?" she snapped.

"Be my guest."

The call was brief. Apparently her shift had been changed from late to early.

"Nice," Zoe remarked with heavy sarcasm. "Now you and old Goggy can scheme till the cows come home."

"Right." Clover marched for the door. Once there, she executed a smart about-face. "I'll be off to my plotting, then. In case you're interested, Sergeant Lewis told me about a report that came in a little over an hour ago. It seems a member of your crooked little band's been shot."

Zoe's head came up. "Torbel?"

Clover merely smiled and opened the door. "How silly of me. I forgot to ask."

Chapter Fifteen

"Damn!" Torbel gave the stuck door of the storehouse an irritable yank. He was soaked to the skin, frustrated and out of sorts with the world.

The neighborhood was waking up, the oily businessmen next door skulking to work in their dark suits and homburgs. Former bankers all, now miserable loan sharks. If he survived this nightmare of notes and rhymes and midnight attacks, he'd expose them for the crooks they were. But only after the nightmare ended and he'd resolved his own complex problems.

Smudge was sitting on the kitchen counter when he got there, calmly dipping her paw in the sauce from someone's forgotten plate of spaghetti. By the size of the serving, Torbel guessed it was Ron's. Whatever had called him away must have been important to make him abandon his food.

He thought of Victoria and Keiran, swore under his breath and dropped into the nearest chair, too exhausted to put Smudge off the counter.

Nothing. He hadn't turned up a single bloody clue, and he'd been prowling the streets for hours. Actually he had found one lead. He hadn't followed it up yet, but he would. As soon as he sorted out the mess in his head, he'd be on it like Smudge on Ron's spaghetti.

He'd been grilling Tito outside Myrtle's when he'd seen a Cockney bum stumble through the door. Nothing remarkable about him really, until he'd looked down and seen the man's boots. Black boots with once-shiny gold buckles—just like the ones Boots wore.

Tito, who'd spied them at the same time, had jerked back as if kneed. He'd recovered quickly and would have steamrollered the man if Torbel hadn't restrained him. With a motion for Tito to stay put, he'd moved in instead.

"Sod off" had been the drunk man's first reaction to Torbel's question. He hadn't been quite so rude with a forearm pressed to his windpipe and his spine plastered against the outer wall.

"If you want to keep breathing, talk," Torbel had said in a tone that made it clear he didn't care which the man chose.

Sensing that, the drunk had mumbled out an unintelligible "I found 'em in a rubbish bin."

"Where?"

"Here."

"At Myrtle's or on the docks?"

"On the docks. Near the broken pier." He chafed under Torbel's grip. "There wasn't no one in 'em, Torbel. They was way inside the bin."

Why did these people all seem to know him? Torbel wondered.

He believed the man, however, and released him without another word.

Needless to say, Tito had been hopping mad.

"You let him go in Boots's boots," he accused, flailing his thin arms. "Maybe Boots was in the bin, as well."

But Torbel knew people well enough to omit that possibility. "If he'd been there, the guy would have given it away. He's dead drunk—his defenses are virtually nonexistent."

"Where's Boots, then?" Tito challenged. "Dead, dead?"

"Maybe. He might have seen something he shouldn't have. You're no innocent, Tito. You know how life works in Dockland. People like Boots disappear all the time."

Tito hadn't appreciated that answer. He went off kicking a beer can along the docks.

A trash bin near the broken pier, Torbel reflected now. Without looking, he opened the fridge and removed a bottle of

Guinness. That was where the old Pierpont Hotel stood, condemned, as he recalled, though not yet scheduled for demolition.

He'd checked out the bin but found no sign of Boots. He'd considered checking out the old Pierpont, but it had been dawn by then and the city was stirring. He'd decided to check in with Victoria instead—by telephone, because he was no fool.

"Keiran's sleeping," she'd told him in a somewhat stilted voice. Then she sighed. "Look, Torbel, why don't you just come back here, and we'll talk about this. I don't think a personal crusade is the answer, do you?"

Of course it bloody wasn't, he thought snappishly. Walking, however, had cooled him down to the point where he felt back in control of his emotions. Not all of them, mind you, but the more destructive ones had finally been harnessed.

A picture of Victoria's exquisite Gypsy features danced in his head. Unfortunately it was tarnished by the overlying shadow of death—and by Augustus Hollyburn's scowling, vindictive face.

He took a contemplative sip of Guinness. How often in the past decade and a half had he seen that old face in his mind, glowering at him? Too many times to count, he decided wearily.

Rubbing his temples with the thumb and middle finger of his hand, he tried to push the image out. But it persisted, and with it came all the words and accusations they'd traded over the years.

Another, less palatable picture took shape, of old Goggy badgering witnesses, of tricking them, and leading them and finally coercing them into testifying in the manner he chose. In other words, he'd been out for Torbel's blood in the past, he still was and he wouldn't rest until he got it.

Torbel's mind drifted further back, to his days at Scotland Yard. It was a stretch to recall the good, but there had been moments. Unfortunately, and thanks in large part to old Goggy, the bad times overshadowed the rest.

Old Goggy... He let his aching head fall forward. Was the judge behind this current horror? Aware of it, yes, applauding it, almost certainly, but was he also the source of it?

Something nagged in his brain, some detail too obscure to be called up. Maybe even two details—at this point, he was too tired to do more than squint at the shelf clock across the kitchen.

Six twenty-two a.m. He wanted to check on Keiran. He also wanted to see Victoria. Badly. So much that he found himself hesitating. He'd fallen in love with her, dammit. What if he couldn't fall out?

It felt real, and so undoubtedly was. But he could not, dared not, tell her that. He and his temper were infamous, to say nothing of inseparable. For the most part, he controlled it, but what of those rare occasions when he'd been unable to, when, if not restrained by Keiran, he would have ripped a man's throat out with his bare hands?

Boots's voice echoed softly in his head. It spoke of the magic he'd inherited from his mother. It should have mentioned the temper that had also been her gift to him. Magic was bollocks. Fury unleashed had deadly possibilities, supplemented in his case by another trait, a deeper, darker streak of—

"Torbel! What are you doing here?"

Ron's exclamation from the doorway cut short the grim thought. Torbel kept his eyes focused on the shelf clock. "Drinking beer," he said, emptying the bottle down his throat. "Keiran's been shot."

"Aye, I heard." The Scotsman sounded more aggravated than concerned. "Er, will he be all right? Who did it, do you know?"

"Probably, and not yet." Torbel tossed the bottle aside and shoved back his chair with his foot. It gave him no satisfaction to watch the other man back up a pace.

"You look annoyed, Torbel," Ron noted carefully. "Out for blood."

"I am. And I mean to have it." Torbel's fingers ran the length of his scar. "Slowly and not, I promise you, without pain."

"VICTORIA? IT'S ZOE."

Victoria glanced at Keiran, sleeping fitfully in his bed, then went to unlock the door. She was disappointed. She'd wanted it to be Torbel.

"How is he?" Zoe asked at once. "Where's Torbel? Not hunting for lunatics, I hope."

"I wish." Victoria rebolted the door. Thank heaven for the hawkers in the street below. They lent a certain measure of comfort to an otherwise freakish situation.

Zoe looked at Keiran, then, satisfied, flung herself into an armchair and released a pent-up breath. "I had another 'visit' from Clover early this morning. I caught her going through my desk. She was searching for Sophie's diary. Do you still have it?"

Victoria produced the book from her backpack. "Oswyn brought my stuff over—" she didn't say from where "—while all the confusion was going on here."

Zoe started to reach for it, paused, then retracted her hand. "Never mind. You keep it. Let me know if you find anything interesting."

"Do you consider an affair interesting?"

Zoe's eyes narrowed. The hand she'd pulled back came reluctantly out again. "All right, give over. Who's the lucky affairee?"

"I'm not sure." Perched on the arm of the chair, Victoria indicated the pertinent pages. "Here she talks about her 'love' looking like a powdery ghost, and old Goggy having the perception of a clay turtle." She glanced sideways. "I gather your grandfather's not always the most sensitive of men."

"He has his moments. What's this about his cunning being no match for her love's?"

"Foxes are cunning," Victoria remarked.

Zoe swore crudely and flopped back. "I can't handle this stuff right now. It's probably a lot of old cobblers anyway. Sophie was a flighty thing to the end. Off to Ireland she flew without a word to anyone. Why the frenzied departure? What was the big attraction in County Clare? Another lover?"

"Maybe she explains herself." Victoria thumbed through the entries, which became harder to read as time went on.

"Don't count on it." Zoe rose with a grunt, bent to peer at Keiran's handsome face and sighed as if in regret. "I have to go. I'm on a new case. Anyway, I'll catch up with you later. Tell Torbel my last report is on his desk, and this one'll be joining it shortly."

When she was gone, Victoria pondered the bizarre situation surrounding the Hollyburn family. Twins at odds, one of them virtually disowned by an ex-high-court judge who'd had the power to affect at least one man's career to a ridiculous extent. And then there was Sophie. Did the answers to this mystery lie in her diary? Or was that a false trail, and they should be concentrating on Robbie's death instead?

She glanced at Rosie curled up in the crook of Keiran's arm and felt her mind beginning to wander. Where was Torbel? Why didn't he return? Would he, could he, love her? What if he could? More disturbingly, what if he couldn't?

Trembling inside and out, she wrapped her arms around her upraised legs, pressed her forehead to her knees and prayed that he would return to her unharmed.

SHE WAS ASLEEP on the sofa when Torbel got there. He stroked the hair from her cheek, tucking it gently behind her ear. She'd been reading Sophie's diary. It lay open on the carpet beneath her curled fingers. God knew what she must be dreaming right now.

Crossing to Keiran's bed, he was surprised to find his friend awake with Rosie curled up on the pillow next to his head.

"You're alive," he noted in a wry tone he knew Keiran would not misinterpret.

"No thanks to that prat with the gun. Did you catch him?"

"Not yet."

"That has an ominous ring to it." Keiran fixed his bleary eyes on Torbel's face. There was more shrewdness left in them than he would have expected. "I don't suppose you've told her yet?"

Torbel glanced at Victoria, then cast an astute sidelong look at Keiran. He weighed his chances of deceiving his oldest friend and cursed the answer.

Keiran chuckled. "That's what I figured. You're crazy if you let her get away. You should know by now what you want in a woman. Me, I'm the Lady Caroline Dester type."

Torbel frowned. "Who?"

"From *Enchanted April.* Polly Walker played— Never mind." His Irish accent blurred with amusement and pain. "You've got a rare gem in Victoria."

"Yeah, a rare Gypsy gem from Bouverie Street."

"You're an incurable cynic. Let it go, Torbel. It'll only bog you down in the end."

The painkillers were bringing out the philosopher in Keiran. That the philosopher might be right, however, was not a thing Torbel was prepared to admit. Not yet. Not with a murderous maniac apparently dogging their every move.

He sat on the edge of the chair and massaged his forehead with his fingers. "Guns, notes, nursery rhymes, forklifts—this one's beyond me, Keiran. Someone wants revenge for Robbie's death. Street's dead. Peacock, too." His brow furrowed at the last name. "Peacock wanted to tell us something about Sophie Hollyburn. Sophie was Robbie's mother. An affair's the best I can come up with. Seems obvious, though, doesn't it?"

"Depends on who she had the affair with."

"What do you mean?"

"Look beyond the obvious, Torbel. There's Goggy's old friend Scratch or Scranton or whatever his name is. And Chivers."

"The butler?"

"Never overlook a butler."

"Keiran, that bullet hit your shoulder, not your brain. Nothing's obvious about any of this—and the butler didn't do it."

He saw the faint smile that quirked Keiran's lips. He also saw his eyes close, and wisely he fell silent.

Slumping back in the chair, he ran a meditative thumb across his lower lip. Never overlook the obvious. It was one of the basic tenets of police work and a lesson he'd learned early on—which was undoubtedly why his instincts had taken to screaming at him lately. Something *was* obvious here. Why couldn't he see it?

"Torbel?"

Her soft question came from directly in front of him. Lifting his eyes, he regarded her in the gray light of dawn. She looked rumpled in his red jersey, which was far too large for her, and faded denim cutoffs that left her long legs bare and tempting beyond reason. The suggestion of a smile played on her lips. Had she heard his conversation with Keiran?

As if in answer, she held out her hands to him. "Oswyn's here. He's going to bed sit for a while."

One of Torbel's dark brows arched. "What about Zoe?"

"On a case. The flat's empty."

Oh, God. His eyes closed briefly as a wave of resignation washed through him. He couldn't fight this anymore. No man was that strong.

"Breakfast first?" he asked, his expression deliberately benign.

A spark of mischief lit her eyes. "Not a chance, Torbel. Sex first. Then breakfast."

He was going to regret this, Torbel thought. Yet even as he took her hand, it occurred to him that he no longer cared.

AUGUSTUS SAT ALONE in his large bed, ate his soft-boiled egg, drank his tea and brooded. They'd stolen Sophie's diary. The dust on her desk had been smudged; he'd spotted it right off. Unfortunately he hadn't thought to go searching for smudges until long after they'd departed.

Blast their meddlesome backsides. And here he'd been so pleased at having located the missing documents in his magazine rack. Now he had a whole new set of papers to worry about. He should have burned all her belongings years ago.

Had she written down anything that mattered to him? His body shook as he struggled to think. The thing spanned five years, from two and a half years prior to Robbie's death until—well, until her demise.

Had Blodwyn's name come up? he wondered, too crotchety now to eat. Had Sophie known about her? No, he thought vehemently, she hadn't. No one had. Damn her evil blood. How long would it taint his life? How long would he have to agonize over past mistakes and errors in his famed Hollyburn judgment?

He tossed his fork fretfully onto the tray. "Curse you," he barked to no one and everyone. "Chivers! Get in here and take this mess away." The butler appeared as if by magic. "Leave my tea. No, not that runny excuse for an egg. And fire the cook while you're at it. Can't even boil an egg properly. He's terrible."

Chivers nodded and took the tray. Augustus watched him leave, smoldering all the while.

Where was Clover? Why hadn't she returned home? A shiver worked its way through his old bones. Had Zoe woken up and caught her burgling her flat?

Rubbing his sore chest, he climbed awkwardly from his bed and started for the bathroom. But even movement couldn't shut out the cacophony in his head.

Sophie, Sophie, Sophie...

She hadn't been as dense as he'd once thought. No, not dense at all. She'd put one over on him, all right. Not that he'd admit it under torture, but the truth was, she'd hoodwinked him good. She'd also flown off to Ireland, and what she'd found there, he shuddered once again to think.

"Blod—" he growled, then stopped the thought cold by kicking the bathroom door barefooted. A new pain shot up his leg. Enough, he ordered himself. Wait for Clover. Maybe his silly daughter hadn't written anything in her book. He'd skimmed the diary himself many years ago. It hadn't made much sense to him. On the other hand, he'd never sat down and pondered the entries, either.

The stabbing in his chest intensified, doubling him over. "Not yet," he snapped through gritted teeth. "I'm not ready yet. I have to see justice served. I have to see the Rag Man and his woman die."

He fumbled out two pills and heaved a sigh of relief as the pain slowly subsided. Justice must come soon. It must. Shuffling to the phone, he picked up the receiver and dialed the number of the Stepney precinct house, where, for reasons still a mystery to him, Clover had requested to be assigned. It was a very odd choice, he reflected, now in middial. A very odd choice indeed....

Chapter Sixteen

"I want to help, Torbel."

"Then stay here where I know you're safe, and keep the door locked."

Torbel jammed the hem of the red jersey Victoria had been wearing into the waistband of his jeans. It still carried the elusive flowery fragrance of her skin and hair.

Three hours of making love, showering and making love again. He felt drugged and dazed—and desperate, mostly to have her again, but also partly to get out while the saner portion of his brain still had some say in the matter.

Unfortunately his sanity was a fast-fading thing. She was angry, walking back and forth across the floor, defiant and glaring in a black silk kimono with a bright red dragon streaming down the lapel. Beneath that, she wore nothing except a pair of black lace bikini briefs and a matching bra. Talk about unfair weapons, he allowed dryly.

"You call me stubborn," she accused, pivoting to face him. "The least you could do is tell me where you're going and why."

"I told you about Boots, Victoria. I'm going to see what I can turn up besides his footwear."

He wasn't being sarcastic, and she knew it. She regarded him through her lashes and finally relented. "Oh, all right, if it'll help find Boots, I'll stay here. I still have a lot of Sophie's diary to wade through. Her handwriting's worse than Lord Hobday's."

Torbel blew out a silent breath of relief. "I won't be long," he promised. "Six at the latest."

"Famous last words."

Her mumbled retort brought a smile to his lips, one he took pains to conceal. Any show of amusement would only annoy her further.

He kissed her but took pains with that, as well. It would be all too easy to wind up back in that softly rumpled bed of hers. It wasn't until he pushed his way into the pub that he began to relax.

Ron was there arguing loudly with Ratz. Torbel caught the words "case" and something about "midnight" before Ron clamped his mouth shut and stomped out.

Torbel shot Ratz a bland look. "Should I ask?"

"It's nothing." Ratz shuffled his big feet. "You know Ron, all talk. He's on a tear. It'll pass."

Torbel's interest, barely piqued to begin with, dissolved. "What's the word on Keiran?"

Oswyn emerged from the back room into which Ron had just marched. "It's good, Torbel. He sent me packing an hour ago. The doctor was there when I left," he added, offsetting any objection Torbel might have offered. "Uh—" he glanced at the back room "—are you on a case?"

Torbel masked a smile at the boy's obvious unease. "Of sorts."

"Can I help?"

"That depends. Do you enjoy digging through rubbish bins?"

Oswyn made a face. "For what?"

"I don't know. I hope not a body."

The boy hesitated, then drew himself erect. "Yeah, sure, I can do that. I, uh, is Victoria coming with us?"

Torbel glanced upward. "She has her own digging to do." Heading for the door, he said, "Let's get to it, then, Oswyn. And hope the only bodies we find belong to mice and flies."

A LOUD CRACK OF THUNDER made Victoria jump in her seat. Her eyes, bleary from reading for hours on end, focused slowly on the lowering black sky. Another thunderstorm loomed, black and sinister—to match the current tone of Sophie's diary.

With a shiver, she slid from the chair, stretched her cramped back muscles and headed through the unnatural darkness toward the kitchen. Another ominous peal of thunder accompanied her.

Her day's reading had been a fascinating foray into the life and mind of Sophie Hollyburn. She hadn't learned anything of practical value, but she did think she understood the woman's inner demons a little better now. In one way, the two of them were very much alike—both dissatisfied with the directions of their lives, yet not quite able to pinpoint the reasons why.

Augustus notwithstanding, Sophie felt she should have been happy and yet she was filled with despair. She'd liked and admired her husband, Duffy; she had a fine home and a talent for gardening, which had won her numerous trophies. She claimed not to have been seeking romantic liaisons; the opportunity had simply continued to present itself. And what better way to escape old Goggy's dominating clutches than to meet her lovers at quiet village pubs and inns?

Victoria heard Zoe drag herself through the door while she was fixing a sandwich and pondering Sophie's somewhat bleak outlook on life.

"Banana and peanut butter," she said over her shoulder. "I'm not in a gourmet frame of mine. It's too hot."

"You look cool enough to me." Zoe tugged off her black T-shirt and fanned herself with a copy of *Majesty* magazine.

Victoria started a second sandwich. Her navy blue tank top, white shorts and bare feet were in fact very cool and comfortable. Zoe wore too much heavy black.

"Did you find anything more in Sophie's diary?" Zoe inquired, setting the teakettle on the stove.

"Nothing that'll help Torbel and me, but there were other things."

"Other affairs, you mean?"

"In the beginning. Later she seemed to stick to one man."

"Not Duffy."

Victoria handed her a plate. "No, but I think your father knew what she was doing. I—" she took a deep breath "—I think maybe he did the same thing."

"I'm sure he did," Zoe said glumly. "I wish I didn't know that, but wishes aren't horses and I do."

Victoria frowned at the odd reference. "That's from an old nursery rhyme, isn't it?"

"Is it? I thought it was just a figure of speech. Anyway, show me what you've found. I might as well know the worst."

Wiping her hands, Victoria retrieved the diary and brought it to the table. Beyond the window, clouds continued to mass. On the stereo, Gerry Rafferty sang "The Royal Mile," one of Victoria's favorites.

"What's that?" Zoe stopped her partway through the book.

"A picture." Reluctantly Victoria went back. "I found it earlier. I thought you might not want to see it."

"Ah, yes, the Hollyburn family—minus Clover. I don't remember why she wasn't there."

Victoria studied the subjects more closely. "I thought that was her and you were missing."

"Nope. That's me. There's Sophie, too. Oh, and Duffy. A real Irishman you'd think, with that red hair and those bright green eyes, but his people came from Norway—which tells you something about Irish history. Those Vikings really got around."

"That must be Robbie." Victoria indicated a small boy. The brown curls surrounding his face gave him the look of a cherub. That and his big brown eyes, as wide as saucers and completely devoid of guile. She noted a mark on the side of his jaw and ran a light thumb over it.

"It's not a flaw in the picture," Zoe told her. "Robbie had a scar. Something was removed—a mole, I think. Anyway, he was about eighteen months old here. This must have been taken right before Sophie took off for County Clare... Good Lord," she exclaimed, then laughed. "Look at old Goggy. Have you ever seen such a pickle-faced old buzzard?"

"He's very distinguished," Victoria remarked politely.

She was cut short by an indelicate "Bull" from Zoe. "He's a flint-hearted old cretin who had Clover cowed from the day she was born. Thank heaven I wasn't as gullible. Sometimes I think it might have been easier for her if our triplet brother had lived, but you never know."

Victoria's eyes shifted to Sophie's pretty face. A blue-eyed blonde, she seemed more sweet than sophisticated.

"Sophie was the reincarnation of Grandma Blanche," Zoe told her. "The rest of us were jumblies. I can't imagine why she kept this particular picture. Old Goggy looks like a member of the Inquisition."

Victoria swallowed a mouthful of tea. Zoe always made it too strong. "Maybe she wanted to remember him the way he really was. My aunt Prudie says there's no point believing in lies. Better to face the truth and get on with your life.

"Clover should have a chat with your aunt."

"Prudie lives in a Florida bayou."

"All the better. The alligators would love my sister, and vice versa. What about the diary entries themselves? Any startling revelations, or just the usual bosh? Funny, I never thought Sophie was the type to keep a diary. Maybe I should have searched her room better."

Victoria tried to read Zoe's mood. How much did she really want to know of her mother's thoughts and feelings? Probably not a great deal.

A horse clopped past on the street. You still saw that in some parts of London; horses pulling carts, bobbies on mounts and bicycles....

Bobbies. Police. Torbel...

Eyes closed, she let her thoughts slide sideways into the one area she'd been desperate to avoid all day. If she couldn't be with him, she was better off not thinking about what trouble he might be in.

Except that he was too smart and self-sufficient to walk blindly into trouble. He'd be watching everything and everyone now. He'd be fine. And he'd be back by six o'clock, as promised. She would hold him to that.

In answer to Zoe's question, she said, "I don't think Sophie intended to startle anyone. She was very guarded when it came to her feelings—and her relationships."

"How guarded?"

"Here, for example." Victoria turned to an entry dated July 23. "This was made the year before Robbie was born. Sophie's been with the same lover she spoke about earlier for several months now."

"The 'even foxier' one?"

"You remembered that?"

"It seems like a funny way of referring to someone."

"I suppose." Victoria set her mounting suspicions aside and read:

"Goggy's on a rampage again, the old bugger. He wants a grandson—pure Hollyburn to the core. I hope he chokes on his roast beef tonight. As if I haven't been through enough since the twins were born, he has to bring that heir-of-the-manor subject up again and rub my nose in it. The loss was my fault entirely, he says, and not nicely, either. I didn't take proper care of myself.

My lover tells me to ignore his gibes. I turn to him and my roses for solace. But I keep thinking that it was old Goggy's fault really, for shoving me into the sitting-room wall. He's a cruel man, and tiny babies can be damaged very easily before birth...."

Zoe looked vaguely like the "powdery ghost" Sophie had mentioned on an earlier occasion. She offered no comment, simply asked, "Is there any more?"

"Not that I've found, but there's quite a lot that's illegible. The next several days are a mess. She was either in a big hurry to record them or too upset to write clearly." Victoria waited a beat, then said, "What did Sophie mean, 'since the twins were born'?"

Zoe appeared to extricate herself from some deeper thought. "What? Oh, that. Clover and I were always referred to as twins. Joey was just a name and grave site." Her expression soured. "Although, in light of Sophie's diary, maybe 'died' isn't the appropriate term." A thud against the outer stone wall brought her head around. "What was that?"

Victoria hated to think. "Should we look?"

"We'd better, or we'll both be jumping at shadows for the rest of the day."

As if they weren't already.

Victoria approached from the left, Zoe from the right. Together they crept to the window, wedged up the warped sash and peered out.

"Nothing," Victoria said in a rush of breath.

Zoe looked up the fire escape, then down. "Must have been a bird hitting the wall. Come on, I've had enough of this stuff. The Agatha Christie mysteries are on the telly. It's Poirot today. 'Mrs. McGinty's Dead.'"

"Better her than us," Victoria murmured with an apprehensive glance at the clock on the bookcase.

Zoe, surmising her troubled train of thought, shook her head. "If you're worried about Torbel, don't. The man's a cat with nine lives."

Victoria summoned her best false smile. But the disquieting question remained. What if he'd used up eight of them?

CLOSE. Far too close for comfort. Mustn't let her see just yet. If she guessed the truth, and she very well might, given a few more of Sophie's melancholy diary entries, the plan would fail miserably.

Because there were flaws—small ones, to be sure—but they could conceivably lead to unpleasant revelations. No, at all costs, the truth must not come out until the appointed hour.

Speaking of which, the tainted tea should start to take effect very soon. At least that had been easy to arrange. Tea for the flat came from Gooseberries. Stores of that tea were kept in the pub pantry. Anyone from bag lady to chief constable could steal into the pantry and doctor the tin set aside for the tenant upstairs. A few more minutes, and the machinery would be set in motion, plan A, backed up by contingency plans B and C.

Because you couldn't count on success where Torbel was concerned. And Victoria had so much luck on her side that she might have been born Irish, as well.

A hand rose in concern to stroke a perspiring jaw, then fell away. Old habits must die, or too much could be revealed too soon.

Nothing to do but wait at this point, think about the picture she'd found in Sophie's diary and hope that what was so painfully obvious within its borders would not be prematurely perceived. What was it they said? A picture was worth a thousand words.

Sadly, in this case, there were pictures, words and slips of the tongue that couldn't be retracted. The possibility of doubt existed—about a person who, by all accounts, should not.

VICTORIA HAD NO INTEREST in Mrs. McGinty's death, or in the tea that Zoe had just refreshed for her. She lingered at the table, leafing through further pages of the diary and listening to the inexorable ticking of the clock.

Five o'clock...five-thirty...six-fifteen. Torbel should have called by now. She looked outside, turning pages at random. Had that thump been a bird? Probably. But she couldn't shed the notion that creepy eyes were watching her, that more was unfolding here than she or Torbel realized.

She forced her attention back to the diary, sipping her tea as she noted the dates. Sophie talked of abdominal pains several times, then finally about the agony of childbirth.

It's a boy, with masses of blond hair that I'm sure will not last, brown, puppy-dog eyes and, unfortunately, his grandfather's mouth and nose. A tiny telltale mark, as well, near his tiny mouth. I will call him Robbie. And this mouth, I shall teach to smile....

Victoria mulled over that statement, took another sip of tea, then moved on.

So far no rain had fallen, but the black storm clouds looked somber and threatening. She glanced at the clock—6:35. Where was Torbel? She'd give him until seven o'clock to call.

In the diary pages, time marched on for Sophie Hollyburn. She made only a few references to Robbie. She spoke briefly of an operation—to remove the mole Zoe had mentioned? She also said that Augustus had commandeered the child early on and that the more time he spent with Robbie, the more fearful she was of the possible ramifications.

Victoria stopped there. Was Sophie afraid that Augustus would turn Robbie into a carbon copy of himself? It seemed the likely answer, yet something about the nature of her remarks preyed on Victoria's subconscious, some elusive thing she could neither identify nor dismiss.

The movie droned on. Zoe sat unmoving, apparently engrossed. Hot, sticky and worried half to death, Victoria clawed the hair from her flushed cheeks and stared at the final few notations in Sophie's book. One of them seemed to leap off the page at her. Again there was no year, only a month and day.

Nov. 17

I have him at last, the old goat. I'm away to County Clare, and when I return he'll eat a double helping of crow. Assuming I'm right, that is, and I'm sure I am.

All those innuendos, those nasty little barbs he tosses out—they're only meant to hurt me. He wouldn't dare breathe a word to anyone else. Oh, no, he's far too desperate for life everlasting as he sees it, and the purity of the Hollyburn line. So he will feign blindness. The fool! Women are precious, too, if he only knew it. But even if he did, he'd never admit it. Better to let me have the blot of birth removed and pretend it signified nothing at all.

No matter, I leave in three hours. Three more to ascertain the truth, and then it will be Father who is at *my* mercy. My lover and I will be free. Rags to riches, so to speak, in a way that old Goggy could never conceive. How ironic life can be . . .

The rest of the words blurred. Victoria's eyelids drooped. She had to prop her elbow on the table and rest her cheek in her palm. Reading must be more soporific than she realized. She wondered how Zoe was making out with Poirot and Mrs. McGinty.

She tried to utter her flatmate's name, but oddly nothing emerged from her throat except a funny sound like a sigh.

Her thoughts wobbled. Where was Torbel? Why had Sophie gone to County Clare? Maybe the killer had followed Torbel, and that's why he hadn't called.

Unable to hold her head up any longer, she rested it against her folded arms on the table. The flat had a weird air of mystery about it right now. A whodunit on the verge of a climax— just like the storm over the Thames. The ghost of Sherlocks past, her cloudy mind proffered. Doyle and Sherlock, Agatha and Miss Marple, Dickens and Scrooge.

There'd been a rag seller in that Dickens novel, hadn't there? He'd bought Scrooge's bed curtains, or would have if Ebenezer hadn't changed his wicked ways. One thing about the Rag Man, he didn't seem to need reformation.

Good Lord, her mind was wandering all over the place. It would wander all the way to Ireland if she wasn't careful.

Torbel knew Ireland; he'd been born there, to an Irish-Welsh witch, according to Boots. Her own da had people in Ireland, didn't he? Not in County Clare, but somewhere like that.

She shifted her head on her arms, her troubled thoughts progressing. Why was Augustus Hollyburn so hateful? Everyone hated him—Torbel, Zoe, Sophie, Keiran, her—so he must be a horrible man. He wanted Torbel dead; he'd made no bones about that. He wanted Zoe out of his life. He'd wanted to control Sophie completely. And yet he'd loved Robbie and maybe he loved Clover, too.

Was that his criterion for caring? Accept the people he could control and reject those he couldn't. Even if those people were members of his family. And why did the purity of the Hollyburn line matter so much to him? Why had Sophie spoken of it so scathingly?

More than weariness assailed her now. Augustus Holly-burn's face bobbed in her head, then Sophie's and Zoe's and Robbie's. The last to present itself was the most wanted.

"Torbel," she murmured.

He didn't answer, of course, but there was something; she saw it without understanding what it was.

Fog enveloped her mind, thick and insidious. She saw Torbel's eyes glitter, blue green and deadly. What was she missing here? Why couldn't she think?

With an extreme effort, she raised her head. It seemed a shadow fell over the table. She tried to look but couldn't locate the source. A weird gray fog swirled in dizzying circles through her entire brain.

The shadow hovered for a moment, then vanished. "Torbel," she said again.

But he wouldn't come to her, because he wasn't here. She made a feeble sound of protest as a black wave of unconsciousness spiraled in on her. Her head fell forward onto her arms. And she was sucked, dazed and unresisting, into a vortex of darkness, danger—and very probably death.

"WHAT ARE WE DOING HERE, Torbel?" Oswyn glanced apprehensively around the narrow, cluttered alley. "No one would drag Boots all this way to hold him or even, you know, to dispose of his body."

Torbel kept walking, his attention fixed on a set of worn stone stairs ahead of them.

"Torbel?" Oswyn said again.

"Quiet. We're here because I saw someone come this way."

"But—" the boy darted a quick look into the deepening gloom behind them "—maybe we should get some backup."

Torbel's gaze remained fastened on the stairs. "Don't we already have it?"

"I think we might have lost—" Oswyn broke off with a start. "I mean, no, of course not."

"So your being with me today wasn't Ron's idea?"

"No." The denial came too quickly. In his peripheral vision, Torbel saw Oswyn wince. "I just think we need backup is all. I keep remembering that guy on the forklift. Anyway, you said you had to phone Victoria.''

''The call box on the pier was out of order, Oswyn.'' Actually the receiver had been ripped right off the chain. ''I'll find another as soon as I know where this alley leads.''

He saw the shudder that Oswyn attempted to hide. It wasn't unwarranted. The alley, like most of the area surrounding the Pierpont Hotel, was infamous. Cutthroats haunted these grimy lanes, and the hovels that crowded both sides housed rats of all shapes and sizes.

One rat in particular had caught Torbel's attention fifteen minutes ago. He'd been about to give up on his quest to find Boots when he'd spotted the figure dressed in layers of black, gray and brown, hurrying along the street toward the waterfront and possibly the old Pierpont Hotel.

He'd searched the first two floors of the hotel earlier that day. But the third had been too rotten and creaky to explore. It was Oswyn's brash opinion that any moron who dared to set foot up there would come crashing through the floorboards and wind up below anyway, so what was the point in going up?

A logical question, but the real reason Torbel hadn't continued his exploration was that it was getting late and he wanted to phone Victoria. He was also hot and sweaty and losing his patience with everything and everyone.

Oswyn had been a leech on his back all day long, and a bloody obvious one at that. The only reason that Torbel hadn't forced the boy to explain his presence was that his focus had been on locating Boots. That, and catching the psychotic git who'd been making his life and Victoria's a hell on earth lately.

''Wait here if you'd rather,'' he said, then added a less testy ''Watch my back.''

Oswyn drew a steadying breath. ''No, I'll come, too. I'm not a coward, you know. I just don't fancy dark alleys. Me da was jumped in one when I was five. Died the next day. There are eyes everywhere here, Torbel. I can feel them crawling over me like bugs.''

Torbel noted a fleeting movement at the bottom of the stairs. Keeping Oswyn at bay with his hand, he moved closer. The door, halfway open at first, swung closed.

Investigate or back off? It was no contest, really. He started for the door.

Oswyn bumped into his shoulder as he tested the knob. "It's starting to rain," the boy noted uselessly.

Glancing up, Torbel pushed his way inside.

"It's an old wine cellar," Oswyn declared at length. "Look at the holes. Shelf pegs must have gone into them once."

Torbel shone the flashlight he'd borrowed from Ratz into one of Oswyn's holes. For something intended to house a peg, it was awfully deep—and large around.

"They run from floor to ceiling in an alternating pattern." His brows came together. "I've seen something like this before. . . . Don't close the door, Oswyn."

"I've got it. It won't cl— Oraghh!"

Torbel pivoted at the choked sound. What he saw made his hands curl into fists.

A lumpy-looking figure, silhouetted briefly on the threshold, yanked away the pole he'd used to ram Oswyn in the stomach, grabbed the bolt and dragged the door swiftly shut. Torbel heard a click and a thud as the iron bolt was secured from the other side.

The moment he spotted the figure, he lunged for it, but the person was agile, and Oswyn, doubled over and staggering, blocked his path. He wound up pounding his hand against a solid three-inch plank and cursing his lack of foresight.

Oswyn's grunts of pain brought him around. He took the boy by the arm and eased him upright. "All right now?" he asked.

Oswyn nodded. "Yeah, fine."

He wasn't, but Torbel understood the necessity for preserving pride.

Still bent from the blow, Oswyn squinted up at him. "What's he got in mind this time, do you think?"

Torbel scanned the ceiling. "Nothing pleasant."

"We're below ground aren't we? What is this place?"

Torbel didn't like the way those holes were positioned. "Not a wine cellar, that's for sure."

"What, then?"

The clank of an ancient mechanism reached them before Torbel could respond. He swung the flashlight up, aiming it at the topmost collection of holes.

Oswyn edged closer, his pride forgotten. "What was that?"

Torbel spied them first, the pointed metal spikes that emerged slowly from three of the walls.

"Get back," he snapped when Oswyn would have crept forward to look.

He heard the boy gulp. "They're coming out of the holes, Torbel." Wide-eyed, he searched for an escape. "What do we do?"

Pray, Torbel thought bleakly. Aloud he said, "Get to the wall by the door and search for a release lever."

Oswyn obeyed instantly. "Have you ever seen anything like this?"

He sounded fearful . . . and with good reason. Crouching, Torbel felt along the base of the wall. "Yeah, I have. We're in Black Sheep Alley. This is part of the old Fleet Prison. They used to interrogate prisoners here."

"Interrogate them how?"

Torbel slanted him an unpromising look. "By torture."

Chapter Seventeen

"Victoria. Come on, luv, wake up. It's Keiran. You have to snap out of it. That's right. Easy now. You've been drugged."

She sat up groggily, holding her head in her hand. "I feel like someone hit me with a sledgehammer." She blinked her eyes. "What was that about drugs? No, wait a minute." She squinted at him. "You shouldn't be up. Why are you here?" She clutched his good arm. "Torbel! Where is he? Have you heard—?"

Keiran's hand across her mouth cut short the panicky last question. "I don't know where he is, but I know the general area. Apparently Ivy's been tailing them all day."

She removed his hand, her mind clearing slowly. "Why?"

"I didn't ask. She lost them near Hangman's Lane."

"Then why...?"

"Because she spotted the person they'd been following running out of the lane."

Victoria's head throbbed. Over Keiran's shoulder, she saw Zoe asleep in the chair. Ron was endeavoring to revive her, fanning her face with a magazine and jiggling her limp wrists.

Pushing herself away from the table, Victoria tried to stand.

Keiran set a firm hand on her shoulder. "Give it a minute," he suggested.

His face seemed unnaturally pale, but of course it would. He'd lost a great deal of blood. By rights, he shouldn't be out of bed, much less wandering around the city.

"Did you . . . ?" She swallowed and tried again. "Did you catch whoever it was that Ivy saw?"

"No. It's more important that we find Torbel and Oswyn."

He'd said "them," she realized belatedly. Oswyn was with Torbel. She wondered, with a surreptitious glance at a scowling Ron if that was good or bad.

This time when she endeavored to stand, she made it, with no assistance or objection from Keiran. Swaying slightly, she walked, or rather stumbled, to Zoe's chair. "Is she . . . ?"

"Knocked out but otherwise fine." Ron didn't look at her.

Victoria fixed him with a mistrustful stare. "Why did you send Ivy after Torbel?"

A moan from Zoe forestalled his reply—which probably would have been a lie in any case, Victoria reflected. She fought the fog in her mind and moved to help her flatmate.

Bits of mud under her knees brought an uncomprehending frown to her lips. She hadn't noticed any mud earlier.

"What was it?" Zoe groaned. "An earthquake?"

"Drugged tea," Keiran supplied from the table. He ran a finger around the rim of Victoria's cup, sniffed, then tasted. "Some kind of knockout powder. Chemist's strength."

Zoe slumped back in her seat. "Only knockout? I feel close to death."

Zoe had drunk three cups of tea, Victoria recalled, to her one and a half.

Her dulled mind returned to Torbel. She regarded Keiran, a blurred figure across the room. He was bent over, leaning his palms heavily on the table. "Does Ivy think Torbel and Oswyn are in trouble?"

"Ivy doesn't know what to think." Keiran's handsome features hardened. "But I think we have to find them. Hangman's Lane is notorious. They used to execute back-stabbers and thieves there. The same types still haunt the place. And there's more."

At Victoria's apprehensive look, he reached into his back pocket and brought out a plain white envelope. "We found this stuck to the flat door."

The pounding in Victoria's head worsened. Fingers shaking, she took the envelope and removed the folded paper inside. This time the note was scrawled in awkward red letters, like a child using blood to print words. Reluctantly she read the message out loud.

"The Queen of Hearts,
She bought some tarts,
And ate them with her tea.
The Knave of Hearts,
Ignored the tarts,
And made a prophecy.
The King of Hearts,
Who had no tarts,
Made shish kebab instead.
The Knave of Heats,
Played many parts,
Bye, King and Queen. You're dead!''

"I CAN'T STOP THEM!" Oswyn cried above the scrape of metal on stone. "What are we going to do?"

Torbel shoved him away from a particularly nasty spike. They were projecting at various rates, but sooner or later they would all reach the center of the room, and then there'd be nowhere left to go. For the moment, Torbel concentrated on keeping his eyes moving. He sidestepped a double spike, pulling Oswyn with him. One of the tips jabbed his arm. He cursed freely, then grabbed Oswyn by the sleeve and shifted him again.

The boy reacted well, but he was scared. Burgling East End flats had not prepared him for an encounter with a psychotic killer.

"Look out," Torbel said sharply.

Oswyn jumped left, yelped and bounced back right. "They're—ow, damn—they're everywhere."

"I know."

Torbel glanced at the far wall, the only one from which the rows of floor-to-ceiling spikes were not emerging. He'd found no release mechanism inside. He hadn't really expected that there would be any, but he'd thought they might be able to loosen some of the stones enough to wedge a hand out and grope about on the other side.

He felt Oswyn plastered to his spine. "Torbel..." The boy appealed to him for a solution he could not provide.

Torbel continued to watch the protruding spikes. A few yards farther and they'd be skewered.

"What about Ivy?" he said, running a wary eye across the ceiling. "She was tailing us today."

"How do you know it was her?" The boy made no attempt to conceal his astonishment.

"I know when I'm being followed, Oswyn. I looked. If we're out of sight long enough, she'll go for help."

"I—I think we lost her."

Torbel's response was short and profane. He thought of Victoria and thanked God she wasn't here. "In that case," he said, once more easing Oswyn to one side, "we should both start saying our prayers. Because at the rate these things are going, I'd say we have less than five minutes until we're run through."

"TORBEL!"

It was Victoria who called to him. Ron and Zoe, who'd accompanied her, stood in somber silence as his name drifted among the cluster of dark buildings and even darker alleyways.

No rain fell now, but the sky above was black with storm clouds. Black and sinister, an eerie backdrop to their so-far fruitless search.

"Torbel!" she tried again. "Where are you?" she added in a desperate whisper.

She wished Keiran had come, but he'd been near the point of collapse and so had appointed Ron and Zoe to go with her.

Ron was ill-tempered, though whether from concern or annoyance she couldn't tell. Zoe showed concern but was strangely subdued.

"Hello? Who's that I hear?"

Victoria squeezed her eyes closed. "Fox," she exclaimed softly. He would require an explanation she had neither the time nor the inclination to provide.

Zoe made no bones about her feelings for the man. Wooden faced, she demanded, "What are you doing here, Inspector?"

He studied her rather curiously before replying, "I'm looking for Clover. She, uh, didn't report in at the end of her shift."

"So the inspector took it upon himself to track her down. Aye," Ron said with heavy sarcasm, "that makes perfect sense to me."

Fox's slender face flushed. "In case it has escaped your notice, Mr. McDougall, I am, for the moment, two people short at the precinct."

"Yes, thoughtless of Peacock to have died like that," Zoe put in, her tone cutting. "As for Clover, you've never given a fig for any other shirker at the precinct. Why single her out?"

Offended, Fox drew himself erect. "My good woman, I'm not searching for her in order to reprimand her. I'm simply concerned about her welfare and too severely understaffed right now to send anyone else out to look."

"So you're not doing this as a favor to Augustus Hollyburn?" Victoria stole a glance into the darkness behind him.

His flush deepened. "Preposterous," he muttered. He puffed up like a bird ruffling its feathers. "What brings you three here, if I may be so bold as to ask?"

"We've lost two of our own," Zoe replied. "We want them back."

"I'd think you would be more concerned about your sister," Fox retorted, his blue eyes coolly critical.

"I'd think you would have learned by now to mind your own business," Zoe retorted.

Score one for her, Victoria thought. Aloud, she said, "You haven't seen Torbel, have you, Inspector?"

Did a peculiar expression cross his face? His lower lip jutted. "Not since yesterday morning."

"And you've noticed no one suspicious lurking around these parts?" Ron asked.

"No, but like you, I'm aware of their presence. Their stares have a similar effect to beetles crawling up your spine."

The burly Scotsman faced Victoria. "I think you should let me search for Torbel and Oswyn alone. No sense all of us asking for a knife in the throat."

Victoria raised a hand to her windpipe, but her resolve didn't falter. "We stay together, Ron," she said. "Where's Hangman's Lane?"

Fox started. "Good Lord, you're not going there so close to dark, are you? I'm afraid I couldn't allow—"

"We don't need your permission, Inspector," Victoria reminded him.

"Right. Fine. Let's go, then, shall we?"

"We don't need your help, either," Zoe said curtly. "Just carry on about your business, Fox, and let us do the same."

Victoria didn't like the glint that appeared in Fox's eyes. Nor did she like stalling when Torbel's and Oswyn's lives might be in danger. "I don't care who comes, I just want to go. Where exactly did Ivy lose them, Ron?"

"At the eye," she said. "That's where the lane broadens out a little." With a grudging look at Fox, he added a gruff "I'll lead the way."

Victoria hadn't intended to bring up the rear, but Zoe's mind was elsewhere, and Fox had the chivalry of a caveman. He marched along a pace behind Ron in the thickening dusk.

The first drops of rain splashed on her head as they wound their way through a maze of crooked alleys. For the most part, it seemed they were heading toward the Thames.

Ron kept up a steady pace that Victoria could have met quite handily if she hadn't noticed a cat trying to claw its way out of a tall trash can. By the time she'd scooped the animal out and turned back, they were gone.

"Zoe?" she called tentatively, then more strongly, "Zoe?"

The only perceptible sounds were those of the rain and the distant hum of traffic. She hated to think what less conspicuous sounds lurked beneath them—the silent pulse beats of the people who almost certainly watched her every move.

"Ron?" She hunched her shoulders. "Zoe!" she tried again. "Damn."

The invisible eyes crawled over her skin, much like the beetles Fox had mentioned. She didn't dare stand here motionless. Ron had been leading them toward the river. If she kept going that way, hopefully she would meet up with them.

The labyrinth of alleys wound, zigzagged and finally spiraled downward to the water. Her nerves, frayed and raw, began to get the better of her. She'd reached one of many spots similar to the eye Ron had spoken of. Nothing stirred, not the air or the rodents or anyone who might be secreted within the numerous shadows. She was about to turn left when she caught a muffled sound coming from the opposite direction. A shout?

Hand and body pressed to the corner of a brick warehouse, she listened. It was a man's voice, possibly, she thought in a spurt of hope, Ron's. She strained to hear. No, not Ron. The accent was wrong. He also sounded young, which ruled out Fox.

Disappointed and with her stomach tied in knots, she turned away. Then she stopped dead as a name shot through her head. "Oswyn!"

Spinning, she pinpointed the direction of the voice. Cautiously she started toward it. Anything was preferable to going in endless circles.

A discarded food wrapper skittered over the chipped bricks. The alley had a spooky aspect to it that brought goose bumps to her skin.

She ventured closer. The air felt suffocating. Beads of perspiration formed on her hairline. She rubbed a damp palm along her bare thigh. One voice—a boy's. Dozens of watching eyes. It was Big Brother with a sinister twist.

"Help! Is anybody out there? We're trapped."

Victoria's heart skipped a thundering beat. It *was* Oswyn, and he'd said "we."

"Torbel?" she called excitedly. "Oswyn? Is that you?"

"Yes!" It was Oswyn who shouted back.

"Victoria?" She closed her eyes at the deeper sound of Torbel's voice. "Is someone with you?"

She started to say no, remembered the shadowy niches and said loudly, "They're right behind me. Ron, Zoe, and Inspector Fox. Keep talking so I can find you. Are you all right?"

"No. There are fifty bloody spikes about to turn us into shish kebab."

A fierce shudder tore through her. "The King of Hearts," she muttered. Where were they? All the doors along here looked the same. Thank heaven the alley, not Hangman's Lane, was a dead end—she hoped.

"There's a staircase near the end, Victoria," Torbel shouted. "On your right and down five steps. Do you see it?"

"Yes."

"Forget the door. Old bolts are tricky. Look along the base of the wall. There should be an opening with a lever inside."

She crouched, her gaze skimming the lower portion of the stone wall. A wooden frame six inches square was the only thing that looked remotely like an opening.

She spied a movement in her peripheral vision. Something metallic glinted in the murk of an alcove. The rain made a soft pattering sound as it fell. "Figures," she muttered, wedging her hand into the hole. Louder, she said, "I found the lever, Torbel." And a nest of spiderwebs, she thought, flinching.

"Pull it," Torbel yelled.

"Torbel!" Oswyn gasped.

"Do it, Victoria. Now!"

She tried, but the mechanism was old and badly rusted. It hardly budged. Five pulls later, it still hadn't moved. Unfortunately something or someone in the alley had. A low murmur of voices reached her ears.

Firming up her grip, she tried babying the lever. When that didn't work, either, she swept the sopping hair from her eyes, set her teeth and gave another mighty yank.

The lever popped—so unexpectedly that she thought for a dreadful moment she'd broken it. But no, it was still attached, and the grinding noise inside had ceased.

"Torbel?" she ventured, terrified her success had come too late.

She heard a scrape of metal, then a weary "Bloody hell" from Torbel.

Forehead resting against the wet stone wall, she breathed a sigh of relief. "Thank heaven . . ."

"Oh, I wouldn't do that just yet," an amused, guttural voice said from behind. "On your feet, lady."

Something sharp and undoubtedly deadly jabbed her in the back. Hot, whiskey-laced breath rushed through her hair. She heard the greedy anticipation in the man's tone.

"One sound, darlin', and you'll be as dead as your friends in the dungeon." He leaned closer. "Or wish you was, at least."

IT WAS NO AVENGING ANGEL who held her tightly against him from behind. His breath poured in sickening waves over her face; his liquor-tainted words flowed into her right ear.

"What should we do, then, you and me, eh?" A knife popped open beneath her chin. "Let me relieve you of your money? Or will you just write me a check? You look well-off." He raised his voice. "Don't she look well-off, lads?"

The surrounding mutter of agreement jarred every nerve in Victoria's body. He planned to rob her. It was better than the alternative.

To her surprise, the man shoved her up flat against the old door. Her nose was two inches from the bolt. If only she could get her groping fingers to the knob.

"Nothing to say, darlin'?" the man demanded roughly.

On the pretext of clawing at his arm, Victoria brought her hands up. She used one to try to pry herself free and the other to grip the bolt.

"Ah, ah, ah, Little Titch." He grabbed her hand and gave it a squeeze. "None of that, now. I know who's in there, right enough. Like a tiger in a bag, that one. Cut him loose, and he'll tear me throat out, all for the want of a few quid."

"He won't." Victoria scratched at his wet arm. "He's after someone else." A thought occurred to her. "We're trying to find the person who murdered Lenny Street. Did you know Lenny Street?"

The man hesitated. Slowly the pressure on her throat eased. "Why would the Rag Man help Street? They was on the outs."

"Not the way you think. I'm not lying. Ask Torbel yourself. If you speak up, he'll hear you."

The sneer in the man's reply was unmistakable. "Yeah? Well, maybe I don't want to talk to him. Maybe all I want is a little cash and a couple of pints. Now, give over."

"No, wait, please." His grip reasserted itself. "Torbel!"

His name was lost in a flurry of unexpected activity. The arm around her throat suddenly slackened its hold, though not enough to prevent Victoria from toppling with the man when his body crumpled. She landed on top of him, struggling even as she fell to wriggle free of his constrictive arm.

She scrambled sideways on the soaked cobbles, terrified and panting. What now? With her hair in her eyes, she couldn't see a thing. But she'd recognize Torbel's angry snarl anywhere.

Through a tangle of black curls, she watched as he hauled the man to his feet and slammed him face first against the still-bolted door.

"Torbel, don't," her ex-captor rasped. "I wouldn't have hurt her none."

"The hell you wouldn't, Merdin. You're a prat with an attitude and dung for brains." He gave the man's arm, already twisted upward at a near impossible angle, a punishing jerk. "Tell me why I shouldn't break every bone in your body right now."

"Torbel . . . !"

Victoria swiped the hair from her eyes as Oswyn tumbled through what appeared to be a trapdoor in the roof. A trapdoor in a torture chamber?

The boy pointed to the north. "It's Ron and a man in a suit."

"Fox," Victoria muttered, climbing to her feet. She touched Torbel's shoulder. "Let him go," she advised. "He'll be free by morning anyway. The jails are overcrowded, and his buddies will back him up in whatever story he concocts."

Torbel's jaw tightened as he gave the man's arm another wrench.

"As awful as it sounds," she continued, "we don't have time to deal with this. That lunatic's still out there. He drugged my tea, tried to make hamburger out of you and Oswyn and left another note taped to Zoe's door."

The first remark captured his attention. Frowning, he demanded, "Drugged your tea? How?"

She wrung out her hair. "I have no idea. Zoe drank it, too— I think." She paused, then shook herself. Of course Zoe had. "We're fine, though," she went on. "It was just something to knock us out. Keiran showed up and said that Ivy— Well, it's a long story. Put simply, Keiran figured you might be in Hangman's Lane in trouble, so..."

"This is Black Sheep Alley."

"Whatever. I just wanted to find you, so he sent Ron out with me to look. Zoe came, too. We bumped into Fox down here, but then I got separated from them. It was sheer dumb luck that I heard Oswyn shouting for help. The rest you know or can guess."

"Yeah. Unfortunately." Giving the man's arm a final hard twist, he released him and stepped away. "Go on, get the hell out of here, Merdin. And take the gits in the shadows with you."

"In the shadows?" Victoria glanced uneasily around. "I thought they scattered when you grabbed their leader."

"They only scatter as far as the nearest hiding spot," Torbel told her, dusting off.

Oswyn jumped from the roof to land beside them. "I wish you'd spotted that old chimney earlier, Torbel," he said breathlessly. "We could have been run through, the pair of us."

"But we weren't." Torbel watched Merdin's receding back, then fixed Victoria with a wary stare. "Why Fox?"

"He said he was searching for Clover. Old favors have to be repaid, you know, especially to a tyrant like Augustus Hollyburn."

"There's Ron." Oswyn indicated the top of the alley. "What kind of favors?"

"That," Torbel said flatly, "is what we need to find out."

Victoria's keen legal mind had no trouble running with that, more so than Torbel might realize in light of the doubts that had been building inside her today. She rubbed the chill from her bare arms, unwilling, for the present, to dwell on such a disturbing thought. Later she would discuss her theory with Torbel. When they were alone and dry, with a bottle of wine, a mock fire and a large, soft, cushy bed beneath them.

Ron marched down the alley like an irritable Scottish soldier. "Women," he declared in disgust. "First this one disappears, then Zoe up and does the same. You look put out, Torbel. Was there trouble here?"

"Nothing we couldn't handle," Torbel told him. "What's this about Zoe?"

"We lost her," Inspector Fox said from underneath a large green garbage bag.

Naturally a fusspot like Fox wouldn't want to get wet. Victoria shook tendrils of dripping hair from her eyes and glowered at Ron. "If you bothered to look behind you every now and then, you wouldn't lose people. Where did you last see her?"

"Near Hangman's Lane."

"Where's that from here?"

He glowered back. "About five alleys over and six down. How you got here's a mystery to me."

Was it also an annoyance? Victoria still didn't trust him. He could easily have poisoned the tea in Zoe's flat, written the note and locked Torbel and Oswyn inside the Black Sheep Alley torture chamber. Unfortunately the same could be said for Zoe. Ditto for Clover and Inspector Fox, and maybe, just maybe, Augustus Hollyburn, as well.

"Pure blind luck, it would seem," she answered Ron levelly.

Removing his black cotton jacket, Torbel wrapped it around her wet shoulders. The look he cast Ron and Fox held little patience. "Zoe's no piker, but I want her found before we leave. It'll be full dark in another fifteen minutes. She's no match for Merdin and his crew."

Fox, whose face Victoria couldn't see under his makeshift umbrella, came to life. "Merdin," he repeated. "I thought he was in prison. The justice system in this country needs a good going over if you ask me."

Not that anyone had, but his ugly tone brought a resistant lump to Victoria's chest. Edging closer to Torbel, she offered a reasonable "Why don't we just accept that Merdin and others like him are out there in force and start searching for Zoe?"

"We'll split up," Torbel agreed, setting a disconcerting hand in the small of her back. "Ron, you and Oswyn backtrack to Hangman's Lane. Go all the way to Gooseberries if you have to. Victoria, Fox and I will keep going toward the Thames."

Fox's eyes came up. Odd how someone who normally came across as a brownnosing wuss could suddenly seem so unpleasant. "I'm sure," he said slowly, "that I'm not the least bit interested in locating Zoe. I came here to find Clover."

On a more menacing note, Torbel replied, "Then you'd be as well to stay with us."

Ron nudged Oswyn. "Let's go, then. We've a fair bit of ground to cover."

Fox shifted the plastic covering his head and suit. "I need to place a quick phone call," he said briskly. "Back in two shakes."

"Pompous ass," Victoria remarked in his wake. "Why did you let him go, Torbel? He won't be back."

His face etched with lines of fatigue, Torbel reached into his jeans pocket and removed a square of paper. "This was attached to one of the spikes as it came out. Can you read it?"

Not well in the darkness, but a silvery light filtering downward from one of the windows above helped.

Baa, baa, Black Sheep,
Your time is past to die.
Still, though, I know,
Your Irish luck is high.
Bring Vickie; save Boots,
A fair enough exchange.
If you survive: the Pierpont,
Tonight, in Blue Fish Lane!

NOTES EVERYWHERE. Nursery-rhyme threats. Robbie had loved nursery rhymes. He'd memorized most of them by age four.

More disquieting thoughts pressed in. Irish luck—Welsh magic. Boots. Another death. Fresh corpse in the river. This was beginning to be too much.

There'd been a number of different personae during the past few weeks. Sweep, beggar, cop. Yes, you could call that last one a disguise of sorts, certainly. It would all end here, tonight. Not a chance that Torbel and his new lady love would escape justice. Too bad old Goggy was going to miss the culmination of two years' hard work and planning.

Street was gone; Torbel and Victoria, for all their blind luck, were as good as gone; Lord Hobday was dead; so, apparently, was his courtroom assistant.

Robbie would rest easier after this night passed.

And so will I, thought the person who waited in the sanctuary of the old lair. An evil smile appeared. Just let Blodwyn's magic try and save her son tonight. It would be done at last. The "eyes" would have it. The stain of birth had been erased, so that could be overlooked. But the eyes. How was it they'd never noticed the eyes? . . .

Chapter Eighteen

"You're not coming," Torbel declared. "I didn't fall in 1—" He caught himself. "I didn't bring you to Stepney in order to watch you die. I'll deal with this alone."

Victoria glared at him across the floor in Zoe's flat. Ron had located Zoe. They'd met at Gooseberries, had an unrevealing confab and gone their separate ways.

It was past nine o'clock now, far enough into the night for Torbel's nerves to be stretched taut. He wanted this nightmare finished. If Victoria would quit being so stubborn about accompanying him to the old Pierpont Hotel, he might stand a chance of achieving that goal. On the other hand, he was enough of a realist to understand that, backup or no, he might also wind up dead.

"You think if you go there with Ratz and Tristan lying in wait on the docks that I'll be safe?" she demanded angrily. "Think again, Torbel. This whole thing started with me coming down here. It isn't going to end with me trotting back to my legal practice unharmed. You could die down there."

"I'm not going to die." Torbel ran an exasperated hand through his hair. "Dammit, Victoria, this is—"

"Serious?" She snatched a folded newspaper from the bookshelf. "Do you think I'm stupid, Torbel? Sergeant Peacock was a seasoned police officer. Read the article on him. Even Fox had nice things to say."

Torbel glanced at the newspaper she'd tossed onto the table. Peacock's photo, unsmiling and typically stuffy, stared back at him. The bags under his eyes must have come from overwork. To Torbel's knowledge, he'd had no personal life.

Not unlike Oliver Fox, or, he reflected with a twinge of disdain, himself. But his own jaded past wasn't in question here. Sophie Hollyburn's "even foxier" lover very well might be. He regarded a poster of Sherlock Holmes in *The Spider Woman* contemplatively. Unless, of course, the answers resided in Clover. Or Zoe.

He didn't realize that Victoria had moved closer until her towel-dried dark hair brushed his arm. "What are you thinking?" she asked. Was that an edge of suspicion in her voice?

"Nothing that makes me happy."

He sensed she wanted to pursue that statement but couldn't bring herself to do it.

"I'm coming with you," she repeated, crankily stubborn. "I know Ratz and Tristan will be there. You'd still need eyes in the back of your head to cover all the angles in that decrepit old hotel. Backup's bull in the end. You could be bushwhacked on the doorstep. In case you hadn't noticed, this person does not fight fair."

He was also crazy. Torbel grimaced. Or she.

Cursing his train of thought, he leveled a glare at Victoria. "I need to know you're safe."

"That's what you said this morning. I wasn't any safer here than you were out there."

His temper began to mount. The force of it no longer concerned him. He'd never become so angry with her that he would lose it. "This is different, Victoria."

"The hell it is. I know we'll be walking into a trap, but if worse comes to worst and one of us gets caught, the other can distract him until Ratz and Tristan move in. That's logical, Torbel. We both know there's no point calling the police. For one thing, neither of us trusts Fox, and for another, any authority figure would send our psychotic note writer scuttling for cover. But only temporarily. He wants us dead, and he means to have his way. He'll try again, sooner or later."

Her blue eyes flashed electric in the soft apartment light. "You're not putting me off this time. I'm coming and that's that. On the way, you can tell me what it is about your temper that sends blowhards like Merdin scuttling for the shadows. And what," she added, more determined than Torbel had ever seen her, "made you decide to leave Scotland Yard."

WRONG. IT WAS ALL WRONG. Dangerous and stupid, a mistake. The Rag Man was too clever by half. He wouldn't die easily, not even caught like a stuck pig. Of all people, Augustus Hollyburn knew that. For years he'd tried his influential best to beat the man or at least beat him down. What had his efforts gotten him? Not a blasted thing.

Scum, it seemed, rose. No doubt it would rise again. And yet, he thought, clinging to that one remaining thread of hope, what if this time it sank? How gratifying that would be…unless his family name wound up besmirched in the process. . . .

The very idea of public humiliation made his knuckles go white on the arms of the chair. He would love to see the Rag Man burn, but would he not risk losing his remaining grandchild over this? Why, oh why hadn't he considered that unacceptable eventuality sooner?

Because he'd wanted Torbel's head on a platter, that's why. Hatred for the Rag Man had blinded him to the more-agonizing consequences of this vengeful act.

Augustus's breath grew hot and painful in his chest. He refused to lose either a grandchild or a knighthood. It must not come to that.

"Chivers!" he bellowed, crumpling the note about sheep and Irish luck on his lap. "Get in here."

The butler appeared, placid and quiescent as always. "Yes, sir?"

"Put on your coat and hat. I've an errand for you."

"At 9:00 p.m., sir?"

It was the first time Chivers had questioned an order. Augustus's hackles rose. "Yes, at 9:00 p.m. You've served me for more than fifty years. You'll do as I instruct, or you'll find yourself another position. And another pension, as well."

The butler's expression remained bland. "As you wish, sir."

"Bloody right," Augustus said huffily. "I want you to take that old black Mini of Sophie's. It still runs. Remove the license plates. Keep the headlights off, and drive carefully to the river."

"The river, sir?"

"Yes, the river. Do you know the old Pierpont Hotel?"

"Yes, sir."

His impatience forgotten, Augustus scowled. "I want you to go there, Chivers, and wait."

"For what, sir?"

The scowl dissolved into a brutish twist of Augustus's thin lips. "A man and a woman." His blue-green eyes, hard as ice and just as cold, strayed to the fire. "Damn you to hell, Blodwyn," he growled. "This was your doing, your curse. I had no part in the outcome. But this I will affect. For the sake of my grandchild and justice, this thing must be done correctly."

"YOU LEFT SCOTLAND YARD because of your temper?" Victoria repeated, incredulous.

"My temper and Augustus Hollyburn." Torbel led the way carefully along the foggy dock to Blue Fish Lane, where the old Pierpont stood in all its dark, decrepit gloom. "A guy I'd worked with briefly at the Yard turned up dead. His name was Tom Potts. I discovered the body. We'd had words on several occasions. Someone with clout tried to frame me for Potts's murder. I'm sure Fox helped him. I found out who was behind the frame and—" his eyes darkened at the memory "—dealt with it."

Victoria shivered, more out of fear for their current situation, he suspected, than his past. "What did you do?"

He moved a vague shoulder, tightening his grip on her hand. "I went to his house in the middle of the night and confronted him."

"With your fists?"

"I was tempted. Old Goggy wasn't as frail ten years ago."

"Why would he want to frame you?"

"He liked Tom Potts."

"That's a pretty feeble reason, Torbel."

"It's as much of a reason as Augustus Hollyburn needs. But, yes, there was more to it than that. He was an unethical judge, and I knew it. He took exception to my having that knowledge."

"How did he know you had it?"

An ironic smile played on Torbel's mouth. "I told him."

"Well, that's one way." Her smooth forehead wrinkled. "How did you obtain this so-called knowledge?"

"Street recruits have plenty of resources at the Yard."

She eyed him warily. "What aren't you telling me, Torbel? Does this have anything to do with— No, that wouldn't work. You'd have been too young."

"For what?"

"To have had an affair with Sophie Hollyburn. Unless she was an extremely perverted woman, which I don't think she was."

"And always assuming that I was a horny adolescent."

"Lots of young men are," she retorted, her mind obviously still shuffling through the possibilities. For the present, Torbel preferred that she not shuffle too close to the mark.

"Priorities, Victoria," he reminded, nodding at the misshapen black monstrosity directly in their path. "That last note implied that our coming here tonight would save Boots's life."

She blew out an exasperated breath. "You don't believe that Boots is alive any more than I do. It's a trap. The only reason we're here is to spring it and hopefully bag the homicidal creep who's behind all of this."

That was putting it bluntly. Torbel admired her grit if not her unwavering resolve to accompany him tonight. It took guts to walk into a death trap, because if the person behind the threats didn't kill them, the hotel itself very well might.

In the poor light cast by the dock lamps, he surveyed the mist-shrouded husk before them. No one would ever have called the place grand, but it had probably possessed a certain air of old London charm once upon a time.

"Yeah, like Charles Dickens's Marshalsea," he muttered dryly.

"His what?" Victoria asked.

"Debtors' prison. *Little Dorrit.*"

She summoned a faint smile. "Good book." She squinted at the building. "What's that?"

He followed her index finger to a second-floor room. A speck of light no bigger than a snow pea passed over the window, then was extinguished.

"Bait," he said flatly, and forced the tension from his muscles.

He didn't dare signal Ratz or Tristan. He would have to trust in their presence nearby. He shouldn't have brought Victoria, though. If he'd had to tie her to a chair in his flat, he should never have exposed her to this kind of lunatic danger.

Their footsteps echoed on the wet pavement. Fog slithered in ghostly tendrils about their heads. The outline of the old Pierpont wavered eerily in the ever-thickening mist. The heat of the previous few weeks had vanished with the light of day. The traditional fog and dampness that was London had returned, bringing with it an aspect of horror that would have done a Gothic filmmaker proud.

They entered by the front door, for the simple reason that front doors made for the easiest avenues of escape. In this case, it also gave them the broadest view of things to come, although in typical British fashion, the lobby was a small affair, the staircase narrow and set well away from the door. Ten psychotic killers could be lurking here, and they wouldn't know it until they crossed the inner threshold.

"I saw a Sherlock Holmes mystery like this one," Victoria whispered, her breasts pressed disconcertingly against his arm. "The villain was an old actor. He wore clothes tinted with phosphorescent paint and ran across the moor like a ghost. Holmes and Watson cornered him in the abandoned hotel."

Torbel forged a path across the sagging floor. "Did they capture him?"

"Not there."

"Good story," he said with more than a trace of irony.

"I wasn't trying to make a point," she retorted, her tone testy. "This place gives me the creeps. I thought conversation might help."

They'd reached the stairwell—if you could call it that. A good one-third of the steps were either broken or so severely cracked that the slightest pressure would splinter them.

Surveying them, Victoria shrugged. "If he got up, so can we."

Torbel squinted into the musty darkness. "He might have used one of the rear stairwells."

"I can't believe they'd be in better shape." She wrinkled her nose. "This place defines the word *rot*. It's moldy and cobwebbed and probably overrun with termites and rats. I can't imagine what's holding it up."

"Faith," Torbel replied, testing the strength of the first step. It screamed beneath his weight. "You ready?"

"No, but let's do it."

Even as they climbed, Torbel couldn't make out the top of the staircase; however, logic told him it would be fifteen, maybe twenty steps up. The trick lay in not falling through and spraining an ankle, or worse, having their attacker catch them in that vulnerable position.

"Hug the wall," he instructed Victoria.

"Torbel..."

He missed the note of alarm in her voice at first. "It's all right," he promised, his eyes focused on a point deep in the murk. "If we're lucky, we'll catch him off—"

It struck him like a lightning bolt, the tension in her grip, the urgency in her low tone, the faint drag on his arm—and beneath that, some finer thing that could only be his instincts belatedly kicking in.

Uttering a succinct obscenity, he closed his eyes.

"Good fellow," a raspy voice, indefinable even at close range, congratulated. "One wrong move, Torbel, and your lady love will resemble a piece of Swiss cheese. Very pretty—and very dead."

A SINGLE, HORRIFYING thought raced through Victoria's mind. Torbel could move or stay put. The end result would be the same. They'd be dead. If not here and now, then later.

The stairs groaned beneath them. Even though she was plastered against the wall, the boards beneath her felt weak. Victoria supposed it would be asking too much for Providence to crack one of them under the person behind her.

She tried to catch a glimpse of him. But every time she turned her head, she was jabbed in the back—with a weapon she *had* managed to see.

It was a military knife, similar to the one her father had inherited from his uncle. Who would make a military knife his weapon of choice?

"No tricks," their captor repeated in a vicious whisper. "Disappear into the shadows, Torbel, and she dies."

He jabbed the knife into Victoria's back again for emphasis.

Torbel's body language said it all. Victoria felt the tension that radiated out of him. No doubt, so did the person behind them. And yet somehow he held all that energy and anger inside. For her sake, she hoped, he simply followed orders and climbed.

He loved her; he must. If she was going to die tonight, she wanted to take at least that much solace to the grave.

Below her sneakered feet, one of the planks gave way. Startled, she clutched at Torbel's arm. He caught her, easing her foot free before she could release the scream that swelled in her throat.

"It's all right . . ." he began, then swore and started downward. "He's gone!"

"How can he be—" she looked behind her "—gone? I don't understand. He was there a minute ago. He poked me in the back with his knife. Where did he go?"

"There must be a hidden door." Torbel drew her to the comparative safety of the second floor landing.

"I hate this, Torbel," she said, leaning against him. "It's demented. Twisted nursery rhymes, a phone message that sounded like it came from a clown played on 78, and now a game of hide-and-seek."

Torbel's blue-green eyes probed the heavy shadows. "More like 'The Farmer in the Dell.'" He took her hand. "Let's go."

She resisted his pull. "Where?"

"Any place that's away from the top of the bloody stairs."
His fingers moved to curl around her upper arm. "Stop asking
questions and move."

"I can't."

"Why not?"

"I'm caught on a nail."

She expected him to reproach her for her clumsiness, but instead he sighed. Turning, he cupped her face and planted a
swift, hard kiss on her mouth. "You," he said simply, "are a
pain."

"Thanks," she murmured as he unhooked her. She looked
back, shivering inside and out. Where had the person gone?

They inched forward. Torbel kept his flashlight beam angled downward. Scrabbling claws spoke of rodents in residence, though none so large as the one wielding the knife.

Victoria's gaze swept the dingy corridor. It smelled like an old
sea chest, dank and moth-eaten. There was even an old top hat
hanging from one of the crooked doorknobs.

She did a shocked double take. "Torbel!" she exclaimed
suddenly, halting him with her free hand. "That hat over there
has the top punched out."

Torbel pointed the beam at the door. "It's Boots's hat," he
said through his teeth. "Damn that unholy sh—"

"Don't," she urged, her nails digging into his arm. "He'll
hear you." At his skeptical expression, she rubbed her arms
with her palms. "I'm sorry. I'm scared. I keep trying to figure
out who it is. I couldn't tell if it was a man's voice or a woman's."

"It was a man's."

"You don't know that, Torbel. You just don't want it to
be . . . someone we know."

The sidelong look he sent her felt like a dagger being shoved
between her ribs.

"I didn't say it was, Torbel," she defended. "Only that it
might be."

He stared past her now, his manner preoccupied.

She wished he would confide in her, voice the doubts she
knew they shared. Then again, who was she to talk? The un-

pleasant prospect running around in her head stuck just as surely in her throat.

They moved on, slowly, carefully, creeping from one gloomy shadow to the next. The floor let out unearthly creaks of protest; the walls, tilted and badly decayed, seemed to shudder around them.

As the seconds ticked by, faces began dancing in Victoria's mind's eye, ghastly, distorted pictures. Of Zoe and Clover, red haired and turquoise-eyed, so alike physically as to be virtually indistinguishable. Of Augustus with his piercing Hollyburn blue eyes, his shock of white hair and his bony finger wrapped around the trigger of his rifle. Of Oliver Fox and Sophie Hollyburn, deceivers both. Of Sophie, pregnant with Robbie. Of Robbie, a would-be black sheep within the Hollyburn ranks. Everyone said he'd been different, kinder. He hadn't thought like them, looked like them or acted like them. He hadn't wanted to live like them despite his grandfather's strong influence and the fact that he'd undoubtedly loved the old man.

Ratz said Robbie had been excited the night he'd died. Zoe had confirmed that.

Victoria pictured Robbie searching for Torbel, his brown eyes eager and shining, his brown curls wet with perspiration and the dampness of the fog. Hunting for Torbel on the docks.

Zoe's voice echoed in her head. *He loved nursery rhymes....*

He'd also wanted to join the Rag Man's agency.

His mother Sophie had died in Ireland. What had she been doing in the land of Torbel's birth? Why had she been so anxious to go there?

Old Goggy would eat a double helping of crow when she returned; that's what she'd said in the diary. She and her lover would be free at last. Free from Augustus?

Victoria's temples began to throb. Too many images crowded in. Of Boots and Peacock, who were probably both dead. Of Lenny Street, who'd been poisoned, and Boots talking of Torbel's magic. Boots believed in magic; Torbel did not.

She thought of Robert Peacock's face. He never wore gold. He was allergic, broke out in a rash if he did, like her da when he ate peanuts. Boots hadn't been allergic to gold. He'd flashed the ring that Tito had given him like a banner. And talked of magic. And Torbel's temper . . .

A feeling of dizziness swept through her. She was fighting it when her ears picked up the barest hint of a squeak behind them. If it hadn't been a protracted squeak, she would have missed it altogether.

Before either of them could react, a shot rang out, whizzing past Victoria's head and into the dusty darkness of the stairwell. She heard the unmistakable thump of a body as it landed close by on the floor. Moving as swiftly as Torbel, she dived for the safety of the opposite wall.

She spotted the fallen man instantly, recognized the tattooed forearm and bald head illuminated by Torbel's flashlight beam. Her breath caught painfully. "Ratz!" she whispered in horror.

"Quiet." Torbel's voice was a hushed growl in her ear. The ends of his hair skimmed her cheek; his warm breath fanned her temple. She took odd comfort in those things, in spite of a situation that threatened all three of their lives.

The big pub manager lay there unmoving. Seconds that felt like hours ticked by until finally another floorboard creaked. From the darkness, there emerged a figure, visible from the torso down. It was dressed in unrevealing black and moved with a casual grace that could only belong to one of two people.

"Oh God, no," Victoria said softly, not wanting to believe her eyes.

The figure chuckled and deposited an oil lamp on one of the alcove shelves. "Oh God, yes," the woman carrying it countered. The barrel of a handgun gleamed in the glass-filtered light. She strolled closer, smiling as her face came into distorted view. Her eyes glittered, emotionless blue green. Hollyburn blue, Zoe called it.

Victoria couldn't help it. She flinched at the fevered expression in those eyes.

"Don't move," Torbel cautioned under his breath.

The woman's smile widened. "No, please don't," she entreated in mock horror. The barrel rose. "A moving target is ever so much more difficult to hit, or so they taught us at the police academy."

Clover Hollyburn's mouth stretched into a grotesque parody of a smile. Double handing the gun, she took careful aim. "Bye-bye, black sheep. Time for you to die...."

Chapter Nineteen

She was mad. She was going to kill them! Victoria froze. She loved Torbel. Dear God, why hadn't she told him that before?

"I love you," she managed to whisper.

His eyes on the unfired gun, he murmured, "I love you, too." Her teeth bared, Clover cocked the hammer. And squeezed...

Two shots blasted out in rapid, earsplitting succession.

Pressing her fist to her chest, Victoria dropped her forehead onto Torbel's shoulder and waited for death. If one of the shots had hit, she didn't feel it yet. She wondered hazily if it was supposed to be like that.

Unsure, she lifted her head. The blood pounded so loudly in her ears that she couldn't hear anything. But she was fairly certain that Clover hadn't fired again.

She couldn't read Torbel's expression, either. Had one of the bullets struck him? She wanted to ask, but she could no longer seem to control her vocal cords. It wasn't until she went to move that she realized he was unharmed. Gripping her forearm, he said sharply, "Don't!"

Don't what? Move? Talk?

Another blast. This time, Victoria heard a thud as something fell to the floor.

Snatching her gun hand into the shelter of her chest, Clover dropped to her knees, her face contorting into a mask of pain. "Chivers," she cried. "How dare you!"

To Victoria's astonishment, Augustus Hollyburn's butler materialized on the fringe of the light pool. Wisps of smoke from his gun curled up to fog his normally bland features.

Utterly confused, Victoria appealed to Torbel. "What is this?"

A small shake of his head preceded Clover's high-pitched shriek of betrayal. "This," she screamed, "is sabotage! You idiot, Chivers. You prevented me from doing the just and right thing." She scrambled to her feet, searching for the unfired gun that Torbel had picked up and tucked discreetly into his waistband. He went to his haunches now, bringing Victoria with him.

Clover's face by lamplight went from chalk white to mottled red. "You're fired!" she screeched at the butler, who looked as dazed as Victoria felt. "Who sent you here to interfere?"

"Your—your grandfather, miss."

"You're lying!" She coddled her wounded hand, her mouth stretching to ghastly proportions. "He didn't know I was coming tonight. He couldn't have. I want the truth."

The butler shuffled discomfited feet. "The truth is he ordered me, er, to shoot a certain woman. And, er—" his eyes shifted to Torbel, then swiftly away "—a man."

"What man?"

"Me," Torbel said quietly from the wall. With a subtle head motion at Victoria, he stood. "Your grandfather sent Chivers out to make sure that Victoria and I would die tonight, isn't that right, Chivers?"

The butler hung his head. "That's right, sir."

"But Chivers couldn't commit cold-blooded murder, even for old Goggy. He also couldn't stand by and watch you ruin your life, so he altered his employer's plan."

"Clumsily so," Chivers admitted, his eyes still downcast. "It shouldn't have taken three shots. I'm sorry, sir, miss."

Victoria didn't know if the apology was directed at her or Clover, but she did know she needed to check on Ratz. Concealing herself in the shadows, she crawled over to him.

Clover appeared not to notice the creaking floorboards. Hatred spewed from her eyes and mouth.

"You snake," she hissed at Chivers. "You're fired. As for you, Raggedy Man, you'll get yours with or without my help."

His gaze hooded, Torbel inquired, "Where's Zoe, Clover? Is she here with you?"

Clover's upper lip curled. "Don't be absurd. We don't hang out together, in case you hadn't noticed."

Confident that Ratz would survive, Victoria joined Torbel.

"We have noticed, Clover," she said. "At least, I have."

"We've all noticed," Torbel confirmed. "Tell me, have you and Zoe ever been in the same place at the same time?"

Her laugh was bitter. "We're twins, isn't that enough punishment?"

Torbel studied her. "Who killed Street, Clover? And Boots? And Peacock?"

"I don't know, Torbel."

He advanced on her, his face set in a determined line. "I think you do know. You set us up tonight and tried unsuccessfully to kill us on several other occasions."

She swallowed under Torbel's intense stare. "You're wrong," she denied. "Much as I'd love to take all the credit, I only read a note. 'The Pierpont,'" she quoted, "'tonight, in Blue Fish Lane.'"

A chill far colder than fear rippled along Victoria's spine. "What are you saying, Clover? That you didn't write those notes?"

Another voice took over. It came from the corridor ahead of them, from a place deep within the jet black shadows. "That," it said in a precise, terrifyingly familiar British accent, "is exactly what she's saying. Good evening, all. Welcome to the moment of truth. And death."

Augustus Hollyburn tottered into his daughter's dusty bedroom. Crossing to the desk, he removed her old photo album.

There she stood, he thought in disgust, pregnant, unable to look her husband or the camera in the eye.

He snapped the book shut. "I won't believe it," he vowed. "Robbie was a Hollyburn on both sides, her son and Duffy's. I won't accept another."

But hadn't he done that already? Accepted one other than Duffy as Robbie's father? All those favors...

He opened the album again, grudgingly this time. He found a picture of Robbie as a child. Big brown eyes, happy, chubby face, red cheeks, brown curls, noticeable scar below his left cheek...

His breath hitched painfully at the coloring. But what did hair color prove? Plenty of brown hair in the Hollyburn family.

Brown eyes, too, for that matter. Why, his own uncle Morris had had brown— No, no, Morris's eyes had been green.

A sudden dryness invaded his throat. He hadn't looked closely at a picture of Robbie for two years now, hadn't been able to do so since the funeral.

Big brown eyes stared up at him from the photo. Familiar eyes? He couldn't be sure. He'd never thought so before, but then, he'd never had thoughts like these before. The suspicions that plowed their way into his mind tonight were born of an unexpected vendetta, one he had approved of if not officially endorsed.

The dryness worsened as horror began to supplant suspicion. The scar on Robbie's jaw. Where had it come from? Surgery, to be sure, but what had been removed to cause it? Not a mole, a birthmark of some sort.

Another face began to swim in his head. He didn't know why, but there it was. A man's face. A man with brown eyes and below his left cheek a—

Pain stabbed his chest like flaming arrows. It wasn't his imagination. A resemblance existed, a strong one. And yet how could it be? All that had happened this past week could not have occurred unless—

He groped for the edge of the desk as an invisible wire seemed to tighten around his chest. His eyes scrunched. His shoulders slumped.

It had been a fake from the start, a clever lie. And they'd fallen for it, he thought with a twinge of black humor. Even the Rag Man. His grandson's sire was a master of manipulation. And as mad as a bloody Hatter.

VICTORIA STARED, shocked, at the man before her. Sergeant Robert Peacock, late of the London police force, Stepney Precinct.

It was impossible—but true.

"Tie them up well, Torbel," Peacock ordered. His fingers rose to stroke the birthmark on his left jaw. "If they escape and interfere, they die. Otherwise—" he shrugged "—what happens to me after tonight doesn't matter."

Torbel finished binding Clover's and Chivers's ankles, stood and faced the nemesis Victoria had been looking at all along. She still couldn't believe her eyes.

"Damn you, Peacock, I was trying to help," Clover barked. She kicked at Ratz's still-unconscious form with her bound and booted feet. "If I escape, I'm hardly likely to turn you in, now am I?"

A knife gleamed in one gloved hand, a gun in the other. "Shut her up, Torbel, then join us over here. You had no idea who was behind the notes, Clover," Peacock retorted coldly. "You harbored no particular love for your younger brother. You hate Torbel because your grandfather despises him. A hatred which, I suspect, goes deeper than Robbie's death."

"It goes as deep as Blodwyn," Clover stated, firing a venomous visual dart at Torbel. She tried to bite his finger when he gagged her, but Torbel was too fast.

Peacock had taken them to a second-floor room. Through the begrimed windows, foggy river water caused the shadows within to ripple. Victoria stared, dry mouthed and with a palpable sense of panic rising in her stomach.

The man was a ghost. He should be dead. And yet, she thought, her brow knit, there had been clues, details she couldn't grasp right now but had been pondering in the corridor when Clover appeared.

Zoe's voice echoed in her head. *We were all named for some ancestor or other. It's a Hollyburn tradition. . . .*

"Robert," she whispered. "'Robbie' for 'Robert'?"

Peacock's gun hand shook. With rage? Victoria sidestepped, closer to Torbel. Apparently she'd struck a nerve.

"You all missed it," he said in a savage growl. "Every blasted one of you. Old Goggy never wanted to see and so blinded himself to the truth. One only had to look at the eyes to know. Duffy's eyes were pale green. Sophie's were blue green. Most unlikely that a brown-eyed child would spring from that pairing.''

Oliver Fox's eyes were blue, Victoria recalled, sliding her hands around Torbel's left wrist. Only Peacock's eyes were brown. And the birthmark that Peacock possessed—hadn't Robbie had a scar in that same place? A scar where something had been removed. Perhaps not a mole, as Zoe had believed, but a telltale mark of parentage. A birthmark to match his father's.

Peacock closed the door after them with a click that echoed ominously through the dilapidated hotel. Fog like a nether-world vapor swirled about the windows at the far end of the corridor. Peacock used Clover's lantern and stayed just out of range behind them.

"Last room on the left, Torbel," he ordered.

His voice, hard as stone, had a passionate quaver in it. So did Victoria's heart. She shivered as Torbel curled his warm fingers around her cold hand.

Images, like unstrung puppets, bobbed in her frightened mind. Sophie had described her lover as resembling a "powdery ghost." Calamine lotion covering a rash that came, not from poison ivy—as Augustus had believed—but from contact with gold. Peacock was allergic to gold.

"In there," he barked at them. "No tricks. And you can forget about your lackey Tristan. He's lying in a pool of his own blood in the lobby. Thus my precipitous departure earlier."

Victoria felt physically sick. Torbel looked ready to pounce. His eyes flashed in the amber light cast by the lantern. She felt his muscles tense, and tightened her own grip to hold him back.

"It's what he wants," she whispered.

"Did you kill Boots, too?" Torbel demanded, ignoring her. "Yes."

If there'd been a veneer of civility before, it was dissipating now. Peacock's mouth compressed to a thin white line beneath his immaculate mustache.

"In the explosion?"

"He took my place—in uniform. He was dead before the bomb went off."

"The gold ring!" Victoria exclaimed, unthinking.

She would have clamped her mouth shut had Peacock not barked "What ring?"

"My da read—"

"Nothing," Torbel interrupted. "There was a gold ring found at the scene of your murder, along with a tie clip or cuff links. None of us twigged at the time, but with your allergy you wouldn't have been wearing gold. We should have realized that."

"An oversight on my part." Peacock walked to the window. "I was abnormally busy just then, plotting not only your deaths and Street's, but my own unfortunate demise, as well." His teeth gleamed with unexpected wolfishness. "One has to make provision for a flaw or two in any plan. I must say I didn't think you'd be so bold as to break into old Goggy's home, otherwise I would never have used Sophie's name as a ruse on the telephone."

The floor creaked loudly as he forced them deeper into the cobwebbed room. The remnants of a bed, heaped with boxes and other refuse, stood directly under the window. Even if Peacock could be distracted, they'd never make it to the outer ledge—assuming there even was one.

"Why nursery rhymes?" Torbel asked. Victoria noticed that he'd eased himself in front of her. A rush of love and renewed terror poured through her.

Peacock set the lantern on what might once have been a dresser. "Because Robbie loved them. He had a scribbler as a child. I visited old Goggy's home on occasion while Robbie was growing up. As a teenager, he had no use for childish rhymes. I doubt if he missed the book."

Clearing her throat, Victoria ventured an apprehensive "You never told him you were his father?"

The quaver returned. "I had hoped his mother would do so in time. I was shocked and devastated when she died in Ireland. I didn't even realize she'd gone there until I heard from one of her old college friends that she was dead. I..." His voice broke.

As if galvanized by an emotion too strong for his mind to accept, he let out an agonized cry, then snapped the sagging gun upward. His dark eyes gleamed with fury and no small amount of insanity.

"It was your fault, Torbel," he said, his voice tight with rage. He took an unsteady step toward them. "Robbie shouldn't have died that night on the docks. He was going to give up a career in law to join your criminal band. I—I couldn't let that happen. I followed him to the docks. I knew I had to do something."

Her eyes focused on his changing face, Victoria whispered, "What's he saying?"

"What are you saying, Peacock?" Torbel demanded.

The man halted, swaying slightly. Perhaps vivid memories made a person dizzy. Or maybe madness did that. Victoria's fingers crawled up Torbel's forearm and dug in.

"I had to stop him," Peacock said, blinking as if at a bright light. "He would have ruined his life. I thought, I'll get rid of the source of the problem. That's what you do, you know. You destroy a creeping cancer at its source. I called the storehouse on a false pretense and was told that you would be on the docks that night. I went there myself with a knife. Difficult to trace, knives. Then I hid, and waited for you. When I saw you, I burst from my hiding place and plunged the knife deep into your spine."

"Oh, God." Victoria pressed her forehead into Torbel's arm.

The chortling laughter of a broken mind bubbled from Peacock's throat. "I know what you're thinking, Victoria. You think that I stabbed my own son, but I assure you I did not. I stabbed Torbel. Same brown curls and wiry build from the back. Same height, same weight. It *was* Torbel." Beads of perspiration gleamed on his forehead and cheeks. "But when I turned the body over, I saw Robbie's face. I knew then that it was true what the locals said about Torbel's magic. He used it that night to trade places with Robbie, just long enough for my son to die in his place."

Victoria was aghast. "You killed Robbie?"

"No!" Peacock's face contorted. "Torbel did it. And Street backed him up. And you and Hobday and that slimy assistant of his aided them." He came toward them, his features alight, his voice a parody of madness. "It was nothing to do with me at all. You people are the culprits. You must pay the price for your crimes."

The gun rose. The floor let out a high-pitched scream and gave a mighty crack.

Seizing his chance, Torbel went for him. But Peacock's finger was already on the trigger. He squeezed off a single shot even as he snared Victoria's arm and yanked her around.

Through a haze of instinctive reaction and splintered floorboards, she felt his knife press into her. Scratching at his face, she twisted free and endeavored to locate Torbel.

She tripped over something on the floor and looked swiftly down. "Torbel!" she screamed, and would have gone to her knees had the long fingers of Peacock's hand not suddenly clamped themselves onto her throat.

He spun her around until her back was plastered to his front. The hand on her throat remained tight despite her clawing fingers. A moment later, the tip of his knife jabbed hard into her breastbone.

"One more sound," Peacock snarled, "and what breath I don't choke out of you, I'll release from your lungs with my knife. Your champion's dead, Victoria. And once we reach the place where my son was taken from me, you'll be joining him."

"TORBEL!"

Dazed and disoriented, he felt someone shaking him.

"Come on, wake up. He's taken Victoria down to the water."

Victoria! Torbel's eyes snapped open. Jaw set, he levered himself upright. His left shoulder felt on fire. His brow furrowed. What the hell—was it Zoe hauling him to his knees?

He couldn't see her clearly, but her clothes were black and her flaming red hair was messily confined in a ponytail.

Grunting, he rolled over. "It's Peacock," he said thickly. "He'll kill her."

With Zoe's help, he climbed unsteadily to his feet. Hair and blood mingled on his forehead. He drew sticky fingers away, frowning. "Which way?"

"Toward Myrtle's, but probably not as far as that. There's a good patch of deserted docks between here and there."

"He'll take her to where Robbie was killed," Torbel concluded grimly. He staggered as he headed for the door. "Bloody hell," he swore, unable now to move his shoulder. "Did he shoot me with an elephant gun?"

"No, a .45." Zoe nodded toward the bed. "He must have dropped it. He had Victoria at knife point when I saw him. And if you're wondering what I'm doing here, I wormed the information out of Ratz's assistant. I, er…" She swallowed. "I also saw Tristan."

"I know." Fighting a spate of dizziness, Torbel groped his way into the corridor. He could not, would not, collapse.

A thump penetrated the fog in his brain. Zoe's head swiveled. "What was that?"

"Peacock's prisoners. Two or three of them." He still wasn't sure of the count, but at the moment he didn't care. "Check them out, Zoe," he told her. "Ratz is hurt. I don't know how badly. See to him, then send Chivers for the police."

"Chivers!" She'd guided him to the top of the staircase. Now she stared at him in disbelief. "What was old Goggy plotting in that warped little mind of his?"

"Same as Peacock," Torbel said bleakly. He brought the stairs into focus and started down. "Old Goggy's reasons are more complicated, Zoe, but dead's dead any way you look at it, and—" he steeled himself to utter the words "—Peacock's got the woman I love."

"JUST A FEW MORE STEPS," Peacock promised in a silky tone.

He was angry again. He'd been alternating between anger and anguish for the ten interminable minutes it had taken to drag her out of the Pierpont and along this stretch of deserted, fog-shrouded dock. It was so isolated that Victoria could barely hear the traffic on West Ferry and Manchester roads.

Her mind worked feverishly. He might not have killed Torbel. In his frenzied state, he hadn't checked, and if anybody knew how to dodge a bullet, it was Torbel.

"Stop dragging your feet," Peacock snapped as she stumbled over a large split in the pavement. "It won't do you a bit of good."

Still clawing at his hand—she knew she'd drawn blood—Victoria made one last attempt at reason. "This makes no sense, Sergeant. Killing me won't bring Robbie back. And..." she choked as his grip on her throat tightened. "I can't believe Sophie would have wanted this." His hold slackened fractionally, and she gasped for air. "I read her diary. She disliked her father's tyrannical attitude, but otherwise she didn't have a vindictive bone in her body."

"That," he said, his mouth next to her ear, "was her problem."

She couldn't stave off the shiver of revulsion that swept over her. How could Sophie have loved this monster?

"Here we are," he announced, yanking her around in an unceremonious arc. "The place where he died. My only son, whose murderer you helped to escape justice."

"He'll still be dead when we're gone," Victoria cried. "What will you have gained?"

His narrow features, what she could glimpse of them, grew mournful. "Satisfaction," he replied, then pulled her tightly back against him and jerked her sideways. Victoria felt his head tip backward. "Soon, Sophie," he promised, "the three of us will be together. And for once in his life, old Goggy will be grateful to someone else."

Victoria's skin prickled. Perspiration slid along her spine. Would he stab her in the back? It seemed likely. But to do that, he would need to create an air pocket between them.

She waited only until he loosened his grip, then, using two parts of her body at once, she brought her heel back hard into his shin and jammed her right elbow into his stomach.

He yelped but didn't release her completely. His fingers managed to catch her wrist in a bloodless grip. Then he stopped. His features froze. A pained whisper emerged from his throat. "Bugger that . . ." he croaked.

To Victoria's shock, he staggered into her arm, unbalancing her. A funny gurgling noise accompanied his drunken movements. The knife skimmed across Victoria's rib cage, slicing her jacket and tank top. For a dreadful, unexpected moment, his hand shot back up to her neck and squeezed, cutting off her breath. Then suddenly it was gone and she was free, panting as she dropped to her knees and fought to refill her lungs.

Before she could scramble away, a pair of hands descended on her shoulders and pulled her sideways. In her peripheral vision, she saw Peacock's shocked face and the military knife hovering uncertainly next to his head. His mouth gaped open; his brown eyes bulged; the knife clattered to the ground.

The last sound he made was a raspy "Robbie . . ." before he pitched backward onto the badly cracked pavement.

Victoria recognized Torbel's touch instantly. On his knees behind her, he wrapped his arms around her shoulders and pulled her firmly back against him.

Feelings of love and relief swamped her, the strongest sensations she'd ever known. They mingled with pity and a residual trace of fear as she beheld Peacock's startled, staring face.

It wasn't until she glanced lower and spied the knife protruding from his chest that she realized what Torbel had done. "Thank you," she said, and turning, pressed her cheek against his.

His mouth moved against her hair. "Anytime."

They remained that way for several minutes, unspeaking, taking and receiving what comfort they could under the circumstances.

"I didn't know you carried a knife," she said finally, wincing as he stood and she spied the blood on his forehead and shoulder.

He gave her a weak smile. "I keep it as a memento of worse times." His fingers traced the line of his scar. "It belongs to Augustus Hollyburn."

Shocked, Victoria breathed, "He did that to you?"

"I told you, he wasn't as frail ten years ago."

She touched the scar, then his injured forehead. "Why, Torbel? What happened between you that made him hate you so much."

Bending, Torbel closed Peacock's lifeless eyes. Crouched there, he brought his gaze back up to hers and said calmly, "Blodwyn."

Chapter Twenty

Torbel wasn't sure why he'd brought her here. Possibly because he really did love her, and he hadn't realized how deeply until he thought he might lose her to a homicidal maniac. Now that the nightmare was over, it was time to reveal to her the single biggest secret in his life.

Even Keiran didn't know this one. His mother had, of course, and so, he reflected cynically, had old Goggy—for more than thirty-seven years.

The old judge, clad in a burgundy dressing gown, shuffled into the parlor of his home to glare at them, or more specifically, at him. Victoria was incidental in this. Torbel was now and had for years been the focal point of his hatred.

"What do you want?" the old man demanded without preface. "Get out!" he snapped at a heavyset man in his midfifties, the new butler, Torbel presumed. It didn't matter. Victoria had used her connections on Bouverie Street to find Chivers a new and far healthier position.

"Would you believe me if I told you we wanted to see how you were doing?" Torbel retorted with exaggerated courtesy.

Scowling, Augustus massaged his chest. "No."

"It's true," Victoria put in.

"Bull," said Clover from the door. She wore a drabber version of her grandfather's bathrobe. "You came to gloat. Admit it. Your testimony got me booted off the force. And what was all that rubbish about my having a split personality? Me and Zoe, one? You're crazier than Peacock, the pair of you."

"And you're lucky that booted off the force is all you got," Victoria countered. "You'd have been charged with attempted murder if it weren't for your grandfather's clout and the absolute guarantee of psychiatric help."

"You little—" Clover began.

"Shut up," Augustus barked. His gaze shifted. "What is it now, Smythe?"

"Another visitor, sir."

"Send him away."

"Her," Zoe said, strolling through the door. She regarded Victoria. "Did I miss anything?"

"Get out," Augustus and Clover ordered as one.

"Not until I'm clear on a few important points." Arms folded, she eyed her grandfather shrewdly. "Just how much of Peacock's plan were you aware of?"

"None of your business."

"It came out at the inquest," Torbel told her. He was grateful for Victoria's hand gently stroking his leg. "Your grandfather received the same notes we did. I don't think he knew it was Peacock before the last night."

"Did he know that Peacock was Robbie's father?"

Torbel shrugged. "I doubt it."

"He was not Robbie's father," the old man choked. "Peacock was off his stick. He didn't know up from down in the end."

"The police found chimney sweep clothing inside a navy trunk belonging to Robert Peacock in a cellar room near the river," Victoria reminded him. "There was also a beggar's outfit—and a red hat," she added with a shudder. "Peacock killed Boots, planned attacks on Torbel and me, poisoned Lenny Street and didn't get caught doing any of it until the end. He knew up from down, Judge Hollyburn. He was mad—who wouldn't be after killing their own child?—but very, very smart."

The old man's lips trembled. "None of that makes him Robbie's father."

Zoe pulled Sophie's diary out of her pocket and tossed it onto the coffee table. "Read this, then," she challenged. "The truth fairly leaps out at you."

"Her 'even foxier' lover wasn't Oliver Fox," Victoria said. "Her lover was foxier than Fox."

"You have no proof," Augustus rasped, desperate to maintain the illusion. "Robbie was not the spawn of a madman. He was Duffy's child, a Hollyburn through and through."

"God, but you're a blind old bat," Zoe said scornfully. "Not to mention a bad example. You had affairs, and Sophie followed your lead."

"I never—"

"Blodwyn." Torbel interrupted old Goggy's heated protest.

It had the desired effect. Augustus's face went white with shock, then purple with rage. Breathing labored, fingers bloodless, he rubbed his chest furiously. "You—you..." He broke off before finishing the accusation.

A wise move, Torbel reflected, since the unspoken word revealed precisely what he was. "Bastard?" he inquired levelly.

Victoria's eyes narrowed. Her gaze traveled from Torbel to Augustus, then back again.

It was Zoe who demanded, "What's going on here? Who's Blodwyn?"

"My mother," Torbel told her.

She frowned. "I've heard that name before."

So had Augustus and, judging from her pinched expression, Clover, as well.

Zoe's uncomprehending gaze met Victoria's. Torbel sensed rather than received the silent message that passed between them.

"Well, I'll be damned," Zoe exclaimed softly. "I have an uncle." Then she threw back her head and laughed.

"HE'S YOUR FATHER?" For all her composure inside, Victoria began shaking Torbel's arm the moment the mansion door closed behind them. "Why didn't you tell me? How long have you known?"

A slow smile crossed Torbel's lips. "God, but you are a pain," he maintained. He kissed her before she could think to become indignant. "I wanted to be sure about us before I told you. I've always known." His eyes fogged. "I think Robbie may have learned the truth the night he died."

"And that's why he came looking for you on the docks, why he was so excited?"

"It's possible. Goggy probably still has the documents proving my birthright. Blodwyn made sure they were delivered to him before she died. He must have confided in Clover."

The door opened, and Zoe came out onto the porch. "He's not long for this world, I'm afraid. Old Scratch is with him now."

"What about Clover?" Victoria inquired. "Will she be properly helped?"

"Count on it. We're estranged, but let's face it, she requested an assignment in Stepney. She might not like me, but I think the sibling love is there deep down." Turning, Zoe regarded Torbel. "So you're my uncle. And Clover and Goggy knew it all along. I got one thing out of her. The truth was in the documents that Clover was searching for."

Victoria brightened. "That's why Sophie went to Ireland. She wanted to find proof of her father's infidelity so he couldn't lord her own over her."

"Ain't we a great family?" Keys jingling, Zoe started for the Jeep she'd borrowed from Keiran. "I'll be off, then. It's a full moon. Go ahead and get romantic. We'll go shopping for offices tomorrow, Victoria."

Torbel waited until she was gone before arching a dark brow. "Offices?"

Smiling, she wrapped her arms about his neck. "I thought you'd be pleased. You could use a good defense solicitor in Stepney."

"One specific defense solicitor," Torbel agreed. His somber eyes—his Hollyburn eyes, she realized in retrospect—searched her face. "Are you sure about this, Victoria? I do have a temper. I lost it once after old Goggy slashed me, and I nearly tore his throat out. God knows what I might have done if he hadn't collapsed before I really got hold of him.''

"So that's what happened. Everyone said you had a temper, even you, but I never saw any real evidence of one. At least, not one that was out of control." Still smiling, she reached up and touched his scar with her mouth. "The answer is yes, Torbel."

"To what?"

"Everything. Anything. I love you, temper and all. I don't care whose son you are or how much magic you have in your veins."

Torbel's smile had a wry tilt to it. "Old Goggy cares, always has. He swears it was Blodwyn's magic, combined with my loss of temper, that caused him to collapse. He insists I'm responsible for his heart problems today."

"That's ridiculous. Anyway, magic can be used to make good things happen, too." She gave him a seductive nudge with her lower body. "How about brewing up a batch tonight? I'll supply the bubbly."

All traces of cynicism vanished. Amusement played on the corners of his sensual mouth. "Fair enough," he agreed. "And in case I haven't mentioned it, I love you, too, very, very much."

"You have, but not lately." She hesitated, then glanced at the closed door. "Do you think Augustus will be all right? He looked a little peaked when we left."

"He'll be fine," Torbel assured her. His own eyes darkened slightly on the lion's-head knocker. "Scratch is with him. That's all he needs at this point." He saw her looking around. "What?"

"I left my backpack inside. I, uh, don't suppose..."

"Yes, fine, I'll get it for you."

"Thanks." Sighing, she shook her head. "You know, for a while there, I thought Ron was the killer. All those secret plans and nasty looks he gave me. I still think he's up to something."

"He is." Torbel's eyes danced. "He's planning a surprise birthday party."

"What?" A delighted smile curved his lips. "For you?"

"Yeah, but don't tell him I know. I imagine he was trying to keep it from you, figuring you'd let it slip to me."

"Some trust."

"He'll come around."

She regarded him thoughtfully through her lashes. "So it's over, then."

"That depends on how you look at it."

"What do you mean?"

"I mean—" he inclined his head until his lips brushed warmly over hers "—as far as I'm concerned, it's only just begun...."

Epilogue

Alone in the parlor, a tight-lipped Augustus finished his story. "That's it in a nutshell," he said angrily. He had to use his knuckles to massage the ache in his chest.

Scratch swirled the dregs of his Scotch. "So justice *has* been served, then—in the eyes of the law, at least."

"The law's a crock." One bony finger stabbed the air in Scratch's direction. "I still want Torbel punished. He's responsible for Robbie—and for my bad heart."

Concealing his amusement, Scratch rose. "Justice has been served, Goggy, like it or not. You offered to sell your soul in exchange for the truth. Well, you got your truth. Stop kicking up such a fuss, and let's go."

Augustus was halfway across the floor before he realized he'd moved. His chest felt as if someone were carving it up with a butcher's knife. "Go where?" he demanded crossly.

Scratch smiled. "Oh, a little place I know. You'll feel right at home there, Goggy."

Augustus searched his pockets. Where were his damned pills?

"Come along, old friend." Scratch took him firmly by the arm. "No point stalling."

Augustus felt himself gliding across the floor. What an odd sensation. Gliding away from his ever-present fire, and yet he didn't feel cold at all. If anything, he felt quite warm. Good old Scratch. He always knew what to do. Good old...

His eyes came up slowly as realization began to dawn. Old Scratch? But wasn't that another name for...?

The tricky devil, to be seen by others, to have gotten close to him, to have listened so patiently. It seemed he'd sold his soul, after all....

WHEN TORBEL RETURNED, he saw Victoria's backpack on the sofa—and Goggy lying motionless on the parlor floor. He crossed to the old man's side. No pulse, and his face had a blue tinge to it.

"I heard you come back," Clover said dully from the doorway. "Is he . . . ?"

"Dead," Torbel finished, his tone as flat as hers. He sat back on his heels, wondering if he would ever find it in his heart to feel any remorse.

Clover inched closer. "Where did old Scratch get to?" she asked.

Torbel regarded Augustus's staring eyes. His arm was stretched out on the carpet, his fingers curled as if grasping someone's hand. "I don't know," he said slowly. "And I'm not sure any of us really wants to find out...."

Merry Christmas, Baby!

A romantic collection filled with the magic
of Christmas and the joy of children.

SUSAN WIGGS, Karen Young and
Bobby Hutchinson bring you Christmas wishes,
weddings and romance, in a charming
trio of stories that will warm up your
holiday season.

MERRY CHRISTMAS, BABY! also contains
Harlequin's special gift to you—a set of
FREE GIFT TAGS included in every book.

Brighten up your holiday season with
MERRY CHRISTMAS, BABY!

Available in November at
your favorite retail store.

HARLEQUIN ®
®

Look us up on-line at: http://www.romance.net   MCB

The collection of the year!
NEW YORK TIMES BESTSELLING AUTHORS

Linda Lael Miller
Wild About Harry

Janet Dailey
Sweet Promise

Elizabeth Lowell
Reckless Love

Penny Jordan
Love's Choices

and featuring
Nora Roberts
The Calhoun Women

This special trade-size edition features four of the wildly popular titles in the Calhoun miniseries together in one volume—a true collector's item!

Pick up these great authors and a chance to win a weekend for two in New York City at the Marriott Marquis Hotel on Broadway! We'll pay for your flight, your hotel—even a Broadway show!

Available in December at your favorite retail outlet.

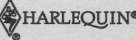

HARLEQUIN®

INTRIGUE®

THE SPENCER BROTHERS

*The Spencer Brothers—Cole and Drew...
two tough hombres.*

Meet

Cole Spencer
Somehow this cowboy found himself playing bodyguard.
But the stunningly lovely, maddeningly independent
Anne Osborne would just as soon string him up as let
him get near her body.

**#387 SPENCER'S SHADOW
September 1996**

Drew Spencer
He was a P.I. on a mission. When Joanna Caldwell-
Galbraith sought his help in finding her missing
husband—dead or alive—Drew knew this was his
chance. He'd lost Joanna once to that scoundrel...he
wouldn't lose her again.

**#396 SPENCER'S BRIDE
November 1996**

*The Spencer Brothers—they're just what you need to
warm you up on a crisp fall night!*

Weddings by DeWilde

Since the turn of the century the elegant and fashionable DeWilde stores have helped brides around the world turn the fantasy of their "Special Day" into reality. But now the store and three generations of family are torn apart by the separation of Grace and Jeffrey DeWilde. Family members face new challenges and loves in this fast-paced, glamorous, internationally set series. For weddings and romance, glamour and fun-filled entertainment, enter the world of DeWilde…

Watch for *FAMILY SECRETS*,
by Margaret St. George
Coming to you in December 1996

In an attempt to shed the past and get on with her future, Grace DeWilde has left her new store and her new life in San Francisco to return to England. Her trip results in a devastating discovery about the DeWilde family that has shocking implications for her children, for Ian Stanley, whose unrequited love for Grace has been years in the making, and for Jeffrey DeWilde, the estranged husband Grace can never stop loving.

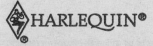

HARLEQUIN®

HARLEQUIN®

I N T R I G U E®

COMING NEXT MONTH

#397 A MAN OF SECRETS by Amanda Stevens
Lawman
Natalie Silver couldn't understand why FBI agent Spencer Bishop
was helping her out. But when she was accused of murdering her
ex-husband, Natalie found herself needing the secretive and seductive
Spencer as much as she had once loved him. And therein lay danger.
Because the more clues Spencer unraveled, the closer he got to
Natalie's secret...and to her son.

#398 PROTECT ME, LOVE by Alice Orr
My Bodyguard
Years ago, Delia Barry had gone to sleep beside bodyguard
Nick Avery, the man of her dreams—only to awaken next to a murder
victim. Knowing she was being framed, Delia fled. But now the past
is threatening her new life. And she has no choice but to turn to the
lover who may have betrayed her—the elusive Nick.

#399 A CHRISTMAS KISS by Caroline Burnes
Eyewitness
In steamy New Orleans, Cori St. John testified against a dangerous
man, and was swept into the Witness Protection Program. Now only
her "handler"—sexy U.S. Marshal Joey Tio—can keep her safe. Joey
fears his client and the woman he's coming to love is in danger, the
target of a husband she'd assumed was dead....

#400 BABY IN MY ARMS by Madeline Harper
With his silky ponytail and unfathomable eyes, Ben Blackeagle didn't
fit Kate McNair's image of a security expert. But then, ever since
she'd inherited baby Amanda, nothing had gone as she expected. Her
attempts to learn the ropes of motherhood had been complicated by a
hit-and-run accident and a drive-by shooting. Ben told her she could
rely on him, and baby Amanda called him Daddy, but what did Kate
really know about him?

AVAILABLE THIS MONTH:

Look for us on-line at: http://www.romance.net

HARLEQUIN ®

Scandals

A passionate story of romance, where bold, daring characters set out to defy their world of propriety and strict social codes.

"*Scandals*—a story that will make your heart race and your pulse pound. Spectacular!"   —Suzanne Forster

"Devon is daring, dangerous and altogether delicious."
                                                          —Amanda Quick

Don't miss this wonderful full-length novel from Regency favorite Georgina Devon.

Available in December, wherever Harlequin books are sold.